LAST CHANCE

A FUTURE APOCALYPSE CAUGHT IN A TRILOGY

DARREN E. WATLING

Last Chance

Tellwell Talent
www.tellwell.ca

ISBN
978-0-2288-8287-9 (Hardcover)
978-0-2288-8286-2 (Paperback)
978-0-2288-8288-6 (eBook)

Table of Contents

OUR WORLD

OUT OF THIS WORLD

INTO THE OTHER WORLD

Based on the short story 'Deception'
by and dedicated to
Jill Stubbs Mills

For Taylor, my son I love, more than my sun.

Last Chance is a humorous book. It does, however, contain references to sexual abuse, alcoholism, paedophilia, necrophilia, child abuse, drug abuse, incest, and cannibalism. Reader discretion is advised.

PART 1

OUR WORLD

CHAPTER 1

THE STORY SO FAR

The year 2125.

The end of humanity approached in the form of an asteroid of biblical proportions, dubbed 'Conclusion'. Hurtling through space the enormous obstacle was growing with every piece of dust, ice, space junk and fragment from other expired planets that adhered to its surface. With all of humankind's technology and resources exhausted, there was now nothing more to be done to stop the catastrophe. Inevitably, Earth was doomed.

A world summit was called. All the leaders, ambassadors and representatives from across the globe gathered in Sydney, Australia, at the headquarters of the World Reconnaissance Organisation for Neighbouring Galaxies (WRONG).

Discussions finally began after the leaders were told, 'Sit down, straight backs and hands on heads.'

"We have but one chance to save humanity," stated the Russian leader, through the interpreter, "and you are prepared to gamble our fate on a space shuttle that has never been tested," directed at the American.

The USA had built, 'The Super Shuttle'. Not only did it possess a new power system, it was also fully decked out, with all the mod cons, topped off with crushed velvet and fluffy dice.

"The reason we are in this jolly awful position," blurted out the English official, "is due to your incompetence," staring at the Russian. "Russian satellite pieces, Russian shuttle debris, Russian God knows what else, has rather left us with the smallest window to fly. . ."

"Do not dare!" interrupted the Chinese. "You pompous English think you are not at fault?"

The white bearded Scott said quite a mouthful but with all the 'Canny's, Mc's and Ock's', not even the interpreter could understand him, so everyone just smiled and nodded.

"Obviously, the Italians played a major part," the Swede added.

"Fark me!" the Australian shouted.

For a brief second, there was silence. The interpreter was not sure how to convey this message to others.

"Golly gosh!" the interpreter transposed.

"You're a bunch of fuckin' morons," the Australian continued. "Does it matter? We are facing the end of humanity as we know it, and still, still, you wish to blame someone."

"You are silly people," started the interpreter.

"History itself is history," the Australian ambassador profoundly stated. "The time we have left is extremely limited. You can all get stuffed if you think I'll sit here and listen to this crap any longer."

With that, he stood up and walked toward the exit, a notable confidence in his stride.

"What do you suggest? Where are you going?" asked the Dane.

The Australian stopped, turned and faced the world's leaders.

"What do I suggest? I suggest you put your pointless blame game aside and get on with a decision. Isn't that and a free feed the reason we are here? Where am I going? Fishing, that's where."

The debate continued without the Australian. After about six hours of back-and-forth discussion and what if, should have and could have, the outcome was finally agreed upon.

The Helsinki-born ambassador entered the establishment. "Sorry, am I late?"

"Hmm, we're near the 'finish'," the Irish woman said.

The Korean ambassador was comfortable with the decisions made to ensure the existence of humankind.

Korea had accelerated ahead of any other nation with the space conquest. In all its forty-seven missions, not one single failure or loss of human life. Outstanding! Intended for another mission and available at this time, the Korean space program had the ideal shuttle in wait. It was agreed, then, that this would be the transport to be employed to save the human race.

The Korean shuttle was designed to carry six personnel: the captain, the co-captain, and four others. Over the next week, the countries of the world were to decide who should go.

The American ambassador had already decided the senate would vote for an American space shuttle, supporting Americans, for good old America to carry the human race into a new American existence. This was to be kept top secret, allowing no other countries to interfere. They would still be a part of WRONG's project, thus avoiding any suspicion.

The American senate did indeed see the ambassador's point of view, upon his return to home soil. The American leaders had also decided that Colonel Steven Joseph Harper was the best choice for ground commander and overseer for this more than vital mission.

The colonel had spent his early years in the police force, rising to inspector in a few short years. He then joined the armed forces and was held in high esteem for his organizational skills, dedication, and leadership qualities.

Conclusion is inevitable.

CHAPTER 2

MICHAEL

At the mere age of two, Michael had arranged his toy number blocks in a way that satisfied him. There were no equation signs, minus or plus, but he was content with the formation of the numbers. Christmas holographs were captured, as a remembrance tool, of the happy occasion. The entire Watson family were present. His mum and dad, sister Kelly, aunts, uncles, cousins—a big family turn out for the festive cheer.

Michael had unwrapped his gifts, but most were still packaged in their see-through boxes. He had received typical two-year-old presents. There were toy cars, clothing, balls, ground-to-air-missiles, games, and the like. The arranged number blocks seemed to be the only gift that interested him. Kelly had received, among other presents, a calculator.

"What's that?" Mike asked.

"It's called a calculator," his eleven-year-old sister returned.

"You'll find out what it's used for when you get a bit older," she said.

Sensing his discontent with that answer, she explained briefly the operation of the device.

"Anyway, enough of school for today," she giggled. "Let's look at the holographs."

Kelly swiped her holographic communicator and bought up the day's still pictures.

"Look, there's Mum and Dad and Uncle Mark. And there is you, with your blocks," she added.

"Calacator here," said Mike, pointing to the gap between numbers.

"Calculator," corrected Kelly.

Kelly looked at the blocks in the image, looked at the pre-arranged blocks on the floor, and then gazed in a mixture of shock and disbelief, with her mouth open, at her two-year-old sibling.

"Mu . . . Mu . . . Mum," she exclaimed.

Her mum was chatting (how unusual) in the kitchen with her husband and other family members.

"Mum!" Kelly shouted demandingly.

The children's mum, Irene, a hot redhead, (MILF, I believe the term to be), entered the living room in haste, with their father and other members closely behind.

"What's wrong, Dear," she asked.

"Look," said Kelly, pointing to the blocks.

They all looked to the floor. Irene tilted her head a few times as Kelly's father walked closer to the blocks.

After a few seconds, Irene questioned, "What am I looking at?"

"Don't you see?" asked Kelly. "The numbers."

"I'm not sure what . . ."

Kelly interrupted, "They are math sums."

"Holly shit!" Uncle Mark cursed. "I see it."

The young cousins and Kelly giggled at Marks's swearing. Michael was unmoved, staring at the blocks.

The numbers in a row, five, six, three, zero, two, seven, nine, five, four, one, eight, two, one and six.

Confused, "I still don't see what . . ." aunty Belinda muddled.

"Five times six equals thirty," Mark explained.

"Yes, and two plus seven equals nine," added Kelly.

"Five take four equals one," stated Rick, the children's father, working it out.

"And eight times two…" started Mark, looking at the entire Watson family.

"Equals sixteen," everyone in unison, except Mike, joined.

"This has to be a coincidence," guessed Aunty Belinda. "A child that young is not capable," she added.

There was an eerie, brief silence, as the family tried to take in this strange phenomenon. (The same silence that fills a room full of orgy swingers when someone says, 'Mum'?)

"OK, OK. Let's muddle them up, add some more blocks, and coax Mike into more supposed maths sums," suggested uncle Ron, Rick's brother, doubting the capabilities of a two-year-old.

At first, Michael seemed to be in a bit of a panic, swallowing audibly. Then, Kelly realised what his concern was.

"It is OK, Mike," she said. "I have a picture of it."

She showed him the image again. Mike was now at ease with the disruption of his arranged blocks.

More block numbers were added to the pile and disarranged. Michael looked at the numbers and then appeared to just gaze at the ceiling for some time.

"I thought as much," stated Belinda, expecting Michael to divert his attention elsewhere.

"Yeah," Ron laughed.

Then, as if something snapped in Michael's mind, he quickly knelt in front of the blocks, several numbers he placed in a row, a gap, several more, a gap, then a larger number of blocks.

"Calcacator," he said, pointing at the gaps.

Mark gasped. "Kelly," he said. "Multiply the first group of numbers by the second."

A twelve-digit sum appeared on Kelly's calculator. Irene, looking over Kelly's shoulder, suddenly became very faint and Rick eased her into a seat. The Watson family were stunned.

***

Now twenty years old, Michael had become America's top-ranked mathematician. Not only had he developed formulae for rocket scientists, but he had also corrected some of the standard equations that were used in various fields to date. He was considered by his peers to be a step ahead of the likes of Einstein, Newton, Goofy, and Pythagoras, and was proclaimed as the best mathematics professor that ever lived, or undoubtedly, now, would ever live.

Although thrust into the limelight, Professor Michael Watson was never comfortable in the company of others. He was a loner and preferred it that way. He was, in fact, a social recluse. As a maths genius at an early age, he had great difficulty understanding people of his own age, and they did not understand him. It is said that people of extreme talent have trouble fitting in socially, and Mike was a prime example. To him, happiness came in the form of crunching numbers. Maths was black and white, predictable, something he could count on.

His father, Rick, had arranged an interview for him with a magazine. *The Nerd* magazine's editors were more than keen to put Michael on the cover, as word got out about the young genius, tall and thin, sporting glasses that could have been mistaken for two bottle bottoms. Rick thought this would be a step in the right direction for Mike to develop some social aspects in his life. Try as he did, Rick was never able to encourage his son to develop any social skills. Mike resented his father for taking his time away from maths. Nevertheless, the interview was forced upon the professor.

After the interview, pushing his glasses closer to his squinting, green eyes, Mike said to his dad, "Don't ever do that again."

***

There was knock at the front door of the Watson house. Michael was the only one home at this time, so begrudgingly, he answered the door.

There stood a tall, well-built, uniform with a man in it…his face had a black growth on his top lip. He called it a moustache. There were two other uniformed men and four black vehicles, in the background. The vehicles contained more personnel.

The professor held the door slightly ajar, peering at this activity.

"Forgive the intrusion, son," the gentleman said. "My name is Colonel Steven J. Harper of the U.S. Defense Force," came the official introduction. Recognising the professor from *The Nerd*, through the small margin of doorway, the colonel asked, "Are you Professor Michael Watson?"

Michael was literally shaking from the unexpected attention.

"Uh . . . uh," muttered Michael.

"Son, this is of the utmost importance," the colonel replied. Again, he asked, "Are you, or are you not, Professor Michael Watson?" The colonel, already knowing the answer.

Michael leant to the side peering over the colonel's shoulder at the vehicles and occupants.

"What is this all about?"

"May I come in?"

"Just you," Michael nodded.

Accepting his invitation, the colonel pushed the door open. As Michael backed into the house, Colonel Harper noticed the place was in a state of disarray, and a slight odour offended, but this was not a priority. The mission was, above all, the one and only concern.

They sat down amongst a mess of maths books, dirty clothes and pizza boxes.

The colonel explained the world's fate and the intention of the last mission: To carry on human existence on planet Y-Zlee.

Scientists had found what they believed to be another life-supporting planet in a cluster of stars. Planet Y-4 was extremely questionable, and Planet Y-C was in complete darkness. However, Planet Y-Zlee was reluctantly chosen as the saviour planet (as there were no rivers of alcohol).

The colonel and his upper lip growth also explained that, at this point, the public has been deceived and will continue to be to avoid mass hysteria.

"Why me?" Michael shrugged his shoulders.

"Son, you have one of the brightest minds on this planet. Maths is a vital part of the mission's success. We have received only a few notifications from astronomers about the asteroid heading for Earth. We have passed this off as a top-secret mission for the USA," the colonel continued. "Believable or not to the astronomers, we have their word of silence."

"I need you, the existence of man, needs you, to come with me right now," the colonel demanded. "Where are your parents, son?" he questioned.

"Dad works in the Arctic on exploration expeditions. He left a couple of days ago and doesn't usually return home for about six months," Michael answered. "He is uncontactable during this time."

"And your mother?"

"Mum went to help a sick friend. She won't be back for a week or so."

"Anyone else live here with you?" the colonel pried.

"My sister was staying here, but she got married and moved to New South Wales, in Australia, some years ago," Michael returned.

"Perhaps you wish to leave your mother a note? Of course, you cannot tell her of what you have learned here today, but maybe you wish to express your love and excuse yourself for . . . about three weeks, should do it," the colonel hinted.

Michael knew there was no point in leaving his father a message for several reasons.

"I understand," Mike nodded.

"I will wait out front for you to pack your bags," Colonel Harper stated.

The colonel noticed that Mike was a bit scattered and anxious about all this, but under the circumstances, *Who wouldn't be?* he thought.

CHAPTER 3

KIRSTEN

Born into wealth, Kirsten lived the life others could only dream of. To say she was beautiful was a vast understatement. Long, gold flowing hair, tight shapely body, gorgeous facial features with eyes that seemed to pierce your soul whenever you were lucky enough to have her look into yours. Blue in colour, with bright white surrounds and long lashes, gave a mesmerising appearance. You just wanted to stare into those eyes, those beautiful eyes.

She was schooled in the most expensive and best-proclaimed educational establishment America had to offer. 'Future School' it was called. In the heart of Seattle, the school was open to anyone that could afford it. The annual fees were excessively high. This kept the middle and lower class, 'riff-raff,' away from the rich. As predicted, over one hundred years ago, there was almost no middle class anymore. The gap had increased between the 'haves and have nots'. This school's students were the children of the upper class of society. The parents did not want their 'pampered babies to be forced to associate and mingle with common peasants,' as it was put. Not only did the parents of the rich refer to the less privileged as peasants; kings and noblemen had done the same centuries before. Some attitudes never change.

In the year 2113, one of the regular school sports was swimming. It was Kirsten's favourite, and any opportunity to swim was capitalised on by her. At the age of fifteen, she was aware that she was somewhat of a sex symbol, both in and out of school. Boys, and certainly men of all ages, were constantly ogling and staring at her. Of course, they did. That is what guys do. She had beauty beyond compare. Wives would slap their husbands to divert their attention. You could still see the men trying to, unnoticeably, obtain another glimpse. She was quite often mistaken to be much older than she was.

Kirsten loved to swim but, more to the point enjoyed parading around in her bikini, knowing she was driving all the boys wild. She loved the attention. She craved attention. Her last name demanded attention. Everything about her was a distraction.

Kirsten's family name had been changed several years before she was born. With the same last name as a publicised serial killer, Kirsten's father opted to change it. In the late 2090s, a psychotic paranoid schizophrenic rampaged on a killing spree. As you would expect, there was worldwide media attention and the name 'Muhasim' [Moo-har-sim)] became a regular topic of conversation. It seemed every household shuddered at the mention of his name. His crimes were of a particularly heinous nature. Kirsten's father, Trevor, had dealt with the misunderstanding for many years. Not wanting his daughter to be subject to the same, he came to a decision. He rather liked the last name of a band that reached stardom for a few decades around the year 2000, but now long forgotten.

Kirsten Van Halen was, naturally, immensely popular. She enjoyed her girlfriend's company. Kirsten also enjoyed the company and attention of one particular student. Elton Harrowday, the bad boy type, had grown through his childhood with Kirsten to reach their adolescent years, once again in the same shared school. There had always been a level of attraction between the two.

Elton pushed a smaller male student from the seat, which faced directly and closely to Kirsten.

"Fuck off, loser!" bullied Elton.

The younger child walked off and did not seem particularly fazed by this action, as being bullied by Elton, was a regular occurrence for him and a handful of other students.

"You are such a prick, El," Kirsten, pointing out the obvious.

"Yeah, but I'm good at it, Kirsty," Elton responded using his pet name for Kirsten.

Kirsten, wrapped in her designer pool bathing towel, giggled, loosened her towel and twisted her hair in a flirting motion.

Elton looked so out of place by the indoor pool. His school shirt was mostly hidden by his leather jacket, with black pants, sunglasses, and a crooner hairstyle. The poolside was not Elton's favourite place, mostly because he could not swim.

"Coming over later?" Elton asked.

"Coming for a swim?" Kirsten replied.

"You bitch," Elton joked.

"Tell you what," Kirsten started, "Jump in the pool with me, right now, and I'll come around after school."

Elton immediately picked up the love of his, so far, short life, as a husband would carry his wife over the threshold (or a freshly dug grave). Elton walked to the side of the pool, Kirsten in his arms, and with a throwing motion, aimed for the heavily chlorinated (to combat the mucus and urine) water. Kirsten gripped Elton's easily accessible jacket extremely tight, and suddenly, the centre of gravity was too powerful for Elton to maintain. Elton toppled over and sank to the bottom. He was unable to reach the surface with no swimming skills whatsoever, and along with his heavy clothing, he obviously required immediate assistance. Kirsten shook off her semi-attached pool towel, revealing her gorgeous bikini-clad body, casually drew a breath, feet first in an upright position, and descended behind Elton. She grabbed, again, his leather jacket and, underwater, shimmied him to the edge and pushed him up. Elton arose, placing both elbows and forearms on the pool's perimeter. Pulling himself out of the water, he was gasping and coughing (likened to the aftereffects of smoking a bong, so I am told). Kirsten retrieved her towel and climbed from the pool as well.

One of the teachers walked past at that time.

"Having fun, Elton?" the teacher sneered, taking in his wet, bedraggled appearance and knowing his reputation for being a bully.

A few students, mainly the ones that were usually bullied, saw this entire event, heard the teacher's comment, and quietly chuckled to themselves.

"Fuck you!" Elton whispered at the, now out of earshot, teacher.

Sitting by the pool, close to Elton, Kirsten giggled at his defiance.

Elton, dripping and placing his left hand in his pocket, seemed to check for something, then sighed with relief.

"See you about four," he smiled at Kirsten.

***

Elton answered the security gate's communicator from inside the massive mansion.

"You are a bit late, Kirsty," he said. "The gate's unlocked. Come on in."

Elton opened the front door and Kirsten entered.

"Is your dad home, El," she enquired.

"Nah, just us," he said with that bad boy look in his eye that Kirsten found so attractive.

"Have you got some?" she asked.

"Does a priest sweat at a kindergarten?" he mused. (And we all know the answer to that).

"If I were in the kindy, he would," replied Kirsten.

They both laughed, and Elton proceeded to prepare his "crash", the drug of the 22nd century. The capsule containing the drug had water stains from the day's mishap.

He passed Kirsten the injector, loaded with crash.

"Party time, Kirsty," the bad boy said, widening his eyes and lifting his brows.

Kirsten lifted the back of her long flowing hair and pushed the injector into the back of her neck.

"Oh, shit! This is really good," she exclaimed. Her pupils dilated, and the whites of her eyes became bloodshot, immediately.

"Yeah, I didn't think it could get any better than the last batch we had," Elton said, retrieving the injector. "This is the best yet. I have already had three hits. But I'm going for another."

He began to load the injector again.

"Hello," a familiar voice came from the gate communicator.

"Oh, fuck!" blurted Elton. "It's your dad, Kirsten."

He quickly scrambled to hide the forbidden substance and utensil.

"Hello, it's Trevor. Is anyone there?" He asked again. "Kirsten? Elton? Anyone?"

The gate was still unlocked from Kirsten's entrance. Trevor walked to the front door as Elton, panic-stricken, tried his best to bring Kirsten out of her crash high. Elton had not even shut the front door since Kirsten had arrived. Kirsten's father stepped into the foyer, beams of sunlight through the window hitting the clean, white tiled floor. He peered around the corner into the room, where both were sitting, trying desperately not to give away their altered state.

Trevor calmly said, "Sorry, honey. Our plans have changed. We must go pick Mum up, from the airport. But while I am here, I just wanted to have a quick word with Elton. Would you mind just waiting in the car for a minute?"

"Sure, Dad," Kirsten managed to reply.

She stood up and stumbled toward and eventually through the still wide open front door.

Within a flash, Trevor's expression and demeanour changed to a form Elton had never seen.

Trevor positioned himself directly in front of and inches away from Elton's face. Elton thought Trevor was going to attack him because he suspected he had been feeding Kirsten crash.

"Does the name Muhasim mean anything to you?" questioned Trevor, staring out Elton.

Elton diverted his eyes, tilted his head slightly, scratched his head and said, "Yes, I know who he was."

Elton was still looking confused.

"You know us now as the Van Halens. Would you like to hazard a guess as to what our family name was before that?" hinted Trevor.

"Ah, I . . . um," Elton stumbled.

With a deep, loud voice, Trevor yelled, "Muhasim!"

Elton fell back into his chair; fear spread across his face.

Trevor returned to his daughter, leaving the front door and gate as he found them. The pair drove off heading for the airport. Nothing was said regarding the obvious to Trevor— the young pair were high.

***

As the morning school bell rang, Kirsten was concerned she had not seen Elton. Although notorious for having days off from school, Elton never missed a

Wednesday. Kirsten and Elton would always meet in the morning, before the bell, and walk to their mutual class.

Kirsten's class had been underway for about half an hour when two identical female police officers, Officer Wolf and Officer Wolf, appeared, bringing sad news. The class was informed that Elton had tragically drowned in his home's swimming pool sometime late yesterday afternoon. The officers questioned the class, and it had come to light that Kirsten was possibly the last person to see Elton alive.

Kirsten was directed to an empty room, where the officers asked her a series of questions relating to the previous afternoon. She realised how this must look for her father, so she did not offer the truth about Trevor being there. Kirsten also did not divulge their crash addiction. However, detectives, as they were, soon it twigged, and they dragged the truth from her.

"Thank you, Kirsten," one of the female detectives said. "Again, our condolences. You may return to your class now."

Kirsten, saddened, to say the least, returned home at the end of the day to find her mother distraught and in tears.

"Mum, what's wrong?" she asked.

"Your father has been arrested for murder," she cried out and collapsed into her daughter's arms.

***

Now, back in 2125, Kirsten moved on with her life, pouring all her energy into her profession. Now, at twenty-eight years old, she had become a skilled surgeon and stood out in her field of choice. She was so exceptional, she had performed delicate operations on presidents, the wealthy (who would only employ the absolute best money could buy), several renowned actors, the canteen lady at the hospital (she made a great coffee), and basically, Kirsten operated on the most important people the world had on its earth, at this time.

Kirsten lived with her mum only now, as her father had been incarcerated for many years. Trevor Van Halen had been kept out of the public eye for fear of his and his family's safety. If word had emerged that they were previously Muhasim, the fear would tear apart an otherwise peaceful, upstanding society.

The doorbell rang at the Van Halen's home.

Kirsten's mum, Vera, had never recovered from the devastation all those years ago.

"Kirsten, will you get that please?" Vera asked as she turned the stove off.

Kirsten was used to her mother retreating to her bedroom, whenever somebody came to their home. She had totally withdrawn from all aspects of life, just wanting solitude.

Kirsten answered the door to find a man with an unusual growth on his top lip, in army uniform standing there.

"Doctor Kirsten Van Halen?" the man asked.

"Yes," she said.

"My name is Colonel Steven J Harper of the U.S. Defense Force," came the official introduction. "Is there anyone else present here at the moment, ma'am?"

"No," Kirsten lied.

"May I enter?" he asked, flashing his ID.

"Sure," Kirsten replied, showing him in.

The colonel informed her of the nature of his visit.

Vera had heard everything and sheepishly made her presence known.

Colonel Harper was a little surprised and disappointed with Kirsten's dishonesty.

"It is OK, Colonel," Vera stated. "I won't tell a soul. I'll be happy to sit here and watch the end."

Colonel Harper contemplated this proposal for a few seconds. Kirsten guided the colonel to a more private section of the room and whispered in his ear.

"Ma'am," said Colonel Harper, turning to Vera, stroking his upper lip growth, "You have my consent to remain as you are."

Not hearing the words whispered by her daughter, Vera was relieved with the outcome. She could stay in her fortress of solitude.

"I'll wait for you outside while you say your goodbyes and pack your bags, Doctor," Colonel Harper stated.

The colonel had noted the appearance of the doctor and assumed she might be under stress and had probably let her emotions take over the clearness of her eyes.

Conclusion moves closer.

CHAPTER 4

JASON

Jason Childs was known as 'The Doctor' to his colleagues. He was a mechanical engineer that could 'make it work, again', but Jason kept a well-hidden, deep dark secret. He was a three-time convicted paedophile.

Bought up in The Bronx, life had not been easy for him. Through the Second Great Depression of 2100, he struggled just to survive like many of the less fortunate. His mother passed away when he was five years old. His drunken, abusive father battled to keep down a job.

Warren, his father, had not always been that way. He was doing quite well for his wife and son, had a well-paying job, was involved with community projects, and Jason admired and loved his father, who always seemed to be in control of his surroundings. Warren was an upstanding member of society. Perhaps, Jason's success in his field was inspired by his father when he was at that impressionable age.

After Warren's wife died, in the year 2108, he hit the bottle, (the bottle never complained), and a violent streak would surface whenever he drank. Jason tried to stay out of sight and would hide under his bed, in the kitchen pantry, or any other place he could squeeze into. It did not matter where he hid; his dad always found him. Warren would hit him with an open hand, sometimes a clenched fist, and sometimes he would throw a freshly finished bottle at him. Jason had been hospitalised several times in his youth. This was the Bronx. Nobody cared. After Jason's recoveries, he was sent home to face his father again. Things got worse before they got better. Warren used to invite one of his drinking buddies to his home. His so-called friend, Chris, was not only interested in downing alcohol, but he also knew Warren would pass out, leaving a young ten-year-old child at his mercy. Chris had never shown himself to be a violent man. He loved children for the wrong reasons.

One particular night, Warren had completed his usual ritual of drinking, attacking his son, and then passing out wherever he fell. Jason sitting at the wonky kitchen table was approached by Chris who had a few under his belt as well.

"Your dad sure makes a mess of himself, doesn't he?" Chris asked.

"It's only been since Mum died a few of years ago," Jason defended.

"Yeah, he has gone downhill since then," said Chris. "He seems to have trouble making ends meet these days."

"Yes, Dad says money is scarce at the moment."

"Have you thought about helping out your dad?"

"What do you mean, Chris?" replied Jason.

"Well, you could earn some money. Maybe your dad will stop drinking then, and you would not get hurt anymore either," Chris suggested, knowing full well this was probably not the answer to Warren's drinking problem.

The suggestion was very appealing to Jason. He wanted his caring father back.

"How will I make money, then?" Jason enquired.

"I could sell some images for you," Chris slyly suggested.

"OK," Jason said, seeing that as a great opportunity. "Which ones do you want?" he so innocently asked.

Chris laughed, "Oh, it's probably best if I take some new ones."

"Of what?" Jason said, continuing the conversation.

"I could definitely sell images of you," led Chris. "It will be fun and easy."

Puzzled, Jason asked, "Who wants to buy holographic stills of me? How do you sell them?"

"I know lots of people that would like images of you," Chris baited. "Don't worry about how to get paid. I will sort that out for you."

"Oh, thank you, Chris," Jason said, appreciating Warren's drinking partner.

Chris thought to himself, *How good is this? The kid is thanking me for what I am about to do.*

"Let's do it now," Jason begged.

Chris pretending it was going to be a chore, said, "I suppose we could."

"Where shall we take the stills, Chris?"

"In the bedroom is best," came the reply.

***

The police and ambulance had arrived at Warren's house at first light. There was no knock on the door. The police rammed the door open to a house scattered with empty alcohol bottles, dishes, food scraps, dirty clothes, and cigarette butts, (which could have been mistaken for a teenager's house). As they proceeded through the hall to the main living room, they sighted a man still snoring, spread out on the chipped, tiled floor. Two officers immediately jumped on top of him, cuffing both hands behind his back. Other officers were already checking the remainder of the house.

"Clear," they shouted as they cautiously searched room by room.

They pushed open Jason's door. There was a young boy, unconscious and still tied to the bed, blood oozing from between his legs.

"Get the paramedics in here now!" the senior officer demanded.

"The tip-off was correct," an officer was heard to say.

Images of the horrific event were spotted on the holographic communicator beside the bed. It was Warren's.

Laws had changed so much over the past century and the boy's testimony was inadmissible in court.

For example, to underscore, back in the year around 2000, a jewellery shop owner's family were sued when the assailant shot dead the owner but cut his wrist on the broken glass he had smashed in an effort to steal the valuables.

The evidence pointed to Warren. However, no DNA samples were taken as the police were sure they had their man, and DNA testing was too expensive for an area such as The Bronx.

Warren was to spend the rest of his years in prison.

In 2110, Jason at twelve-years-old, was without parents and traumatised for quite some time. He was a ward of the state and soon put in the care of a foster family. The family he lived with for the next few years were involved in, and unbeknownst to the courts, a paedophile ring. Jason grew up accepting this as 'the norm'. On three separate occasions, Jason had been convicted of indecently dealing with a minor. Because of 'Fire Night', (the night a huge fire swept through The Bronx in the hot summer of 2116), all police and court records were destroyed.

Jason, barely passing lower school, took an interest in vehicles. Close to his paedophile ring foster family home sat a garage which had, in its employ, an older gentleman. Jason made his presence known to the kind-hearted mechanic. Kye had been working as a mechanic for most of his life. He was of the 'old school'. If it broke down, he could fix it. Jason spent many weeks at the garage with Kye, helping him with repairs and the like after his upper school classes had finished for the day. Kye had seen potential and interest from Jason, and soon he was employed part-time. Jason continued his schooling, learning mechanics at both school and the garage. With Kye's help, he studied mechanical engineering and earned a degree. Kye knew nothing of Jason's horrific ordeal as a child or, indeed, how Jason spent his free time. As mentioned before, laws have altered over the years.

Paedophiles were no longer allowed to be named and shamed. It seemed the law was to protect the criminals more than the victims.

Jason moved out of his questionable foster home sometime later and lived in a modest unit alone. He was recruited by NASA, and it was not long until he became an expert in the mechanics of rockets, space shuttles and alien craft that officially never existed. He had become, in his own right, a master of mechanics. It was here he was referred to as 'The Doctor'.

The present, 2125; Returning from work for the day, Jason swiped his communicator open, stared at his collection of images containing his victims and reminisced, reliving some of his hideous crimes.

A knock on the door required his attention. Standing before him, a distinctive uniform, filled with a man of distinction with that thing on his lip.

"Sir, my name is Colonel Steven J. Harper of the U.S. Defense Force", came the official introduction. "Are you Mr. Jason Childs?"

The stubble faced Jason replied, thinking his gig was up, "Yes, I am he."

Jason started to present his wrists.

"May I come in, please, sir?" the colonel requested.

Jason kept swinging his hands forward, integrating his fingers, to appear as if a natural movement.

"Please do," Jason responded with semi-relief.

Once again, the colonel explained the situation.

"Who else will be on this mission to Planet Y-Zlee?" asked the engineer.

"A pilot, co-pilot and five others, including yourself, sir," was the reply.

"Is it at all possible to accommodate an extra passenger, Colonel?" enquired Jason.

"No, sir," the colonel sternly replied.

"Not even a small child?" the concerned engineer asked.

"No sir," again, the answer.

"Can I, perhaps, meet you at the base in a few hours?" Jason persisted.

"Sir, what can possibly be more important to you than saving humankind?" the colonel inquisitively asked.

"Oh, it's just that I . . . ah, just wanted to . . . ah . . . say goodbye to someone," Jason answered.

"You can board one of the vehicles out front. My men will drive you there," the colonel insisted.

"Um . . . it doesn't matter. Forget it," Jason responded.

"Very good, sir. I will wait out front for you to pack your bags," stated Colonel Harper.

Jason was consumed with his current victim. He had a young boy tied up and gagged in his bathroom. He wanted to sneak him onto the base, so he would not lose his plaything. He wanted to take advantage of his prey for as long as possible. The thought of not having his toy on takeoff was most alarming to him. He had a picture in his mind of no child contact, ever again. He did not want to get his freak on with a fully grown female. That would be too weird for him. What was he to do?

After a short period, the engineer walked out of his unit carrying two large suitcases.

CHAPTER 5

SHANARA

Shanara [Shan-ar-rah] was the next specimen of the elite. Her father had been noted as the best scientist in the world at the present time. The WRONG project had already recruited Professor Adam Harding. The USA, still deceiving the world project, were not too concerned with this loss, as Adam was in his later years, and it was speculated that his health could be a major setback to the United States project.

Adam, a notarised scientist at the time Shanara was born, conducted many experiments in his homemade laboratory. His daughter was fascinated with her father and the experiments that Adam had performed during Shanara's youth. She was like a magnet to metal and a 'Tom-boy' at heart. A button nose and medium length black hair, styled just so, which she would keep through her adult years. Always by his side, the professor would involve his daughter as much as possible, sensing her keen interest. Her favourite experiments involved using the

Bunsen burner. It did not really matter to her what was being introduced to the naked flame, as long as something was being heated up or burnt. Sometimes chemical reactions were enough to engage the child's somewhat obsessive behaviour. Adding chlorine to brake fluid was her most treasured memory of spending time with her father.

Adam's wife, Leah, was not Shanara's biological mother. Adam had always considered himself a lady's man. He had many affairs whilst married to his first wife. One of those rendezvous was responsible for the conception of Shanara. Adam tried his best to contain the scandalous situation from his then-wife. His lover refused to terminate. But (and that famous, direct, sensible quote from . . someone from the 21st century), 'Shit happens'. His lover had died while giving her secretive birth. Adam had very few options. He came clean to his wife about the affair and his newborn daughter. She did not take it too well to convey it mildly. (Phrases like, 'cheating fucker', 'unfaithful piece of shit' and 'please put the knife down', were used in their adult discussions). It was a very messy divorce. Some years later, Adam met Leah and introduced Shanara. Leah was your 'gold digger type'. A willowy blonde, always plastered with makeup and overkill on jewellery. She despised Shanara, calling her an 'illegitimate little brat' on more than one occasion and the venomous feeling was mutual. Shanara knew Leah was only in it for the money. She was a kept woman. Never worked a day in her life. Leah was not a particularly good example of a loving wife. Except for parting her legs for Adam, she did truly little else for him. But she made Adam, perhaps not entirely happy, but content with his much younger new wife and his altered life. Shanara seemed to resent Leah a little more every day.

At the age of twelve, in 2113, (Adam now married to Leah for two short years), Shanara was amid her fascination with science experiments and, indeed, fire. The young, yet-to-be, scientist began her own secretive experiments pertaining to the effects of fire on all three states of matter, i.e., liquid, gas and solid. She loved to watch the changes the flame made to different solid obstacles. The melting of plastic, the instant eruption of flammable materials and the short-lived intense heat from paper she found extremely exciting. The power of one small flame could be responsible for a major and even explosive, attentive scene.

Early on a spring morning, Leah had been arguing with Adam, within earshot of Shanara. They were on the topic of money as usual, and as usual, Leah wanted more from Adam.

"Sweetheart," continued Adam, "Our credit card is almost maxed out."

"Can't we just get another one?" said Leah.

"I'm not sure if I'm too comfortable with the extra repayments, honey," Adam debated.

"I'm sure you can deal with it," Leah, almost without a split-second thought.

"I'll sleep on it, darling," Adam replied.

"OK, you sleep on it. While you are sleeping on it, you will not be sleeping with me," threatened Leah.

"I suppose I could delay the equipment I was going to purchase for a unique experiment," Adam quickly pondered out loud.

"Conniving bitch!" Shanara whispered to herself. "I will fix her little red wagon."

Leah's favourite pastime was shopping. She would return home on many occasions with a second vehicle following behind, be it a shop courtesy vehicle or taxicab, full and even bulging with gifts and packaging boxes. Whenever Leah went shopping, she would religiously leave the house carrying her favourite handbag and place it on the passenger's side floor of her expensive, red sports car, which, of course, was paid for by Adam. Shanara had mentally noted this and a devious plan was formulated by the young avenger.

Shanara filled a small balloon with brake fluid. She placed it carefully into the outer side pocket of Leah's unguarded handbag. The spare car key's location was known to Shanara, and she took possession of it. On the passenger's black floor mat of 'the super bitch's' car, she smeared an odourless, black liquid chlorine, which she had concocted in her dad's private laboratory. Saturday mornings were Leah's regular shopping spree days. Shanara waited near the driveway with a small steel skewer concealed in her hand. As Leah was leaving for her expedition, Shanara walked toward the front door, passing Leah at close range. No words were said, just glances of hatred between the two. Shanara diverted her direction to ensure she passed on the side of Leah that supported the bag. She thrust the skewer, unnoticed by Leah, into the side pocket containing the brake fluid. Shanara entered the house and peeked through the entrance curtains to watch her scheme unfold. Leah's habits paid off for her nemesis. Placing her bag down, a volcano-like eruption spewed out hot chemicals and smoke. Shanara, now holding the spare car key, pressed auto lock. Leah was momentarily trapped. She unlocked the vehicle with her keys, which had just been inserted into the ignition, slightly before the eruption.

Shanara again pressed lock before Leah could open the door. Smoke was beginning to limit vision and began to fill the interior of the vehicle. Leah now had burning chemicals attacking her body as she panicked to press unlock again. Shanara was not finished yet. A third time, she pressed lock. Leah, with her hand still on the key, quickly retaliated and managed to open the door, falling out of the vehicle, screaming and coughing. Adam heard the commotion and rushed from his lab to the scene. He yelled to Shanara to call an ambulance. She stood inside the house, filing her nails for a few minutes. Then she called back to her dad; the paramedics were on their way. She then returned the spare key to its previous location. Adam was comforting his expensive wife out the front and was none the wiser as to what Shanara was currently doing. Adam took a moment to look inside the car to try and piece together what had happened. He could surmise from the aftermath there had been some sort of chemical reaction within the interior of the vehicle. Leah was now lying unconscious, overcome by the fumes and pain.

"Where's that bloody ambulance?" he desperately shouted.

"I'll dial again, Dad," his daughter returned.

Shanara casually dialed nine, one, one and said there had been a bit of an accident, and reluctantly, gave the address.

***

Some months had passed, and Leah was still recovering in the hospital. She had burns to sixty per cent of her body. Her vocal chords were damaged, she had been unable to talk and her once unmarked face was deeply scarred. She endured painful skin grafts and would be dis-figured from this day forward. She lay in the burns unit, with Adam by her side as she began to speak for the first time since the alleged accident.

"Can you tell me what happened," Adam softly asked.

"It was your fucking bitch of a daughter that did this to me," she angrily cried out.

Adam leaned over her, his face a few inches from her unsightly features.

"When you are well enough to leave the hospital," he softly spoke, "Fuck off and don't ever come back."

He never questioned Shanara and never spoke of Leah again to his lovely daughter.

***

About four years and two months later in 2117, Shanara now sixteen, was well on her way to becoming a recognised authority in the scientific circle. She was also venturing out further from her home suburb, exploring her expanding world. One evening, she had her father's blessing to travel to a neighbouring suburb, The Bronx, to hang out with some friends. She rode a taxicab, disembarking out front of a friend's house, but she did not make contact. She noticed a sign for a huge factory. It said, *Quintex Paper*. On either side were other factories. There was also a police station, bank, post office and courthouse further down the road.

Her inner firebug was getting restless. She stared at the paper roll factory for a few moments, and the evil urge consumed her clear thinking. She cased the factory for about half an hour and could not see any security of any substance. She would jump the locked gate, reach into a previously broken window on the side of the building, away from the clear view of others, unlock it and enter.

She had a box of matches in her pocket, which was a little unusual for the general population. Matches were rarely used anymore. They phased out about twenty years ago, but you could still get them if you knew where to look. Shanara had her own supply. She had purchased a quantity pack containing fifty boxes approximately six months prior. She still had a handful of boxes left. The moon was rather bright, and through the factory's glass windows, she could see surprisingly well. She could see huge rolls, flat packs, and bins full of wastepaper. She squatted, making herself comfortable with her back against a wall. She retrieved from her pocket, a box of fire lights. She placed the ignition end on the striker, the other end wedged against the tip of her finger. She flicked the match with her free hand. The lit match stopped short of a roll by about then inches, situated at the bottom of an enormous rack filled with pre-rolled paper. The match extinguished itself. She repeated the process, flicking a bit harder this time; the match landed about two inches from the same roll. A third time she tempted fate. This time she used two matches, side by side, and flicking even harder, the matches found their fuel. A small flame took hold. Not any bigger than the size of the matchbox . . .

at first. Then suddenly, the flames grew in height at an accelerated level.

The factory had a high roof, and roof vents were in abundance. The smoke began to cloud the underside of the roof and then pour out through the vents, keeping the inside of the factory relatively smoke-free. Shanara was in a trance, just watching this spectacle. She would have stayed in the factory longer, but the heat became overwhelming. It was time to evacuate. She ran out of the establishment, using the same route for escape, and scaled the gate, but as she raised herself above the gate's height, her head connected with a small drone hovering about twelve feet from ground height and sent it crashing down. Shanara hung from the gate, and then, with a shallow jump, landed next to the now immobile drone. She picked it up and noticed the rotor blades were broken and a tiny camera was attached to it. She was staring right at the lens. She immediately threw the flying menace over the fence toward the burning building, knowing it would not withstand the intense heat. She ran about fifty metres away from the scene, turning down a secluded alley. She turned her jacket inside out, tied back her black hair and made a few minor adjustments to her appearance so as not to be recognised in case somebody had been watching. She then casually returned to the scene, joined a growing crowd of onlookers and listened for any hint of her discovery. *She was in the clear,* she thought. Emergency teams were arriving. A slight breeze was in the air, sending the hot ambers and lit pieces of paper toward nearby businesses and homes. Fire Night was making its own history. She was never again to be responsible for a blaze of this proportion, (try as she may).

Shanara finished her college studies, obtained her degrees in the scientific field and was considered a reputable scientist. In America, she was, without doubt, science's number two, surpassed only by her father.

She lived with her current lover, but it was an on-again-off-again relationship. It had been off again more than on lately. Shanara's partner had already packed her belongings, and the split seemed a foregone conclusion.

There was a knock at the door . . .

Conclusion on its way.

CHAPTER 6

JOHN & JILLIAN

The 'Js', as they were known to their friends and colleagues, had been childhood sweethearts. It is exceedingly rare in this day and age for a couple to stay together for such a long period of time. They attended the same schools, played the same sports, and were inseparable by all accounts. Originally from Germany, they travelled to Spain, married, and then moved to Dallas, Texas in 2110, about fifteen years ago. They applied to NASA almost immediately, hoping to be employed as a husband-and-wife team, pilot and co-pilot, for any and all space shuttle missions. The company's decision was instantaneous. They had been schooled in the best aero-nautical facility the world had to offer at that particular time. The pair were extremely intelligent, with IQs in the 190s. They were also cyber geniuses. This made them an extremely valuable asset to the space conquest. They had piloted several secret space missions over the past years for America, and their experience was rated second to none. Colonel Harper did not have to concern himself with WRONG attempting to recruit them, as Korea and other countries had many pilots to choose from as well. The colonel was not sure the world organisation even knew of their existence, as all their missions had been top secret.

***

The blonde-haired, blue-eyed couple had been in constant debate about children for about six months. The topic was not whether to have children but rather which way. It was still lawful and acceptable to have a natural childbirth, but certainly not encouraged. Jillian wanted to give birth, but John was convinced, 'The Program', was the safest and most efficient. A couple could basically buy a baby from the Authority of Population Control (APC), selecting the genes they considered to be of importance. A designer baby, it was referred to.

"There is no need for further discussion about our method of birth anymore," Jill stated, sitting at her vanity unit, the mirror containing John's reflection to the side.

"I knew you would see it my way," John declared. "The Program has been so successful . . ." John stopped his speech short. "You are pregnant, aren't you?" John sensed.

"You know I am," Jill replied, turning to face John.

"So, the possibility of a child with defects is an acceptable risk?"

"You said it yourself, John. A possibility. I want our child, not a factory-made designer baby."

"Have you forgotten where we come from?"

Jill tilted her head forward and looked down.

"All right Jill, you win. I'm sure it is going to be a normal healthy baby, and we will be the best parents ever," John said, lightening the mood.

"Oh, I love you so much, John," Jill said running her eyes over that strong jaw she loved to stroke.

"And I love you, Jill," her six-foot husband said, looking down at his wife.

"Do you think our past will ever catch up with us, John?" Jill solemnly asked.

"Which part?" John jested.

They both laughed and took a moment to reflect on their more than ordinary lives.

While on their honeymoon in Spain, the couple were yearning to participate in something different, something out of character, challenging to their skills and minds, and something of a daring nature. The thrill seekers came up with a plan. They would rob a bank. But not in the usual way. No balaclavas, no guns. In fact, they had planned the heist, so they were not even near the bank. They would have an air-tight alibi.

They chose the least frequented bank. They would not even enter the bank. There would be no closed camera footage to identify them, no fingerprints, no voices, by all standards, no evidence connecting them to the robbery. Even if their timing were unfortunate or their plan failed, they could simply walk away. They had booked their flight to the USA, so ideally, they would put their devious plan into action, just before leaving Spain. As honeymooners, they had a reason to be travelling.

They had a flying drone in their possession. The pair brought the drone with them from Germany. As one of their favourite recreations, they were rather proficient in the use of drones, model planes, the non-returning boomerang, helicopters, and basically, any flying object. Studying aeronautics was a huge advantage for this type of pastime. These objects were a lot easier to fly than a space shuttle. The drone was homemade, so no serial numbers, nothing stamped into the metal components; the other components were so common that it was virtually impossible to trace where they had originated from, even with up-to-date forensics. They were convinced that if the drone were caught, it could never be traced back to them. They added a small, light mechanical device, a hook and a black plastic capsule. The pair of yet-to-be bank robbers also bought two holographic communicators from a nearby shop.

Came the day of their flight to America. They were booked on a midday flight and would need to leave their area around ten. They packed their suitcases, and it was time to rob a bank. So, they walked downstairs, across the road, to a busy coffee shop at approximately nine thirty a.m. and ordered coffee, and let their presence be known by intentionally knocking one of the cups to the ground. A number of people heard the crash and turned to witness the pair sitting in a booth under a clock with their backs against a wall. The mess was cleaned up by a waitress and another coffee was served. The Js, took out their holographic communicators. Jillian, who was better with the small tech, had altered the communicators to fly the drone. She had devised a way for the drone to be dual controlled by the two communicators. Between them, they remotely started the drone. The camera on it was noticeably clear, with no interference, and the drone, overall, responded very quickly. They knew the maid's schedule, and so left the drone on a desk and the window open to their vacated room. The drone flew out toward the bank about twenty feet above ground height. In the coffee shop, the pair appeared like everybody else—obsessed with their holographic communicators. The drone was now hovering lower to the ground, outside the bank. The Js were able to see the tellers and, concerningly, six customers. They realised that the longer the drone was in the air, the greater the chance of the whole operation failing.

John, with a devilish smile, looked at Jill and said, "I'll be back in a minute."

Jill replied, "Good idea."

John left the coffee shop and jumped in the line of a fast-travelling vehicle. The car swerved to avoid the pedestrian, and then crashed into a parked vehicle. The noise and commotion created a scene to attract stationary motorists and a substantial amount of interest from people close by, including those customers in the bank. All but one had raced outside to see the spectacle. John casually returned to the coffee shop.

"OK, dear?" Jillian asked.

"Yes, just a bit of congestion, but it should clear soon," John smirked.

As the bank's only customer finished his business, the glass sliding doors opened as he presented himself to the sensor. He walked out and headed toward the scene of the accident to join the other spectators. The Js guided the drone down and through the bank doors before they automatically closed again. They could see a young female teller with long brown hair, tied in a ponytail, via the camera on their communicators. Hearing a noise from the rotors, the teller looked up. The drone hovering directly in front of her, about two feet away, unrolled a note from its mechanical device.

The note read, 'My black capsule is filled with deadly nerve gas. Put twenty thousand credits in a bag and hang it from my hook, or I release the gas'.

The teller's face turned white. Her eyes widened and darted around the bank. She briefly turned to a colleague. The neighbouring teller did not know where to look. The drone dropped at gravity speed to about six inches from the ground, then slowly rose in front of the teller's face, positioning itself directly in front of her. It was obvious to them what would happen if they did not obey the note. The teller knew the emergency security screens would drop if she raised the alarm but was uncertain if the supposed nerve gas would be contained. She immediately followed the instructions, stuffing a bank bag with two bundles of money, each containing ten thousand credits. She then cautiously and nervously attached the bag to the hook on the drone. The drone flew toward the glass doors, but they did not open. It seemed that the drone was not large enough to trip the sensor. The 'getaway vehicle' hovered momentarily. As expected by the Js, a customer proceeded to enter the bank. The glass doors opened, and the drone flew out and straight up until it was barely noticeable. The bank's alarms sounded, and all access ceased. A complete lockdown of the establishment.

John and Jillian casually walked out of the coffee shop, appearing natural to others, with two communicators and two suitcases in their possession. They hailed a taxi and traversed to the airport, all the while guiding the drone high above their position. They arrived at the airport, retrieved their cases from the taxi and walked past the entrance. They found an out-of-the-way area with a couple of half-filled dumpsters in it. They summoned the drone. John and Jillian stared into each other's eyes as it made its final descent. Without breaking eye contact, Jillian presented her palm, the bag of money and the drone, landing safely in her awaiting hand. The couple discarded the money-filled bag into the dumpster, and then destroyed the drone, throwing it, too, in the garbage. They placed some of the existing rubbish over the top. The Js, then picked up their suitcases and strolled back to the airport entrance. They were grinning ear to ear. They did not care about the money. It was the thrill.

***

The married couple had landed their dream job, and after residing in the states for about six years, they once again reminisced about their time spent in Spain. They relived their wedding day and chatted about it for a short time. They then spoke of their ingenuity, technical brilliance and the excitement of their 'withdrawal', from the Spanish bank.

"I've assembled another drone, John. It's smaller yet more powerful than the Spanish collector."

"I knew you were up to something."

"What do you say?" asked Jillian, winking playfully.

"I say I've already found our mark."

"I knew you were up to something, too, John."

"We will have to travel again, but this bank is by far the best choice. Would you like to up the ante?"

"You know me so well."

John explained, "This time we send the drone in, but only to unlock the front door."

"We are going to walk right in?" Jillian asked.

"You know me so well," John answered. "This operation will require a bit more cyber-tech, but I have complete faith in you."

Came the day, and the pair had made their way to The Bronx. They booked a room for two days relatively close to their hit. They brought the new super drone and all the tech equipment. Late in the afternoon, the drone was tested. Once again, the camera attached to it presented a crystal-clear picture, received directly to their room television. The controls were bulkier than usual, but they only needed to operate it from their room. Once the drone had unlocked the door to the bank, it could stay there until the couple picked it up a short walking distance away. It was all set. Now they just had to wait until dusk. The couple, dressed in dark clothing, stayed in their room, anticipating the heist.

With the coming of night, John asked, "Ready, my thief?"

"You know I am," Jillian replied. "Do you smell smoke, John?"

"No, but further up the street is a place called *BBQ on a Stick.* Perhaps it's the wood-fired oven you can smell."

"You may be right, John. It sounds like if you take me there after the hit, technically, you have taken care of dinner."

"It's a date," John smiled.

They started the drone, Jillian on the controls. Out through the open window it flew, then straight up, the couple glued to the television.

"Most of these buildings look similar in this area, but I think it's this one, Jill," John said, pointing to an establishment on the screen. "You will have to descend so I can be absolutely sure."

Jillian, now lowering the drone noticed it was responding intermittently.

"We've got a hiccup, John," Jill calmly stated.

Jill negotiated the controls to hover, but it continued descending. The camera remained in focus, relaying the drone's movements. It descended closer and closer to ground height. Forty feet, thirty feet, twenty.

Without warning, the control function returned. Jill managed to regain control of the drone as it fell about another eight feet and hovered above a locked gate. The camera was facing a burning building. The Js, still watching intensely, could see a young girl running toward the drone. Jillian manipulated the controls in an upward direction. The drone did not move. They could see the girl beginning to scale the gate, and then suddenly, the drone fell to the ground. The camera was recording, even though it showed evidence of imperfections, but Jillian had no operational power over the drone at all. As they stared at the television screen, much to their surprise, they were looking at a close-up of the girl's face. They had witnessed the culprit who set fire to a factory, they surmised. They did not realise at the time, but they had an ID on the arsonist of Fire Night. Then the camera seemed to spin very quickly, seconds before the screen blacked out.

"Pork or beef?" John asked, with a hint of disappointment.

CHAPTER 7

ISOBEL

Isobel Murphy was raised in an orphanage on the outskirts of Dublin in Ireland by several sisters of the faith. She then found herself in Hawaii in 2102when she was about six years old.

In the year 2087, all religious acts were banned in the entirety of the world. The WRONG establishment in Sydney hosted 'The Great Debate' two years beforehand. All world leaders were present. There were also priests, rabbis, fathers, mothers, brothers, sisters, the Pope, archdeacons, holy men and others of significance to the religious cults.

"So, let me get this straight," the Australian who had attended the world summit. "You believe everything in that bible book?"

"My son, it is all true," a clergyman of the Catholic faith replied.

"So, this God fella made the earth, rivers, mountains, and the likes in six days?"

"That is what the good book says."

"Have you ever heard the term 'science'?"

"God made science, my son."

"Six days . . . and then he turned on the lights? He liked working in the dark? Wouldn't it make more sense to make the sun first? 'Let there be light'."

"God works in mysterious ways, my son."

"Is this your same God that watched the Egyptians enslave a race for four hundred years? What was he doing for so long that he deemed more important?"

"God can't be responsible for man's doings."

"He made us in his image, didn't he?" the Australian retorted.

"God is almighty, my son."

"You honestly believe people turned into salt pillars instantly? You believe his son walked on water? You believe he parted the sea? You believe a woman gave birth without having intercourse? You believe his son died and came back? Who did Adam and Eve's children have intercourse with to reproduce? And blessed be those who do not question the faith. That is to stop you from asking yourself these logical questions. There are a thousand more ridiculous, unbelievable statements in that fantasy book. Did you know there were more apostles' writings? We, humans, edited it. And look at you in your polyester gown. You are not supposed to wear mixed threads. What about the large number of priests that use young boys for their pleasure? You preach, but you do not follow."

"You have lost your faith, my son," the clergyman said, frustrated.

"Oh . . . fuck off," the Australian ambassador exclaimed.

He turned toward the exit.

"Where are you going, my son?" a father enquired.

"Fishing," said the Australian, with a confident walk.

The Great Debate continued without the Australian.

"Infidel," the Imam cursed. "Blasphemes heathen."

"Heretic. He's the son of the Iblis," another Muslim leader joined.

"Oh please," the Frenchman opposed. "Have you actually read your Quran?"

"Muhammad is the one and only prophet," the fanatic returned.

"Chop off their fingers. Chop off their heads. Humiliate them. This is what you preach from your life book."

"Muhammad will take me to heaven and give me seventy-two virgins."

The Frenchman laughed, "Le idiot. And you believe this Muhammad, flew to the moon and cut it in half with a big sword," the Frenchman laughed again. "You allow your faith to kill. Bombings in cities, suicide bombers, you bombed our newspaper office, records show, because you did not like a cartoon. You savages!"

And one by one, all the religions of our world were dismissed. There was not one single shred of evidence. Nothing concrete from any corner of the world. The world council declared the total abolishment of all religious sectors. Any person or group caught still practicing these insane forms of brainwashing, shall be subject to prosecution. All assets and funds associated with churches were seized, including some luxury mansions owned by religious leaders. The funds were distributed throughout the world, and for a number of years, the less fortunate were looked after properly. Children were no longer hungry or in need of expensive medicines or operations anywhere in the world. Proper care was given to the elderly. The homeless had a roof over their heads (some were fortunate enough to live in a mansion), clean drinking water and warmth—all provided by the 'caring church's' view of material objects. But as time passed, the corrupt and greedy raised their ugly heads, and soon a large percentage of the world's wealth was held by those who did not deserve it, again.

***

The sisters at the orphanage continued their holy vows. It was not long until the authorities apprehended all the defying nuns, except for one, 'Sally', (she flew away in search of a greener 'field'). All the children were dispersed to other orphanages except Isobel. Isobel had met an older woman from Hawaii. Patricia had taken a fancy to her, and she was currently in the process of adopting. The authorities agreed to the proposed arrangement, and the pair flew back to Patricia's home beside the ocean. Pat loved the sea and, in particular, the marine life. Isobel discovered the same love for aquatic wonders. The new mother and daughter were often diving, snorkelling, or simply wading in the shallows. With Patricia's undeniable love, Isobel grew into a kind, caring, generous and lovely person. She volunteered to help the community four nights a week, worked at the local orphanage part-time, and if she had any spare time, she would visit the hospitalised children. Isobel, all the while studying, soon became a marine biologist, and the time spent in the sun gave her a characteristic sun bleaching to her long brown hair. Patricia was terminally ill and drugged out of her senses most of the time and was a lot older by the time Isobel earnt her degree, requiring assistance with her day-to-day living. Isobel was a shining light and had made quite a name for herself in her profession. Most of her pay would go to the less fortunate. The aura around her was so calming and pleasant. Not a bad word did she utter.

There was a knock on her door. There stood a distinctive uniform, filled with a distinguished man, that had something on his lip. The future was explained, but Isobel was concerned about Patricia.

"Ma'am, I will organize a carer immediately," Colonel Harper told Isobel.

The colonel called his contacts.

"It is taken care of, ma'am", the colonel reported. "Secrecy is a must when you say your goodbyes, Miss Murphy."

"I understand, Colonel."

'I will wait out front for you to pack," the Colonel stated.

CHAPTER 8

CAM

Cam was neither male nor female. He/ she/ it was an other. It could don a suit and appear as a handsome man or dress in a skirt and assume a woman's personality. It was a master of disguise.

Conclusion draws closer.

CHAPTER 9

MEET & GREET

Isobel was the last to be escorted into the compound. Security was tight. Guards patrolling the gates and perimeter carried rifles, but some sported heavier equipment. Tanks and trucks were mounted with artillery, scattered in divisions, throughout the confines of the lengthy electric fence. This was a serious show of weaponry.

The convoy of black SUVs came to a halt.

"I'll take you in and introduce you to the rest of the team," Colonel Harper informed Isobel.

"Are you expecting a war, Colonel?" she asked, noting the firepower.

"Indeed, I am, Miss Murphy. This way, ma'am."

Colonel Harper marched toward the entrance. Upon his approach, two guards opened the door with Isobel in tow. A short walk down the corridor and the colonel opened a door and invited Isobel to enter.

"Sergeant, assemble the rest of the team," he ordered.

"Sir, yes, sir."

At this point, the team had not been introduced to each other, and none of them knew the identity of the other.

The sergeant marched further down the corridor. He gathered a small detail and retrieved the new guests of the compound.

Michael, Jason, Kirsten, Shanara, Jillian, John and Isobel. The fate of humankind lay heavy on the shoulders of these seven people.

As they were getting comfortable in the conference room, Colonel Harper introduced the elite, one at a time. He sees seven young, drastically different people, (except for the Similburgs). Each has their own skill, vital for the mission's success.

"Professor Michael Watson, mathematician." – bottle bottom glasses, messy house.

"Doctor Kirsten Van Halen, medic." – drug addict.

"Isobel Murphy, marine biologist." – long sun-bleached brown hair, caring person.

"Shanara Harding, scientist." – tom-boy, black hair, fire bug.

"Jason Childs. 'The Doctor', mechanical engineer." – paedophile.

"John and Jillian Similburg, the Js, pilot and co-pilot, tech whizzes." – bank robbers, married, blonde hair, blue eyes.

The crew shook hands with one another and, by all accounts, seemed to be a pleasant greeting. The Js persisted in glancing intermittently at Shanara, more so than the other members. She seemed familiar to them, but they could not recollect where they had seen her. Kirsten, too, paid attention to one. Michael.

"Is there something wrong?" Shanara asked the Js.

"No. Excuse us. Have we met before?" puzzled Jillian.

"I don't think so. I would remember you two. You have an uncanny resemblance to each other," Shanara replied.

The pilot pair diverted their eyes to the others and the ground or anywhere but straight at Shanara. They also glanced at the colonel to note any suspicion cast at them. The colonel appeared indifferent, or his attention lay with others and was oblivious to the comments.

"Your attention, please," the team silencing as the colonel began. "You are known to my men as 'Crew Seven'. It is our responsibility to train you for the forthcoming events. You will be trained in all aspects of space travel and surviving your new planet. It is also our duty to ensure your safety in the remaining time you have here on Earth."

"Our safety?" Kirsten questioned. "During our training?"

"Did you see the artillery outside, Doctor?" Jason pointed in the direction of the front gate.

"Colonel, what is going on? There is an impressive display of firepower out there. Are we at war?" Isobel asked, tying back her sun-bleached hair.

"People have no illusions about this. When word gets out, and it will get out, there will be rioting in the streets. Rapes, murders, drinking your own vomit with a straw, nothing is out of bounds. We, in the intelligence and armed forces, are prepared for a civilian attack on this compound. Here lies the only means of escaping certain death. What wouldn't you do in their situation?"

Isobel could not believe what she had just heard. Her puppy dog brown eyes looked down briefly, then made direct contact with the colonel.

"You would gun them down?" Isobel reluctantly asked.

"If the situation develops into a compromising position, we must prioritise," the colonel formally stated. "We are going to cram years of astronaut training into two weeks. You will be trained separately for some of the course as time is still precious. Each of you will learn a different aspect of your mission. You will be relying on each other to survive."

The crew looked at each other, realising the importance of one another.

"Doctor, I request you to perform a full medical check on all your crew. Blood tests, DNA, physicals, mentals, the works, yourself included."

Some hearts were beating faster than others, with the mention of a medical analysis.

Jill's face drained of colour.

"Pilots Similburg."

"Yes, sir," the Js responded.

"As the pair of you are already trained in this field, you will assist the others and start familiarising yourselves with the latest technology onboard our super-shuttle."

"Sir, yes, sir."

"Shanara, Doctor Van Halen, and Isobel, it is also your duty to prepare the population pods and samples from The Program," Colonel Harper added.

The colonel continued. "Crew, the United States of America and humankind are counting on your success. We, the U.S. Military, will do everything in our power to ensure that outcome."

The seven were orientated around the compound and living quarters.

After familiarising themselves with their surroundings, they had a meal and retired to the common room, except Michael. After dinner, he bid goodnight and returned to his room. It was only a matter of minutes and Jason, carrying a doggy bag, retired as well.

As light conversations passed, John and Jillian were still focusing on Shanara, unbeknownst to her. Night had set and the remaining crew called it time. They returned to their rooms and tried to be at peace with everything they had learnt that day. Shanara was not at ease with the Js added attention, and Kirsten thought Michael seemed familiar. They had not spoken much as Michael was quiet and clung to the background most of the time.

***

Jason was the last out of his room in the morning. The seven were assigned their training tasks and proceeded to break up into their assignment training areas. An elevated walkway surrounded the areas. From here, the colonel had access to view all progress of the trainees.

"Sir, Colonel Harper, sir," a soldier requested. "There is a call for you, sir. It is Special Agent Chapman, sir."

"I will take it in my office, Sergeant," the colonel replied.

"Sounds official, Chappy. What's up?" Colonel Harper enquired.

"Hi, Harp. I know you are busy, but I have two dead bodies. It looks like the guy left in a hurry. He is on the run. I'll send over a photo ID and all the information."

"I'll keep an eye out, Chappy."

"Appreciate it, Harp."

The day's training continued. Kirsten had the first of her patients, and the doctor began the examination.

"Have we met somewhere before, Michael?"

"You don't even recognise me, do you?" Michael said with a serious look on his face.

"I'm sorry, no."

"I was one of your boyfriend's kick-around toys," Michael admitted.

It then dawned on Kirsten.

"You were that young kid in my maths class for about three weeks. You did the entire year's assignments in three weeks. Now I think about it; I'm not surprised to see you here."

"Elton deserved it," Michael blurted out, with a coldness in his eyes.

Kirsten's composure vanished immediately.

"He resembled an upside-down turtle, sinking to the bottom," Michael added.

"What do you mean?" Kirsten reluctantly asked.

"When he was in the pool."

Kirsten assumed he was talking about the time Elton fell into the pool with her. She remembered Michael's younger face as the small boy Elton bullied that day.

"Being so high on crash, he probably didn't even know he was drowning," Michael casually added.

Kirsten's heart sank. She knew Elton had never crashed at school. *He had it on him all the time, maybe to big-note himself,* she thought. His addiction was never officially released, but he was high when he drowned. Kirsten remembered him saying, "I've just had three . . ."

He must be referring to his drowning, the doctor thought.

"How do you know he was high, Mike?" Kirsten prompted.

"I took care of him for you. That one was no good for you. After you and your father left Elton's house that day, I traversed into his front yard due to the minus of a lock. I circumnavigated my way around to the backyard. Elton was lying perpendicular to the pool with his feet dangling in the water, plus crashing hard. I then divided the good from the bad. I pushed him in for you. I stood adjacent to the pool, just watching. Bubbles exiting his big mouth multiplied at first, then they zeroed out," Michael, in true math style, so coldly divulged.

Kirsten stares at him, jaw open, not believing what she is hearing.

"You murderer," Kirsten yelled, seeing no remorse from the killer.

Michael could not understand that Kirsten did not appreciate his efforts.

"My father...," she sobbed.

As she sat, bent over with her hands covering her face, her hair had divided to reveal the years of crash abuse on the good doctor's neck.

"Your eyes were the apex of my attention. You had such beautiful eyes. I would have done anything to be in their sight forever," he sweetly remarked.

"Now. Now they are pale. Your whites are no longer, your hair is a mess, you look like a sixty-year-old junkie," Michael characteristically added.

Kirsten knew Michael would keep their secrets. Although Michael seemed somewhat (the only way to put it) out there, he was fully aware of his situation. He was certainly not stupid or helpless.

"Bend over now, Michael," the doctor said, the snap of a surgical glove the only sound in the room.

***

The pilots were busy in the cockpit of the super shuttle. There were more switches than a light gallery and more flashing lights than one may find . . . possibly . . . in the same light gallery. The games room at the rear of the shuttle boasted a pool table and indoor heated pool.

They both stopped their tasks and looked at each other.

"It's her," they said in unison..

"What do we do?" Jillian concerningly asked.

"Maybe just keep that thought alight for now, Jill," suggested John.

***

The days passed, and the crew became more familiar with each other. Shanara had noticed Jason spending a lot of time in his room. Being the inquisitive type, she picked out a bottle of wine from the kitchen's supply, two glasses and knocked on Jason's door. Shanara could hear a shuffle, and then Jason answered, slightly cracking the door.

"Drinks, Doctor?" Shanara hinted.

"Ah . . . well . . . I'm sort of busy right now," he replied.

"Busy with what? We are surrounded by four walls," she laughed.

"Oh, you know . . . just . . . stuff," he flustered.

"Come on," insisted Shanara. "Just the one," forcing the door open with one shoulder against Jason's resisting stance.

Jason wore only a pair of boxer shorts, and Shanara could tell he was aroused. She glanced at Jason's bed and noticed a pair of small feet protruding from the covers. Jason quickly grabbed her by the arm and forcefully swung her away from the door. He turned, shut and locked the door. He slowly turned again to face Shanara.

"Oh, you . . . sick prick," she cursed, moving further away from him. "Is she alive?" Shanara asked.

"He is very much alive," Jason corrected.

Shanara was sickened. She reached forward to reveal the victim, grasping the bed covers. Jason lunged forward, securing the covers around his prey.

"I told you he is OK," Jason insisted. "I'm not a necro. I'm not crazy."

"I must inform Colonel Harper," Shanara stated as she gestured for the door.

The 'uncrazy', positioned himself with his back against the locked door.

"And then what do you think will happen? You need me. We need each other. I am going to be on that shuttle. We all die if the colonel locks me up."

The doctor stepped aside from the door and sat on the bed's corner, next to the covered, unmoving body. He knew he had the upper hand. Her silence was a given.

"Now, about those drinks," he said, patting the bed.

"You pathetic excuse for a human being. You are a sick fuck," Shanara said.

She unlocked the door and marched out.

***

More days had passed. The time was nearing. Training was underway when the colonel received a call from the front gate.

"Colonel, you best come down here," the sergeant informed.

"What is it, Sergeant?" the colonel asked.

"Sir, a large gentleman in a limousine says he knows about the mission."

'Very good, Sergeant, escort him through to the conference room," Colonel Harper immediately replied.

The colonel sat in wait, lips pursed, staring at a single spot on the ground. He raised his eyes to witness a large man with a deep demanding voice, a large woman with short red hair that accentuates her chubby face, and two large children dressed in identical clothes and bowl haircuts, waddle into the room. They each carried two briefcases.

"How did you find out about the mission, sir?" Colonel Harper demanded.

"Well, I was not sure until just now," the man said. "I'm Theodore . . ."

"Sir, if you don't tell me how you come to be here, I'll have you and your family thrown into confinement," the colonel interrupted, with that peculiar top lip rising up, as he pointed his lips.

"I'm trying to tell you, Colonel," the man replied. "I'm Theodore Edmund Ridgeway."

There was a brief silence.

"And?" the colonel prompted.

"Well, don't you know me? I'm the richest man in America."

Another brief silence.

"And?" the colonel said, now yawning.

Theodore signalled to his family. They all placed their cases on the tables, opening them to exhibit the goods. They were full of diamonds, cash and gold.

"This is all yours, and there's more where that came from if you put my family and me on that rocket," the man offered.

"Sergeant, escort Mr. Ridgeway and family to the cells," the colonel ordered.

'OK, wait, wait. I will tell you," the obese man submitted. "When you are as rich as me, you can afford an exceptionally powerful telescope. In fact, you can afford an entire observation station. I bought my son one for his birthday."

"A telescope?" The colonel quizzed.

"An observation station. We noticed what appears to be an extremely large planet heading for Earth. I was not sure of anything else until just now. What do you say,

Colonel? Do we have a deal?" Theodore open-palmed to the exposed suitcases.

"Sergeant, place these people under house arrest. Give them the freedom to use the facilities but guard them and no communication with the outside world," Colonel Harper ordered.

"Colonel, you can't do this," Theodore protested. "Then, how about just let me board?"

His family showed disappointment, which seemed to reflect a common occurrence.

"Theodore Edmund Ridgeway," Colonel Harper began, "America's richest man. Got his start by running crash from Korea, then moved on to swindling properties from the terminally ill, then invested in a toxic sub-station that mysteriously lost all of its 700 sea containers of toxic waste, thus avoiding billions in clean-up fees. You have spent your life conniving, swindling, scheming and becoming disgustingly rich and fat. What good is your life's work now? What good is money now?"

The colonel marched out.

"So, he does know me then," Theodore said to his wife, who was looking around for something sharp.

***

Isobel was the next patient for the doctor. Doctor Van Halen asked Isobel to disrobe. She noticed her breasts were rather small.

"Is there something wrong, doctor?"

"Nothing alarming. Have you been taking any hormone tablets?" the doctor enquired.

"Oh yes, actually, I have an overactive gland," Isobel confessed.

"No problem, the tablets will show in the blood tests," the doctor stated. "I seem to be having some false readings with your DNA . . . strange. I'll send the samples off for a better result. Other than that, you are in fine health. Must be all that time in the ocean."

The doctor noted her, surprisingly pale skin.

More time passes. Conclusion: a bit closer. Launch day: a bit closer.

***

Training continued and in mid-afternoon, the colonel was informed of a delivery.

"Colonel Harper, sir," said the sergeant. "I have a package addressed to 'The Doctor.'"

The package had passed through security, deemed safe as it posed no biological, cyber, or explosive threat.

"Probably medical supplies. Open it carefully, Sergeant."

"Sir, it appears to contain racks of capsules."

"Thank you, Sergeant, leave it outside the doctor's room," Colonel Harper ordered.

By now, another training day had passed. Jason was first back to his room. Lying in wait was a box-like parcel outside his door. 'The Doctor' was addressed on the package. Accepting the package, he entered his room. He fondled his little boy. Shot some more heroin into the child sex slave, then sat back and contemplated how to keep his desires fulfilled. He then remembered the unexpected delivery. He opened the pre-opened lid. He immediately knew what it was. These were capsule racks of the drug crash.

These were meant for Doctor Van Halen, he thought. *I will be back in a moment, my poor prey,* his thoughts directed to his victim.

He knocked on Kirsten's door. And again. The doctor finally answered, but obviously to Jason, her eyes were bloodshot, and her irises appeared pale.

"I think this is yours," Jason said, handing Kirsten the box. "You look like shit."

"It's been a rough day," Kirsten replied.

"What are those capsules for?" Jason enquired.

"They are samples from The Program," Kirsten lied.

"Bullshit! I know crash when I see it."

"Please don't tell the colonel."

"Don't sweat it, Doc. I want to live as much as anyone."

The Doctor returned to his sex dungeon. The doctor returned to her crash.

***

The next morning it was the pilots' turn to take the medical. John and Jillian reluctantly gave samples of their DNA. The doctor performed a procedure while the pair waited. Kirsten examined her findings. She made a double take at the results.

"Want to tell me about it, Js?" the doctor said, staring at the pair, waving a printout in their direction.

"About what, Doctor?" Jillian asked.

John, sitting beside his wife, placed his hand on hers and shook his head slightly in a negative motion. John knew they would have to tell of their origins.

Changing their names, upon arrival to America in the 20th century, they were born Gunther and Esther Heidenburg in Dusseldorf, Germany, but not in the usual way. With the end of the second world war, all experiments on humans ceased (officially). However, a few scientists remained who were fanatical about their work. They continued in secrecy, concentrating on their fascination with altered gene babies. The cruel, yet advancing procedures, gave new light to producing the 'Master Race'. With the inevitable third world war approaching, efforts to succeed were encouraged, and indeed, demanded by the new German Fuhrer. It was widely speculated that the German leader was himself the product of these trials. It was rumoured the leader was biologically a descendant of Adolf Hitler. The warmonger is now an almost forgotten, psychotic, paranoid schizophrenic, totalitarian leader of Germany. His desired to introduce his master race and rule the world.

Failure was part of the learning process. There were horrific outcomes. Synthetic life babies were deformed in the most grotesque ways imaginable. However, it is recorded in history that without the mad German scientists, our medicines would not be nearly advanced, and there would be no designer babies today.

"We are a special experiment," John confessed. "After doctors conquered the life-giving process, they naturally continued to the challenge of twins, triplets and so on. Jillian and I are one pair of those twins. Our genes have been altered to increase our brain cell function. One of the side effects is actually an asset. Jillian and I sometimes share the exact same thought patterns. It's like a link to the mind."

"Actually . . . I was talking about Jillian's pregnancy," the somewhat stunned doctor replied. "You are twins, essentially? Brother and sister? You are married and pregnant?"

John looked up to the ceiling closed his eyes, drew a deep breath wishing he could take back everything that he just said, exhaled and opened his eyes again.

"It was just a natural phenomenon," Jill defended. "We are connected in so many ways."

"Please don't tell Colonel Harper," John pleaded.

"Which part?" the doctor jested, placing her palm on her forehead.

"Oh, please, can't you simply fix the results," Jillian begged.

"If we do not board the shuttle, we all die here," John put it bluntly.

The doctor sighed.

"I understand what you are saying. I suppose . . . I could . . . keep the results from the colonel, in the interest of humankind," said Kirsten, justifying her actions.

The couple exhibited a great sense of relief and then returned to their pre-checks.

The good doctor shot herself with crash, ticked all the boxes, and signed herself off as fit.

***

Isobel returned to the medic's examination room.

"Sit down, Isobel," the doctor instructed. "Do you want to tell me about it?" she asked, face-to-face.

Isobel knew it was time to reveal her secret. But what secret could this well-mannered, caring, kind, gentle, volunteer working ray of sunshine, with an aura of contentment, possibly be hiding?

"I'm an identity thief and an 'other,' it confessed.

"I had been following the movements of one, Miss Patricia Wyallu, [Y.-al-lu], in Hawaii. She owns a large estate and cash and a life insurance policy to die for. She would surely leave everything to 'Miss Goody Two Shoes,'" it continued.

The doctor sat, glued to this story, eyes wide.

"Isobel was so predictable. She got wind of a miracle cure for Patricia's ailment. Straight on to a plane, and she would have now been climbing a mountain, somewhere in the Himalayan Mountains, looking for a well-hidden opening to a cave, which contains a flower blessed by monks. Ha, I can't believe she swallowed that."

The doctor's jaw lay open at this point.

"How do I know? I am the one that called her. As timing has it, there was a huge landslide near one of the villages she was known to be in. She was only stopping there briefly, it is understood, to help a child walk again. Can you believe it? What a patsy! What a sucker!" Isobel's voice sounded a bit deeper.

The doctor was now hardly blinking at all. Jaw still open.

"Well, then, it was easy. I posed as Patricia's nurse. Izzy had called a nursing company and expected the nurse. I told you she was predictable. I met the nurse out front of the sick dear's house. I told her she was too late; the old biddy had died. It was a close call the day Harper picked me up. The 'Good Fairy' just left me alone, leaving me to assume her identity, and take advantage of the fully drugged-out rich bitch," it carried on. "And here we are; you know the rest."

Doctor Van Halen, jaw still open, eyebrows raised, her eyes redder in colour than usual (from not blinking), snapped out of it and stated, "I was talking about your blood test. You have a low sugar count."

It sat there, jaw open, eyebrows raised, not blinking.

"So, you are an 'Other,'" Kirsten confirmed.

It snapped out of it, replying, "Yes, I am a product from 'The Program'. "My parents couldn't decide what sex they wanted for their child and so left the box blank. Well, clerical errors and . . ."

"I see," said the doctor. "Well, you are not alone. I understand The Program has its share of problems. It is estimated that one in every ten human beings is an other. Although, I have never had the privilege of examining one. The Program has its own specified doctors, which you would be aware of. Mind you, I have noticed at shopping centres, hotels, laser theatres, in fact, in any public place, there are male, female and other toilet cubicles."

***

Over a century ago, yet another world summit was called at the WRONG premises.

"Please stop referring to them as homosexuals," the Mongolian leader requested.

"But they are, aren't they?" the Australian ambassador answered with a question.

"Yes, but we need to change our attitudes. We must adapt with the times," the Chinese recommended.

"So, you are suggesting we call homosexuals...what?" prompted the Australian."

"I have a suggestion," the Swiss representative offered. "We need to be politically correct. We don't wish to offend. I am suggesting 'The sexually challenged'."

"Oh, that has a lovely ring to it," the English agreed. "It's rather...effervescent."

"Och! Ubsolutely gdate," the Scott declared.

"Oh, it's just ducky," the Welshman said.

With the blink and wink of an eye, the mallet descended to connect with a flat piece of wood, making everything official. The chairman took control of the meeting.

"From this day forth, homo . . . um . . . ah . . . those previously known as something else will be referred to in politically correct terms. The Sexually Challenged is an acceptable upgrade."

"Which brings us to item number two, on today's gender . . . excuse me . . . agenda."

"Should . . . a sexually challenged . . . person . . . and another be able to enter into the sacred bonds of marriage?"

"Are you fuckin' kiddin' me?" the Australian enquired.

Silence in the court.

"Where does it end? So, let me get this straight. You want me to call him (glaring at the English) them . . . a ducky name, and condone a relationship that requires both of the same gender. What about if I get the hots for . . . for instance, a block of cheese?"

A few countries giggled; the Dutch were loudest.

"Well, you are going to permit physical and psychological relationships between two parties. These two parties are not of the opposite sex. I want to marry, not of the opposite sex. I will take out a life insurance policy on a nice-lookin' vintage block, hmmm, Swiss, I think, wait for my sexually challenged partner to grow old, bury. . . it . . . next to the Anti-Alcohol Faction's (AAF) burial ground, hold a funeral, and claim the insurance."

The American, Italian and a few others chuckled to themselves.

"Heat is best to be rid of the body," the Italian, offering his experience.

"I say just females should be allowed to have same sex sex," a perverted little sub-continent representative said.

It's fair to say, all the males in the room were down with that.

"Oh, you sexist," the Balinese attacked.

All the males reconsidered, had a change of heart and agreed with the Lady from Bali. Some say the fire from her nostrils took the focus from her scaly snake-like skin.

"Next, they will want a right to display public affection for each other," the Australian rhetorically suggested.

It's fair to say all the males in the room were totally down with that, too, as they fantasized about female orgies in the street. That is, of course, until the evil ice dragon, drama queen bitch from hell, politely offered a glare of a possible endless living nightmare beyond any pain and suffering imaginable.

The Balinese woman whispered, "Don't forget the man-on-man picture in your head."

There were a few gags, coughs and ah hums as the yearning, daydreaming leaders of men were bought back to reality. There were a couple of female leaders still daydreaming.

"You aren't kidding . . . Oh . . . fuck off!" the Australian said, offering directions.

With that, he turned and walked confidently toward the exit once again.

"Where are you going? What about the importance of our vote?" the sexually challenged from Sao Paulo enquired.

"Seems to me all this homosexual talk is nothing more than a pain in the ass. Goin' fishin.'"

And so, laws were made.

The very next day an emergency summit was called, again at WRONG's headquarters in the desirable city of Sydney, NSW, Australia.

"The Australian has excused himself from this meeting. Once again, politely offering directions," the chairperson started. "A decision must be made as to what we call those with no sexual organs. 'Cockless freaky fucker' is out, apparently, as is 'little itty-bitty titties.'"

Named by the sexually challenged, the cockless freaky fuckers did not want to be confused with the sexually challenged. It was agreed then that they bear the referral name 'Other' or 'it'. And a mallet hit a piece of wood and laws were made.

***

"Those politically correct cubicles are not going to be there much longer," it stated. "What do you say, Doc? Best keep my secret, a secret?"

Kirsten knew what she had to say.

***

It walked out and returned to its duties, still posing as Isobel. It passed Colonel Harper's office on its way. It noted a small stack of papers on the ground, which had been shot out of the office printer, and it could see a photo ID on top of the pile. It recognized the picture. 'Twas Michael. It retrieved all the paperwork associated with him and hid them in its blouse. It made its way back to the comfort of its room.

It had just finished examining the paperwork from the colonel's office. There was a knock at the door . . .

"Hey Isobel, I knocked earlier, but you were not here. What have you been up to?" Shanara asked.

"Oh, just seeing to some paperwork," he, sorry she, sorry it, Cam, slyly suggested.

"We are having drinks in the common room. The colonel has an announcement," Shanara informed it.

Conclusion is nearer.

CHAPTER 10

THE ANNOUNCEMENT

Crew Seven gathered in the common room, along with mixed feelings. Spirits were high from their accomplishments. Kirsten, of course, was higher than anybody else. Colonel Harper stood in the room to face the seven in a semi-circle, centre of attention position. The crew were seated and relaxed.

"Crew Seven, your training is complete. You launch in T minus forty-eight hours," the colonel informed human's hope. "You have twenty-four hours grace. The last day to enjoy our planet. Enjoy your night; the bar is open."

The colonel left the space travellers to entertain themselves.

In this year, 2125, alcohol is still promoted and consumed in large quantities by a generous portion of the world. In the years before, an organisation who called themselves The AAF tried to stop this crippling society drug. They originated in Ireland but were quickly run out of their own country. Next, they travelled down under, all the way to Australia, looking to set up a base camp for their plight. They were quickly run out of there too. (Some say the Aussies were pissed, while running the AAF out of the country). They bounced from country to country, finally setting up shop on the shores of the Arctic. The AAF would fight for fifty years.

To give credit where it is due, the AAF held a sensible argument and for an extremely brief moment, a famous politician was subconsciously almost contemplating giving consideration of thought to what they were saying.

They spoke of the excessive numbers of Alcoholic Anonymous meeting places. (One can conclude there are an excessive number of alcoholics). They drove the point of the number of alcohol-related road deaths. They touched on the alcohol-related child abuse cases and fired up at the mention of alcohol-fueled wife bashings. The hospitalised, the alcohol-responsible cancer patients, the effects it has on the liver, kidneys and almost every other vital organ needed for existence. They fought a long, good, worthy fight, but alas, they were extremely outnumbered. The dream of the world adopting the same attitude as religion was lost, buried somewhere under the Vodka bottles with the members of the AAF that drank themselves to death in protest.

The joyous occasion had been underway for a few hours. Everyone was getting on fine. Conversation was light and happy. A pleasurable time was being enjoyed by all. Empty beer glasses and bottles of spirits started to mount on the tables.

"It is your buy," Michael rounding up Jason.

"Sure, kid," Jason obliged and waited at the bar for more beers.

Shanara spoke quietly to the remaining crew, alight with information, "The Doctor is a paedophile."

'I am not a bloody paedophile," Kirsten dribbled out loud, crashed and tipsy.

"Shhh . . ." Shanara smouldered. "No, Jason is a paedophile. He has a young boy enslaved in his room."

"Fark!" exclaimed Michael, with a number under his belt.

Everyone was disgusted at the mental picture. Jason returned with a couple of beers in his hand.

"Oh, thank you, my friend," the soon to be pi eyed Michael said.

Everyone smiled at Jason.

"I have to go to the powder room," Isobel fluffed.

She left with a dance in her stride.

"She/he/it is an other," Kirsten declared. "And an imposhter," she slurred.

"Who? Isobel?" asked the pilots, in unison.

"Yes," the doctor confirmed.

"Fark!" Michael exclaimed again, putting two and two together.

This news unsettled the crew.

"I'm going to the bar for more drinks," Shanara said, ablaze with excitement.

A few moments passed, and the other returned.

"Shanara was the arsonist of Fire Night," the Js, quietly threw out to the conversation, revealing their newly discovered secret. "Remember the great fire of 2116?"

"Fark!" Michael exclaimed once again, adding it all up.

The crew were concerned about this news. The pilots told the crew they would be back in a moment. Jillian was giggling, and John had his hands all over her. Shanara returned with the promised beverages.

The drugged and drunk doctor gossiped, "Those two are brother and sister. And she is pregnant."

Michael again, "Fark!" calculating the factors.

Everyone was sickened by (the above, excuse me) . . . the incest arrangement.

"Can I get you a drink?" John asked, returning with a smile on his face and his sister/wife still dressing behind him.

"Yes, please, my good friend," Doctor Van Halen answered.

Just then, the doctor appeared pale and sweaty. She suddenly arose, holding her stomach and ran for the politically correct toilets.

"The doctors' a junky," Isobel slurred in a deep voice.

"I am not," Jason insisted.

"No, I mean Doctor Van Halen."

"I knew that," Michael announced, adjusting his glasses.

The doctor returned, wiping vomit from the side of her face, with her T-shirt.

"Michaels buy," the pilots agreed.

"Yea, all right," Michael said, managing to communicate socially.

As Michael strolled to the bar, it stood up, moved closer and leant forward to the crew, who were seated around a table.

"I'm terribly sorry to inform everybody, but I feel it is my duty. It seems Michael is a serial killer," It said, continuing to masquerade. "He ended his parents' lives and left them in his room."

"Fark!" everybody but it said in unison.

"She killed my boyfriend, shoo," the doctor slurred.

"Fark!" everyone exclaimed, less the doctor, who was having difficulty talking at all.

"Here is your drink, Isobel," Michael handing a drink to it.

"Oh, thank you very much, fine man," it said appreciatively.

So, there they were. The absolute best humans our world could produce. The best in their fields. A mathematician, a doctor, a scientist, a marine biologist, two mentally advanced pilots and tech experts and a mechanical engineer. All with their dark secrets.

"Get us a fuckin' drink, mate," the marine biologist slurred as light intellectual conversation continued and a friendly little drink veered toward the so common, so predictable.

"Fuck off! Get your own!" the good doctor retorted.

"Oh, mate, I love you," the mathematician declared to an empty chair.

"And I really blame my mum . . ." the mechanical engineer cried, wiping his eyes.

"And don't think we are all oblivious of your little fetish," the pilots shouted, with a German accent, to possibly, the ceiling. Some say the comment was intended for their maker.

It seemed to be that the more alcohol they drank, the more aggressive, unaware, disorientated, unbalanced, loud, speech impeded, odour offensive and mentally unstable they became. Who would have thought? One cannot help but think of the plight of the deceased AAF.

America's last hope had consumed an excessive amount of alcohol and was still consuming when temperatures started to flare, and rage was prevalent in all seven. Push and shove succumbed to physical attacks, and pieces were broken from the furniture to act as weapons. Just at this point, Colonel Harper's men burst into the room and subdued the situation. Somewhere around this time, it was nearly agreed that almost, perhaps they had, maybe, probably, could have, had enough to drink, possibly for one night.

Crew Seven dispersed, staggering, swaying, vomiting and muttering back to their rooms.

***

Sunshine was in abundance the next morning. The birds chatted in the trees, the fresh smell of a brand-new day filled the air, and there was that bodily feeling of goosebumps. It was great to be alive today, here on Earth.

Kirsten woke in a pool of vomit. She opened her room door, lurched in the corridor, shot herself with crash and returned to bed. The rest of the team slowly arose, one by one, meeting in the compound's diner. The diner for some architectural acoustic reason had a rather bad echo. After some time, Kirsten staggered to the eating area, still in the night-before-clothes. She passed the common room, noticing broken furniture, smashed bottles and glass, vomit, blood and a half-smoked reefer sitting on a still-standing table. She grabbed the joint and continued to sway her way.

"What happened last night?" Kirsten quietly asked the gathered members.

"Shhhhh . . . not so loud, Doc," Jason with longer face stubble said.

"I don't remember anything," Shanara stated, holding her head.

"It's just one blur," Michael replied, staring at a wall.

"How did you get that black eye, Shanara?" the pilots asked.

"I don't know," was her answer.

The good doctor hid her right knuckle under her top.

"Are you sure there is no paracetamol left in this compound, Doctor?" Isobel politely asked.

"Yeah, my head is killing me, too," Jason complained.

"Ours, too," the pilots added, almost in unison. "And the echo in this room is almost unbearable."

Colonel Harper burst into the room with a detail of fourteen men, women and possibly others. The crew instantly groaned together.

The colonel began to announce, "Ladies . . ."

Everyone interrupted, "SHHHH…".

The colonel continued, louder still, "Ladies and gentlemen, we are under attack. You will remain in this room, where your safety will not be compromised," his voice echoed, and some of the seven stuck their fingers in their ears.

"Guard them with your lives," the colonel ordered as he and that unsightly growth on his top lip, gallantly marched into battle.

***

Theodore Edmund Ridgeway is just another greedy, selfish, all too common in this year, capitalising at any expense, ashamed to say, human being. He and his type care not for anyone else or their environment. But to make matters worse, this particular greedy pig does not like anyone else to succeed.

Theodore, as a young man, already bordering on obese, began running crash from Korea. His attitude dictated the atrocities he inflicted on his fellow man. Theodore's 'Life Teacher' was a kindhearted gentleman and taught Theo how to survive in this unforgiving world. 'Gully' was also going blind. He had recently returned from a hiking expedition in the Himalayas. He had found a rare flower that grows in caves, but unfortunately, he inhaled some of its pollen when picking it, and the effects started almost immediately. His condition soon turned into a highly contagious disease. And, of course, the yet-to-be filthy rich was immune to it. And, of course, worse than that, Theo was also a carrier.

Gully owned several private planes and did very well for himself. Theo would be an aviator, taught by Gully. Planes were Gully's life. He especially liked sky writing in the biplanes. His favourite biplane, he nicknamed *Ben O' Fitz*', after his wartime friend Benjamin Orlando Fitzsimmons. He promised Theo it would be his one day. Time passed and Gully's vision deteriorated. He could no longer enjoy the passion in his life. *Never again could he take control of an aeroplane*, he thought.

"Gully, we will take a flight each and every week. I will get us up, up and away, and then you can take control from the front. I will take the rear seat controls; in case we get into trouble," Theo connived.

"Thank you, Theo. You remembered your old friend in his time of need," grateful Gully professed.

A couple of days later and Theo came good with his gesture. The pair were airborne, and Gully took over the plane's controls at Theo's direction. Gully, although blind, could feel the spray from the sea, and the aroma of the ocean. Theo offloaded some floatable packages into the vast expanse of ocean and then flew around with the skywriter in action. The pair returned to the hangar. The soon-to-be fat, rich prick, or these days to be politically correct, the horizontally challenged, disgustingly, excessively wealthy walking penis, then consumed a large amount of alcohol and got blind drunk as usual. This process was repeated several times. Luckily (and wow! That was a close one), Theo had two spare fridges. Enough room to contain more alcohol.

There was a knock on the hangar door . . .

"I am Special Agent Chapman, FBI. I have a warrant to search the premises."

Behind him and navigating their way to the front were two identical police officers (Officer Wolf and Officer Wolf), with two identical sniffer dogs, both called 'Devil'. Obviously, products from The Program. The police dogs did their job.

"Gilmore Sullivan, you are under arrest for possession and supply of an illegal substance," the giant of a man, looking down at aged, blind, infected Gully, declared.

The accompanying officer placed cuffs on the blind man, being the unpredictable, hardened criminal that he was.

"And you, sir. Did you have anything to do with this?" the short-statured officer looking up at Theo enquired.

"No, I'm totally innocent," he declared, looking over the officer's head (it has been said it was a helmet he was trying to focus on), swaying from the grog.

"Son, are you blind? A blind man can see; this blind man is a blind man. He did not fly that plane by himself. Is there anything you wish to tell me?" he paused. "If you confess to merely helping, the law dictates you will both walk away free men. If you claim this blind man flew a plane and dispersed drugs by himself, the new law dictates he will get a strong sentence." (To underscore: Laws have changed).

"I know nothing. I hardly know this man," Theo responded, pushing Gully into the arms of the sniffer dog officers.

"Well, it's off to the prison for you, old Sullivan," Special Agent Chapman confirmed.

Theo continued his drug running, employing several people to fly Gully's planes full of crash. He did, however, cease skywriting the GPS location of the drugs, and he paid for an expedition team to travel to the heart of the Amazon jungle to search for a witch doctor who may or may not know the whereabouts of someone who may or may not know where 'The Medical Tree' shows itself for its bi-annual revealing in moonlight, for a cure for his infectious disease. He also took ownership of the desired plane. Analysing Theo's movements then, he 'blindly' succumbed to 'the Devils' and threw his best friend to 'The Wolves' for his own 'Ben O' Fitz' . . . A-hem.

Before Theo arrived at the compound, he instructed one of his human servants to plaster all over social media the fate that was about to be bestowed on earth if he and his family, mainly he, did not return from the defense base.

CHAPTER 11

THE LAUNCH

Oversized asteroid—Conclusion, as it was named—was now visible to the naked eye. There was no denying the masses anymore. With the masses comes hysteria.

Over a century ago, a new, highly contagious virus was injected into society. It was a widespread belief that it originated from a plant, only found in the heart of the Amazon when the moon was exactly right. And then, some believed it was intentionally made in a lab.

When this information was released, it created a worldwide panic. Chaos reigned; confusion set in. And a mere coincidence, perhaps, but a second disease gripped the world at the same time. Anyone who caught this second contagion instantly transformed into a self-centred bulk buyer. It is accepted that this disease was responsible for 'The Great Toilet Paper Depression of the 2020s'. The infected would load their two shopping trolleys with the same produce, leaving none for anyone else. As an analogy, imagine all the Doctor Jekylls of this world turning into

Mr. Hydes. With the end of the world aligned, the general population had an opportunity to show dignity, honour, love and respect for his fellow man, and a general exhibit of kindness to the glorious end.

***

"Smash that fuckin' window, Zeke," Ma Cartwright said to her inbred son, signifying the shop signed as 'Little Israel'.

People were running riot. Rampant acts of horror left a trail of destruction. Some confused souls still robbed the tills.

'Steal that car', 'Hold her down', 'Hold him down', 'Hold him/ her/ it, down' were all demands witnessed by others. 'Put a stone in front of that wheelchair, occupied by that invalid, elderly lady' and 'Kick that extremely young newborn, extra cute looking baby in the mouth with your steel capped boots until its jaw separates from its head, Dad' were regular abusive terms heard in the vicinity of Little Israel that day. Some hippies thought it a bit heartless to stone the wheelchair and not them. 'It should run free', they claimed, removing the rocks. But mania prevailed, and that particular wheelchair lady was stoned to death by a confused panic-stricken mob consisting mainly of hospital orderlies.

From the rear of the broken-windowed shop *Little Israel*, a man was late, but he did come forth. Jessy dressed in a full-length robe with a jacket over the top. With long hair and a beard, he could have been mistaken for one of those weirdos that carry a sign that reads, 'The End is Nigh!' Minutes before the world population erupted into one giant orgy of rape, theft, pillage, orgies, child rape, elderly rape, animal rape, masturbation, yet more orgies, murder and not genuinely nice words screamed, especially from those who were being raped (words and phrases such as fuck, ooh it's so big and baa), Jessy was collecting for an organisation called 'Green Orchid Donations'. These workers were known as 'Sons of the Green Orchid Donations'. In essence, 'Sons of GOD' supported those who needed it most. Jessy was quick with a comforting word and was known to nurse the sick back to health. As a foreigner, he had crossed oceans and mountains to get to his destination, most of which the travelling was done at night. With all the night navigation, it's a miracle he returned at all. That is miracle number one. He had arrived at the promised land. It was said that Jessy had planted a thorned tree on his journeys in the heart of the Amazon and built a water fountain to keep the tree appearing young. Jessy had many allergies. Thorns were a headache for him. He displayed a sneezing or hissy fit (some say) whenever coming into contact with them. His guide was rumoured to have remarked, 'Bless you' as Jessy sneezed into the water well, droplets of his mucus finding their way onto the surface of the previously drinkable water. All of his guides died on their perilous journey out of the jungle, as they had no drinking water.

As he exited the rampage-torn shop with a stale loaf of bread in his hand, he spoke to those that would listen.

"Let's have us a feed," Jessy so profoundly and historically suggested.

The bread was broken as it was so stale, and then excessively large amounts of wine were consumed. After

Jessy's usual belching and flatulence outbursts caused by eating, everyone stood back. Jessy then refused another piece of stale bread and the audience sighed with relief and moved forward again.

Jessy had arrived home the night before and switched on a lamp (which now seemed like an intelligent thing to do), turned on the laptop, and stayed glued to the screen to get a glimpse of Conclusion plastered all over social media channels.

"Good people of this city," the man of aura began.

The gathered crowd, consisting mostly of bored housewives and gossiping older women, became silent—miracle number two.

"I have seen the light," referring to his loungeroom lamp. "I have seen a vision."

Big deal. It was on his laptop.

"I promise I will lead you to the land of NASA."

A couple of hours walk down a gravel road, veer left at the fork.

"I shall follow the signs."

It is not difficult. 'NASA this way, mate' signs, twelve feet high, every ten yards.

The saviour turned to face the destroyed shop and bid it farewell. Doing so, he had revealed his jacket to the now exceptionally large group of what appeared to be interested onlookers.

Over the years, Jessy's jacket had faded in certain areas. Only the capital letters were visible. To view his jacket from afar, it read, 'SON OF G . . .O . . .D'. With that, strange old men that carry around signs that say, 'The End is Nigh' drew deep breaths and sighed. They said things like, 'Thank fuck for that', 'I'm so over this', and 'I can't go on'. With religion being banned decades ago, the mass of humans listening to this guy realised that following him would be the wrong thing to do. They were considering returning to merely rape and pillage, but after careful consideration, maybe if they got their faith back, and said some quick apologies with the term 'Father' in it, they could still make heaven if all that jargon turns out to be real. So, just in case, they followed this man called Jessy, who had a couple of minor miracles added to his name.

As he began his journey, the people followed him down the NASA road. He took his people out of Little Israel and led them to the promised land.

Colonel Steven J Harper of the United States of America Defense Force poised, with guns loaded. The distant sound of an army of civilians. The sounds get nearer.

Voices could be heard. 'Perhaps we shall sit down, enjoy a cup of tea together and negotiate our conflicting actions', 'I'm sure they realise we are unarmed,' and 'Stand in front of me, son, in case the shooting starts.'

This massive crowd of two hundred thousand people or more, or less, lots less possibly, well, there was a lot, followed Jessy to the pearly white gates of NASA.

Jessy stood inches from the electrified pearly white gate. He knew one wrong move could send everyone down to the deepest, darkest corners of hell to endure an eternity of punishment from a two-headed dog (probably from The Program) for the sins of all humankind.

He stared at the colonel. The colonel, not backing down, stared straight back through the wire fence. Standing on a tank, legs straddling the gun barrel, the colonel looked out at a sea of civilians. Through his binoculars, he noted some faces with an intense stare. Those faces had eaten some of the stale bread and the anus's that belong to those faces were now letting out a putrid gas. The tension was so thick it could be cut with any knife you had on you.

"Ready men," on Colonel Harper's order.

All of a sudden, the two leaders seem to recognise one another. The atmosphere was overcome with a sense of forgiveness. A sense of compassion for every precious living soul. The world's beauty cascaded in a light of forever changing warm colours and glistening streams of honour and chivalry, carrying deeds of goodness through the hearts of men, women and others, multiplying the feeling, (almost reaching climax) that enticed golden angels of the heavens to melodically play their generous harps of peace and love to a soft lullaby and lay down on white clouds, with fluffy things.

"FIRE!" the colonel yelled his order. "Kill every one of the lower than the filth under my scrotum, brainwashed, fanatical fuckin' heads, kill, kill, fist . . . fuck."

Then he took a breath.

As Jessy lowered his arms with a sense of forgiveness, he turned to face his people, the back of his jacket exposed to the army.

"We kill extremely tiny, insignificant little people like you all the time, maggot."

The colonel opened fire on the 'threatening' civilians. For an extremely short time, Jessy felt the sting of a mortar shell enter his back, cutting through tissue, muscle and veins, probably an artery or two, penetrating his spinal cord and basically blowing him to pieces. There were fragments of brain tissue splattered as far as the mess. His head was separated from his torso and his limbs were scattered from the politically correct cubicles to the far side of the children's playground.

"Is he dead?" a private enquired.

"FIRE," the colonel, needing to reassure. "Mow them all down. Sergeant, get those tanks up front. Gunnery Sergeant, mortar now." He pulls an army issue communicator from his hip. "This is Colonel Harper. We are under attack; we need back up now, keep those grenades on them, chemical warfare activates now, send in squadrons ten to four hundred, protocol zebra green light, repeat green light, Thunderbirds are go; annihilate their asses."

***

The seven, still in the room of echoes, still hungover, were extremely pleased the forty-eight-minute attack on helpless civilians was over. The senseless murder of so many people was incomprehensible, and the noise was unpleasant. The remainder of the day was spent eating and laughing and partner swapping. Tomorrow the rockets would fire. Conclusion is closer.

In the morning, having returned to their own rooms, the seven were called together for a pep talk.

"Who's holding out on the peps?" Kirsten asked, still crashing.

None were found, so the colonel began his to-be-expected, long-winded save humankind, the future, blah, blah . . . speech.

"Crew Seven . . . good luck." The colonel saluted them.

Colonel Harper also informed them of their time schedule. They would need to board the shuttle by one p.m. They can each take one suitcase with them. Lift-off would commence about two hours after they board. Conclusion had accelerated and was due to hit Earth approximately thirty minutes after the lift-off of the super shuttle with its anti-gravity power.

The colonel left the seven as they prepared for their journey. He was on his way to view the audiovisual of the party the crew had the other night. All rooms on the base are monitored. He was interested to see how successful the social experiment with the crew had gone.

The crew returned to their rooms and packed one bag each. Jason gave his child-toy a quick touch-up, then a large heroin dose, before folding him into his case. The good doctor loaded hers with the crash capsules she had received. Shanara packed the rest of her fire lights, chlorine and brake fluid. The Js packed nappies, dummies and a rattle. Michael loaded his with alcohol, and Isobel stole one of Theo's cases of diamonds.

'It' dressed as a male. Borrowed a uniform, walked, talked and acted like a male.

"G'day, mate. I've just hung it out in the pisser," it stated. "Yea, just doing inventory. My balls are itchy."

"Yeah, I git what cha mean. Word, man, word," the soldier so intelligently replied.

It waited for the highly intellectual soldier to vacate the room and then took the case of diamonds. It returned to its room, then dressed as a female. And one does wonder, how could you ever win a politically correct argument against that?

'The time has come'. Rumoured to have been said by a walrus.

Crew Seven and important cases boarded the shuttle. The Seven took one last look at the earth. Jason was standing in dog doo. They looked toward the sky and breathed deep. This was it. Off to save human existence. Humans had put forward the best specimens of society for this offering. The worthy, the ultimate, up-to-date, fully progressed, look what we've become, aren't you proud to be human, can't get any better, look at me, look at me, were in their allocated positions to be fine examples of human beings.

Colonel Steven J Harper marched to the control room a little slow this time. He had a blank stare on his face and was so expressionless. It has been said his face had not appeared like that since he was informed his favourite pastime, the war, was over.

He stepped into dog doos and wondered, *How did that bloody dog get in here?*

He then wiped his boots on a private's privates and stepped into the ground control room.

The best of humans and others have come down to this, the colonel thought. *These 'people' will start a new world.*

Their actions shall dictate the structure of their society. They shall be role models. They shall not steal. They shall not kill. Hey, this is not bad. Perhaps someone should have written it down in a book. Too late now.

CHAPTER 12

CONCLUSION

Colonel Harper ordered ignition. The rockets roared louder than any other. The crew were pleased they were not in the room of echoes now.

The colonel was watching the future unravel. He was horrified. Not because he had just killed hundreds of innocents, men, women, children and 'other' but because he was sending these seven people to 'start again'.

A paedophile, a murderer, an arsonist, two genetically altered, incest-participating thieves, a junkie and the only decent human being amongst them, has been replaced by an imposter/con-artist/thief cross-dressing it thing.

The best of.

The colonel casually wandered to the control console. Everyone affixed to the launch, through the viewing window, the colonel altered the trajectory by one degree. No one would even notice the slight alteration. Over that huge distance, the shuttle would be tens of thousands of miles from its mark—the life-sustaining Planet Y-Zlee.

It would still navigate through the layer of space junk, but then, out of our galaxy and head into an endless void called the universe, fuel permitting.

Colonel Steven J Harper of the United States of America Defense Force sat back in his chair, smiled, and waited for Conclusion. He wondered if WRONG's project was a success.

***

And on the other side of the world:

The Australian ambassador looked to the sky, sat back in his deck chair and baited his last hook . . . and stabbed himself with the hook, creating a large gash in his finger as he was staring at the incoming asteroid.

Crickey! That's a big one, he thought.

PART 2

OUT OF THIS WORLD

CHAPTER 1

A NEW START

In the end, there was the beginning. So, in 'Conclusion,' we will start at the finish.

After the birth and death of planet Earth, there didn't really seem to be much at all. Not much to do. A lot of debris flying around the galaxy, but apart from that . . . oh, there was one little space shuttle that made it out of the exploding planet's domain. WRONG had gotten their shit together, it seemed. Oh . . . sadly, and unfortunately the Korean space shuttle, with such an outstanding performance record, could not be started (they could not find the key). It's 2125 and the WRONG crew are frantically searching for the Korean shuttle key. Luckily, the indigenous folk on the lost Island of Pukka Uppa, (who had rarely come in contact with civilisation), had a spare shuttle, sitting next to their canoes all this time. Not the WRONG crew but the right crew swapped some spit with the chief of the tribe, who said they could borrow it if they brought it back. More bodily excretions were swapped, and a deal was made.

The Lucky seven, carrying one case each, awaited in the shuttle. The chief stood by with a lit match as the remainder of the lost tribe were waving, popping confetti bombs and igniting fireworks.

As the original crew of six from WRONG were occupied (still looking for the key), and time was nearly at an end, the Swiss Ambassador had a contingency plan. It had a few holes in it, but it just may work. He randomly selected six characters from the street. The street was in total chaos as the end of Earth approached. There were all sorts of different individuals running riot. Most establishments were now, dysfunctional. No electricity, or running water, or security . . . The ambassador instructed the six to pack one case each with any items from the riot-stricken superstore across the road. He would get the bill. Amidst the mayhem, the six returned. The Swiss whistled a taxi and told the driver to deliver the passengers and their cases to the mysterious lost island of Pukka Uppa.

"Is that the one with the space shuttle on it?" the driver enquired.

With a nod, the ambassador said, "People, you are our last chance. Do the human race proud."

A world in total chaos and panic. Crazies ran rampant, shops were looted, people and animals were raped and murdered in the streets.

"How's your day been?" the driver asked, turning on the meter.

"Yeah, fine, except I had to cancel my nail appointment today," one replied. "I was not able to reschedule. *So* inconvenient."

The taxi drove on, the long way around, of course, light conversation filling the audible gaps.

"Oh, look at that one. Cor, that one's lost its head," the passengers gazing out through the vehicle's windows noted the human body count stacking up. "That one's dead and got no brains."

"No, no, that's one alive. Oh . . . it's . . . my twin brother."

***

The driver had noticed the current situation. It was then it occurred to him that they were bodies he had been driving over every few yards, not speed humps. He quickly threw a mental plan together as he didn't want to be a speed hump or a body. He would retrieve his case at the same time and simply walk on to the shuttle with the other passengers and hope nobody counts. He thought he was prepared, if necessary, to take a hostage or a life. Could he do that? Take a human life? Maybe. After all, it was the end of Earth. There was no god to answer to, apparently. A thousand thoughts per second screamed through his head. As the seven exited and unloaded the vehicle, the driver, with his suitcase in one hand and hostage held at gunpoint in the other and tickets in another . . . ran for the shuttle. The Pukka Uppa tribe and chief stood in awe as the event unfolded. The other passengers, unfazed, left a tip in the taxi, struck a deal with the chief, then casually walked up the ramp and into the shuttle, joining the other two. The taxi driver realised at that point; this shuttle could support seventy-eight passengers for 900 years. The chief had great bargaining power; it was the deluxe model. The driver holstered his weapon and then appeared a slight bit closer to stranger-friendly. The chief, with his match, had lit the rockets, igniting the last chance for man to exist. Aboard:

'The Lucky Seven' and seven cases.

CHAPTER 2

THE CASES

Oliver Charles, who was known as 'The Count', Deacon, or 'OCD', to the closest thing he had as friends, had OCD (Obsessive Compulsive Disorder). He was a young man of about twenty-five, short, rounded face and a tad unbalanced. Not only was he struggling day to day to maintain his sanity, but now a giant asteroid had blown up his home planet. I think it is fair to say he was having a rough trot.

Tall and lanky, Rodger Philips' allergies ruled his dull existence. If it blew in the wind or sat in a vacuum-sealed container, surrounded by impenetrable concrete and steel, he would break into sneezing seizures on a calm day. The doctors declared this to be in his head.

"A nervous reaction to anxiety," they claimed.

It is said the doctors had not consumed copious amounts of alcohol on that particular day.

Jeff Richardson was a top bloke. He was compassionate, brave, caring and kind. It is noted that his origins lie in Australia. Doctors had confirmed he has untreatable Tourette syndrome.

Venus was the only name anyone knew her by. A self-confessed nymphomaniac; quite a piece of eye candy. Self-administered to the psycho farm, the doctors immediately classified her as a long term-patient and had a bed readied for her.

'The Kid', a bald mute, child of mystery.

Reginald Hargraves has suffered the latter part of his life with phobias. It has been said because of his claustrophobia and agoraphobia, he would spend hours at his outdoor/indoor doorway.

Enrique—the Spaniard—was the first to escape, stole the taxi. A satanic cult leader and sadist.

As fate had it, all of these patients broke out of the 'Fruit and Nut Friendly Psychiatric Hospital'. After rioting took hold, no electrical power or functional backup generators allowed the doors to swing open and let natural things take their course. As the patients left the hospital, they turned to say goodbye to their old home. Staring over the signs that said, 'Electricity is our friend,' the appropriate gestures were made with a few fingers, and the mentally insane made their way to town and stayed together, yet mingled with other looting mobs, remaining inconspicuous. Looking quite natural. Blending in. Enter the Swiss.

***

On board the shuttle, Enrique asked OCD how many stars were on his side of the shuttle. That question kept The Count busy for the duration of the trip . . .

which was two years. Except for Venus and Enrique and the kid, the other four, Reg, Rod, Jeff and Oliver, were familiar with each other and their annoying compulsions and habits. But as brotherly love shone through, each man feeling the pain of the other, feeling the heartache their fellow brethren had to endure, they made agreeable compromises that derived from a mutually acceptable, beneficial arrangement.

"Nah, fuck off," quoted Jeff, to no one in particular.

"Nah, fuck off," now directed at the allergy man, Rodger, sneezing on Jeff, causing his eyelids to be dampened by incoming mucus droplets and throat excrement.

Venus was still situated in the same pilot's seat as takeoff.

She claimed, "The vibrations are sensational."

Reginald was freaking out about earwigs, reacting extreme, nearly bashing his own head against the shuttle structure, carrying on like a real pork chop, agonizingly screaming- Immediately after Enrique talked Reg into taping his fingers together and then put the earwig, he found, in Reggie's head. Guided it straight into his ear, then popped a cork in his earhole.

"Settle down, sunshine," Jeff demanded of Enrique. "Duck in the ass," he added.

Now Reggie was connecting with the structure.

Venus took pity on him and popped his cork. And this was good.

The kid, in the meantime, had collected his case. He knelt in front of it, opened it and exposed the contents for all to see. He had a case full of books. There must have been about 200 books in this container. There were books on fishing, mechanics, cooking, how to fly a deluxe model space shuttle, and just about everything you could think of. Hidden amongst these books was an old-school bible. He selected it out of the case and presented this finding to the crew. Rodger long-range sneezed, his expelled fluids landing on the book. There was an uneasy tension in the shuttle. Not because Venus had returned to her vibrating chair but because religion had been banned from planet Earth years ago. The child calmly lifted the great book above his head, then smashed it down hard and caught an earwig by surprise.

He lifted the book a second time, now sprayed with mucus and pieces of earwig insides squashed into it, and proclaimed in a lot of hand gestures and lip reading, grunts and snorts, and loosely translated, "We shall follow."

There wasn't anyone opposing, really. They looked at the kid and thought it a bit weird that he was standing with a book above his head, grunting, groaning and flapping his arm around.

Enrique touched Reginald's back, stating, "I really should not have wiped that on you."

Reg flew into a state of panic. Similar to a dog chasing his own tail. Around and around, Reg turned. Rodger continued openly sneezing, and Enrique pointed him in Reg's direction.

"Damn, I've lost count," Oliver declared, pointing out the window. "I'll start again. one . . . two . . . "

Rodger had inadvertently turned and now faced Jeff. Rodger once again covered the Tourette owner's face with unwanted droplets.

"Are you shittin' me?" Jeff asked, unhindered by an uncontrollable outburst.

Enrique sat, thinking of new ways to play Rod and Reggie.

Venus arose from the pilot's seat and declared, "I'm done with that ride. Where's my case?"

She collected her case, sat in a secluded area and opened it. She kept an item well hidden, disguised, and secretive as she retrieved it from her case.

"I'm going to finish myself off with this vibrating dong," she stated and headed off to her personal quarters.

"Haven't you got some sort of rag to stick up your nose?" Jeff asked Roger. "Ass felcher."

"Actually, I do have something," he answered. "I'll go get them."

Rodger returned with his case. He opened it up to reveal a case full of toilet paper. Rod had been a tad confused amongst the turmoil and mayhem of shopping at the superstore with the mentally sane. He had flashbacks of the Great Toilet Paper Depression of the 2020s, which saw everyone at the shelves, and he loaded up his trolley. Rod pulled a roll out, tore off a couple of sheets and bought his hand to his nose. Unfortunately, he had not grasped the paper very tight. He sneezed, sending the mucus-loaded projectile into Jeff's face. Jeff now stood with mucus- and toilet paper stuck to his face.

"Yeah, that's better," Jeff eased. "Sucker of cock," he continued.

Enrique, who was still entertained by Reggie's phobias, offered to pull the Botflies out of his scalp. Reggie took to driving his skull into the shuttle structure again.

Enrique had left the nut farm with his personal belongings. He was fond of his collection, and it usually went everywhere he did. He casually walked off and returned with his black case. He revealed the contents. A sacrificial, satanic symbolled knife was the first item he pulled out. As a symbolic remembrance collection, the remaining items were also typical of what one would take from Earth. Chains, whips, gags, ropes, and inverted crucifixes all had their place in a new world for Enrique. He could see himself as the devil on his own planet. He was sick of playing second fiddle to Satan.

Kill this, kill that. Stick a rock in front of that invalid elderly lady's wheelchair. Bah! I'll be the one true leader now, he thought.

"Shall I dislodge them with this?" Enrique asked Reggie, showing him the blood-stained knife.

Reggie hit his head so hard he knocked himself out. Jeff then collected his case from the baggage floor, returned it to the crew and displayed its contents. An AC/DC CD and a receipt for a year's subscription to a monthly magazine entitled *The Nerd.*

Enrique, reaching for the CD, offered to inject the CD player with Jeff's music. The shuttle, being the deluxe model, had a loud surround sound system.

"This is 'His music,'" the Spaniard stated.

Hells Bells began to play at a deafening level. Enrique stood at attention, holding an inverted crucifix to his chest. The vibrations from the music were so loud that parts of the shuttle began to vibrate. Venus stuck her head out of her quarters and asked if it could be turned up a notch. Oliver's brain vibrated against his skull, causing him to lose count again.

"Damn," he said, shaking his head and looking out the window again. "One, two . . ." he continued.

Reginald regained consciousness and immediately turned the music off to satisfy his phobia of loud noise. He then turned it back on to accommodate his fear of silence. He turned it off again. Rodger turned to see the commotion, sneezing on Reginald once again. Instead of collecting his case, Reg was now occupied with finding the foreign substance on his body. The kid was still fascinated with his book while Jeff counted his lucky stars that he survived Earth. Enrique sat down, still clutching his cross. Oliver kept counting, and Venus continued with her love of vibrations.

***

Oliver stated one morning, "2, 400, 082."

It had been two years since lift-off. Oliver straightened the other cases to a dead-straight line. He then retrieved his own case and revealed the contents to the interested onlookers. The interested onlookers were no longer interested.

Over the past two years, the child read up on the operation of a deluxe model space shuttle. He had plotted the course of a planet, which could possibly sustain human life, into the navigation system. The thrusters engaged automatically, and the craft began to slow. Using the correct manual lifting technique, the child then placed the big book on a podium for all to see. The crew gathered at the front of the podium as the child, standing behind it, pointed and grunted at the book and through the gaps of hardened mucus on the shuttle's window, the visible planet.

CHAPTER 3

JEFF

The craft descended and Oliver stated, "We are going down."

Venus smiled and shuddered. Enrique could see Reg becoming extremely tense and offered to nail his hands to the ceiling to help control his phobia of depths.

"The ship's gauges indicate suitable atmosphere outside," Rodger stated after wiping the gauge clean.

The shuttle landed safely, and the crew took the lift to the bottom floor. The keys were taken off the key hook (a lesson for the Koreans, there), placed into the keyhole and turned. (It wasn't that difficult, really). The door swung open to a new world.

Jeff was the first to step foot into the unknown. He drew a deep breath and remembered how life was before he was committed to the mentally insane asylum. After three years of confinement, during which time his wife never visited, and his only contacts had been with those deemed mentally unstable and then another two years on the shuttle, he was finally free. Tears welled in his eyes as he thought about his life prior to the incarceration.

"Linda, I've got the job," Jeff said, eyes wide open, in the spring of 2123.

"That's great news, honey," she answered, flicking her blonde hair to the side. "The APC is a good company to get in with."

"I may be able to apply my theories of gene alteration and become head of the company."

"Don't get too far ahead of yourself, Jeff," Linda said, looking across the kitchen bench at her well-built, short haired, top bloke, Australian husband.

"Stone the crows. I thought you wanted me to climb the ladder?"

"I do, but one step at a time."

"Yeah, sure," Jeff agreed.

Some months into his new job, Jeff approached his supervisor, Doctor Von Schneiden. Dressed in a black coat, white Panama hat with a floral hat band and 'pink shoelaces' that really offset his tan shoes, Doctor Von Schneiden listened to Jeff's pitch on gene alteration.

"I shall have a look at vem, ven ist a goot time for mein," says the doctor, who ranked highest in his English class.

"OK, sure. Thank you, Doctor."

A few weeks went by, and Jeff asked Doctor Von Schneiden if he had looked at his ideas.

"Nein, nein. Vee hast bin very busy," he almost answered in English.

A few more weeks went by, and still the doctor was too busy. Again, more weeks passed. Could this be the time? Could this outcome launch him up the company ladder?

This time, an unexpected conclusion from the doctor.

"This ist nein goot. Vee cannot. Ist useless," said the doctor, making his English clear and throwing the file back at Jeff, hitting him in the chest.

Jeff knew, in a nutshell, basically, that the doctor was full of shit. Jeff believed in his own work and theories.

Later that day, Jeff heard whispers in the cafeteria of a new breakthrough gene-altering additive.

Jeff thought, *This cannot be a coincidence. I don't believe in coincidence. No one has ever made an additive before.*

He needed to get into the main laboratory and snoop around. Or a square. He wasn't fussed.

Most people had gone now, from all levels of the APC building. There was one security guard on each floor. Shift change was four p.m. Every day at five p.m, the three guards would look over, make eye contact and laugh. There was something symbolic about the ring of the five o'clock bell to them. They were distracted for about fifteen seconds. That would be just enough time for Jeff to leave his office, and quickly, but in stealth mode, three doors down, he would be able to activate the door security system with his swipe card. The bell rings. The guards laugh. He follows the plan. The door won't open. Of course, it won't.

"Going home Mr. Richardson?" Goliath, the guard asked.

"Yea, just going home," Jeff said, relieved with that outcome.

Rumour has it those three guards kicked a really cute, extra young baby in the mouth with steel cap boots until its jaw came off because, and quote, "It provoked us. It was self-defence, Your Honour."

Jeff returned home, and as usual, his wife was due about half an hour later. She worked in a private company as a gene analysist.

"Hi, honey," Linda entered. "I really have to shower."

"Sure, babe," Jeff answered. He was a little suspicious of this action, showering immediately when arriving home. He had heard it was a possible sign of an affair. While Linda was soaping herself up, nude, lookin' oh so fine, with bubbles running down her shapely, sexy, perky. . . (ahem). Jeff entered the bedroom, which lay adjacent to the ensuite shower. On the bed, under Linda's clothes, Jeff could see the corner of a security card for the APC. He pulled it into vision and noticed it was a higher rank than his. He took the card. He thought Linda would not ask him for it. Why would she have that? He had been married for six months, and everything appeared fine. Why was Linda having a shower before even a hello kiss? Unfortunately, there is no recording of any sexual activity that night. No mental picture. No momentary arousal (sigh).

The bell rings. The guards laugh. He follows the plan. The door opens. Safely inside the main lab, Jeff takes a closer look at their experiments. Some notations on the desk relate to his work. He digs a little deeper as digging higher is frowned upon. There amongst the paperwork was a copy of his work. The following notations were the practicable application of his work. They stole his theories. Stunned, he knew he had to leave there, for now, before security did their rounds. But how was he to get out? He could only hope the security guard was momentarily looking in the other direction. He cracked the door and peered out. He was in luck. It was only a couple of seconds, but that was all he needed. He quietly crept around the corner out of view. This was not the normal way out, but he could deliver an alibi if necessary. He passed the company's head office. The door was open. An aroma and an object he glanced at for a split second caught his attention. The smell was a distinct, familiar body odour. He knew the smell of Linda anywhere. He knew the smell of betrayal. On the CEO's desk lay a pair of knickers. Lace, with the initials L.R.; the pair Jeff had bought Linda for Valentine's Day. Jeff steadied himself against a wall and regained control of his breathing. He made it outside and into his car.

Then he was heard to have yelled the words, "Golly, gee whizz. This is simply not peachy keen," or something similar.

On the drive home, he concluded the guards were laughing because they knew the CEO was with his wife in the office at five p.m., nearly every day. He was absolutely devastated. He drove home a lot slower than usual (which pissed a lot of motorists off).

Linda's car was in the driveway. Jeff walked in, determined to get the truth.

"You want to tell me about it?" Jeff, straight to the point.

"What are you on about?" Linda said, apparently confused.

"This is your one and only chance to come clean."

"I'll get some soap tomorrow, but what are you talking about?" Linda said, getting desperate.

Jeff slowly takes her underwear from his jacket pocket. She sees the colour. The initials. He hurls the underwear at her feet.

"So, you know then," she suggested.

"Why don't you tell me, anyway," said Jeff, with a glare in his eyes.

"It was Paul's idea. We have been together for five years. I studied you, incognito, for six months before we met. I learnt all about Jeff Richardson and his gene expertise. We weren't supposed to get married, but you wouldn't take no for an answer. I couldn't afford to lose you, for Paul and me. There's a large fortune at stake with the development of a gene additive. Paul and I are going to be rich," Linda laughed throwing her head in the air, (not literally) and performing a pirouette, (literally).

"I was talking about your affair. I didn't know you were involved with stealing my work."

"Well, now you know," she so coldly replied. "Where are you going?"

"What do you care?" Jeff remarked, heading back to the laboratory.

"Paul, he could be going back there." Linda rushed to her holographic communicator after Jeff's car screeched out of the driveway. (Some say it was the sound of the cat from under the wheel).

***

Jeff would be able to enter the building the same way he escaped earlier. It was now on dusk as he crept through the establishment. The guard had his back to Jeff as he swiped Linda's card and entered the lab. He noticed a scraping pattern on the floor in a semi-circular form. He could see light at the bottom of a section of wall and bookcase. It was a secret door. He found a hidden latch behind a book and pulled it. The door opened to reveal several cloaked cages. He could hear strange whimpering as he moved closer to one of the cages. He slowly lifted the cover. There is no comparison of horror to what he saw. This looked like a dog with human limbs chained to the small cage. He lifted another cover. He could see another dog figure, but this one appeared more human, having a shorter snout. He lifted another. He threw up on the floor at the sight of this. No, it wasn't his mother-in-law. It could be described as a dog with an extra head. A human head.

"Vell, Vell, Vell." A familiar voice, in impressive English, echoes behind him. "Vot are vee going to do wit you, Heir Richardson? Paul oont I ver vondering ven you vould vake up."

The three guards from the deepest, darkest, pain-suffering corners of the bowels of hell grabbed Jeff. Two held him as Goliath sent one to his stomach. As he bent over in pain, the guard bought his knee up to Jeff's face and knocked him out.

***

Jeff awoke in a cell. For two weeks, he had no contact with anyone. Food and water were pushed under the door hatch. He could see nothing but, and, to quote a famous Australian band about 150 years ago, 'Four walls' a sink and a bed as well. For some reason, Jeff started uncontrollably swearing. He realized the food had been tampered with. Probably some sort of drug, he guessed. He stopped eating for three days, but the smell of cooked bacon was too much to resist. He could no longer control his hunger or verbal outbursts. At this point, he was taken out of his cell and delivered to The Fruit and Nut Friendly Psychiatric Hospital. He was admitted by his lovely wife, Linda. She told the doctors he became delusional, distant, and he claimed his work had been stolen. But he was a janitor. This would be the last time he would see her.

Jeff tried to speak but could only say profanities, similar to the treacherous, conniving, lowest form of filth, purest-of-evil dragon bitch, bum and cheating wife. Over time, the Tourette's would wear off, eventually.

CHAPTER 4

OLIVER

The crew ventured out into a possible new life, an opportunity to start a civilisation, a new and exciting world. The beginnings of wonder and delight. The start of beauty and fulfillment. Their optimism could hardly be contained.

"Hmmm, not much here, is there?" Oliver asked.

"Yeah, nah, looks pretty barren, Olly," Jeff stated. "Ass," he gracefully added.

Being called Olly tickled him. No one has called him Oliver or Olly in a long time. Oliver's mother gave him away at birth. She was a crash junky and could not look after him. He was raised by his Uncle Max and Aunty Doris. They were kind, decent people and cared for Olly a great deal. Olly had a near-perfect photographic memory and was obsessed with counting. And he would count anything. How many steps to school, how many cars pass, how many ants in a garden, how many talentless musicians made it big and so on. Of course, his card counting skills were exceptional.

"Olly, are you ready?" Rob, the son of Max and Doris, asked.

"Yes, let's go," Olly replied.

In 2116, the pair were going to the casino as it was Olly's eighteenth birthday. Rob fancied himself as a card player, and he knew OCD would be counting cards at any table he sat on. Olly understood the game of blackjack and Rob positioned the pair on a player's table. Rob would start to wager more as the card decks came closer to a re-shuffle.

"What do you think, Olly? Sit or flip?" Rob was dreading fifteen.

"Flip. The chances are eighty-five per cent; it is under seven," Olly said, rocking in his chair.

Rob drew another card, and a five presented itself. The dealer had eighteen.

Later, Olly told Rob to put everything on the next hand.

"Everything? Are you sure?" Rob was instantly and extremely fond of the 25, 000 they had just won. He was considering marrying it.

"Yes," Olly simply answered.

Rob had it all on the cards. They held their breath.

"Blackjack," said the croupier.

"Leave it all on there, Rob."

Rob didn't even question this time.

"Blackjack," again the croupier called.

The young adults left the casino that night, three hundred and fifty thousand ahead. They returned every second night for two weeks. Another patron had been watching the pair from the first time they walked in. This particular night, the patron stood behind Rob and bet tenfold on Rob's bet. The gentleman wore a suit that appeared to have the design of countless small dots. But not countless for The Count. Oliver was preoccupied with the suit. He wasn't paying attention to the fall of the cards at all. Rob and Olly lost seven hundred thousand that night. The patron was extremely upset after his loss. He thought Olly purposely lost. The gentleman walked sharply to the security office and demanded an audient with the chief of security. He informed the chief that they were counting cards. The security officer checked the surveillance footage and confirmed the accusation. The chief also noted the upset man had been backing their bets, as well.

"Get out and don't come back, or I will have you thrown in jail," the chief stated to the patron. "You suspected they were doing something illegal, and then you participated in it."

The gentleman obliged and exited the building, but he was not happy with that outcome. He had to blame someone for his misguided fortune loss. He positioned himself in his vehicle, and his immediate focus of attention was on the car driving by, taxiing Rob and Olly. He followed them home, parked across the street, sat and observed. He witnessed two separate bedroom lights switched on. It was fair to assume the rooms were those of the teenagers. After a brief time, the house was reduced to darkness. The gambler made a phone call and then navigated his way across the road, carrying an object and cased the house for an entry point. With barely enough light, he entered via an unlocked window to the lounge room. He made his way, silently, creeping through the house to the door of one of the previously lit bedrooms. He slowly opened the door and saw a figure under the covers in the bed. He raised the baseball bat and struck down on the head of the figure. A third and fourth time, he struck with rage. There were blood-soaked sheets and brains oozing out of the crushed skull and onto the pillow, (A good pre-soak before the wash is recommended for future use of the linen). Olly, hearing the commotion, turned the lights on and ran to Rob's bedroom. The gambler caught Olly by surprise and smashed his skull, as well. Olly lay unconscious as the gambler swung the dripping bat over Olly's limp body, giving Olly the appearance of being involved. He then placed the bat in Olly's hand. He exited the house and sped off in his vehicle. Max and Doris were still asleep, their bedroom situated on the other side of the house. They woke up to the sound of sirens. The police had Olly in cuffs, and Rob lay dead.

Olly found himself in court, but he was declared mentally unfit to stand trial. On the trial day, the prosecutor wore an identical suit to the one the murderer wore. Olly, in the witness box, was fixated on the suit. The courts placed him in the loony bin. This place he called home for seven years.

CHAPTER 5

REGINALD

"Where's Reg?" Olly asked Enrique as he joined them outside on the new planet.

"Reg was combatting his fears. I think he may have nailed it this time," Enrique answered. "The kid was looking for a claw hammer to help him out."

Reginald Hargraves fought in the third world war of 2,103. His squad were assigned re-con. As the English soldiers walked down the battle-torn town of Helsinki, Finland, they realised they were in the wrong country and flew to New Zealand. Having gotten it wrong again, they made a phone call and then proceeded to the war in another country.

Reg's squad made their way cautiously toward the young girl lying face down in the street. The bodies surrounding her suggested a nearby explosion not too long ago. The girl was weeping, and it seemed her leg was trapped under a concrete slab, which had, no doubt, fallen from the adjacent building. As the soldiers entered the area two of them tried to lift the concrete but to no avail.

"We need a hand chaps," one soldier stated to his comrades.

After they finished clapping, three more soldiers joined the struggle, leaving Reg and two others guarding them. The three lookouts moved out further to enhance their viewing range, now about ten metres away from the concrete. As the girl rolled over, now laying on her back, the soldiers sighted an arrangement of explosives strapped around her chest.

"For the Program," she whispered before she pressed, in her hand, the detonator.

Body parts scattered the area. A few heads were kicking about. One hand blew into a palm tree, an eyeball into the optometrist shop and an exceedingly small digit into a sex shop. Reginald felt lucky. Not only were all his digits in working order, but he was also alive.

"Drop your rifles," came the demand.

The enemy had them surrounded. The other two soldiers that remained alive after the explosion got themselves dead. Not a sought-after and desired state of being for most sane people.

Reg thought, "Screw that," and threw his rifle down.

Unfortunately, the rifle fired a shot as it hit the deck, hitting the enemy's leader in the neck. The leader started gagging and carrying on, holding his throat with a weird look on his blood-covered face. It did not do any good holding his throat or making a face.

The soldiers escorted prisoner Reg to a heavily guarded compound. He was placed in a cell, of course. The next morning, two enemy soldiers roused him to a laboratory in the compound. The site on which the camp lay, was used as a hospital before the war.

Reg was strapped to a chair.

"Vell, vell, vell," a voice Reg was going to get familiar with. Not because they were going to swap spit in a nudist camp, but because this was the voice of a cruel, heartless, mad scientist with an accent that verges on speech impediment.

"Vee haven plans fort you, mein soldier-boy," a young Doctor Von Schneiden, so close to speaking English, declares. "Put him in zee glassen cube."

Sitting in the centre of the laboratory floor was a glass cube about three cubic meters in volume. There was a small access hatch on top of the clear lid, about six inches by six inches. The soldiers followed orders. They lifted the lid and threw Reg in. The doctor started his experiments on human limits. Reg endured days of glass cube confinement with visitors. Spiders, centipedes, and scorpions, all had their time with Reg. The cube itself was filled almost to the top with urine on one occasion. The soldiers stood there laughing at Reg, just 'taking the piss'.

With the invasion of the camp from the English, about two years after Reg was captured, Reg was rescued, but he was a different person. No one could blame him for his phobias, but life would never be the same for him. He heard Doctor Von Schneiden escaped capture by the English army and with some rats, trailed off to Argentina. Upon returning to home soil, Reg was honourably discharged from the army and admitted to the nut farm.

CHAPTER 6

ENRIQUE

The new planet appeared quite bare. Desert like. No water or trees to be seen.

"Do you think there is any life here?" Enrique asked Jeff and Olly.

"I reckon so," Jeff replied. "Asshole," pointing down.

The crew looked down to see a footprint in the yellow dust. They weren't alone. They could not agree, though, if it was an animal or human footprint.

"Either way, I will kill it if I have to," Enrique said, summing it up.

"Easy, possum," Jeff retorted. "Prick".

Enrique had always been fascinated with the other side. He was hoping only to live long enough to witness his own death. He had always been around death. His father was previously a taxidermist, and his mother ran a funeral parlour. In 2118, at the age of eighteen, Enrique realised he had a special gift.

He was invited to a séance to join the hosts, Travis and Prudence Benson. Also, Gary Wentworth, a mutual friend of the three, sat in for the experience. Madam Clover had run an advert in the local paper for many years. Travis and Prudence contacted her to conduct a séance at their home. Prudence had lost her sister to an extremely rare event known as Spontaneous Human Combustion (SHC). There has only ever been a handful of cases recorded. After five years, Prudence was still not convinced of the facts pertaining to the autopsy report but was unable to have the case reopened. The night then was centred around contacting her deceased sister with the help of the medium.

"Gary and Enrique, your seats are there, opposite Travis and me and Madam Clover will be at the head of the table," Prudence organised. "She should be here any minute now."

***

A few minutes passed, and there was a knock on the door, as expected. Travis answered the door.

"Ooh, yes, I can feel a presence," the medium stated as she glided through the doorway.

She was in her mid-fifties and wore a long flowing, loose, dark green dress with astrological symbols embroidered on it. Her sleeves supported trinkets and symbols of safety and goodwill. She had 'bottle bottom glasses,' and her hair was greying and quite straggly.

"I can sense someone close to you has passed away recently," she fished at Travis.

"The deceased was closer to my wife than to me, really," he corrected.

"Yes, yes, but you knew her," the Madam said.

"Come in Madam Clover. Is there anything you need?" asked Prudence.

"I will set the table with my Ouija board and candles, and if you would please turn the lights out," Madam Clover directed. "Now, who is the person we are trying to contact?" she asked.

"My sister, Faith," Prudence answered.

"We must all hold hands, and no matter what you see or hear, do not break the circle. Am I clear?"

The new afterlife seekers agreed.

"Faith, are you with us, Faith?" Madam started and she rolled her head around. "I'm getting an intense sense. I can feel her presence."

Everyone kept the hand circle. There were a few sweaty hands.

"Faith, is there anything you want to tell us?" Madam Clover asked the spirits.

"Yes," the medium's voice had changed to a higher pitch. "My death was a tragedy. A very unusual phenomenon. I love Prudence and Travis. Gary and Enrique will help you through this challenging time."

"She's a con artist," Travis blurted out, looking at the medium. "Faith and I did not see eye to eye on many things. The truth is we tolerated each other for Prudence's sake."

"He's right," Gary said, backing up Travis. "The unusual, supposed, SHC was in the records. Anyone could have found that out."

"It was nobody's fault. I simply burnt from the inside out," the medium stated in her Faith voice.

Enrique had let go of his grip, and he seemed to be in a trance. The room suddenly became extremely cold. He stood up, and with his arms by his side, palms forwards, he levitated about a metre from the ground. His kneecaps were almost level with the tabletop. His eyes closed and his head tilted back. He then straightened his neck and opened his lids to reveal deathly black irises.

Looking down, Enrique spoke with an evil, distorted, dark, chilling voice, "You lying bitch! I killed her. I tied her to a chair, stuck a tube down her throat, into her stomach, then connected a funnel and poured fuel into it."

The séance gang had retreated from the table and were pressed against a wall. This was some scary shit!

"I lit a match and, well, what can I say? My sense of humour was on fire," he so wittingly remarked.

"I am Muhasim! Bow to me."

The expressions on their faces resembled that of a second-rate porn queen actress, at the sight of a large penis . . . so it is believed.

Enrique then collapsed. The coldness had left the room. Gary and Travis cautiously approached Enrique, still unconscious.

"Muhasim died about one hundred years ago. How could he have killed Faith?" Gary questioned.

"He possessed Enrique. That is not to say this is the first time he has taken over another soul," Madam Clover explained.

Enrique awoke, aware of all the preceding events.

"He's a real in-your-face type of guy, isn't he?" Enrique threw out there.

"So, he must have possessed someone else in order to continue his reign and murdered Faith," Prudence pointed out. *But who?* she wondered.

"Yes, there was someone else in the room with her that night," Travis added.

"We need to find out who," Prudence demanded.

"I have a suspicion," Enrique stated. "I'll see what I can find out tomorrow."

Enrique had always been fond of Faith, but his feelings had never been reciprocated. When he finally found the courage to tell her, she informed him she had found a gentleman friend. Enrique knew only one person that fit Faith's description of the gentleman. The morning came, and Enrique sat opposite his father, at the breakfast table. They ate food and talked, which was quite disgusting, really. They were spraying pieces of toast and bacon on the table and at each other, and they should have taken cover with every P word, that particularly pertained to the pronunciation.

"Dad, do you remember a girl called Faith from about five years ago?" Enrique slipped in, not realising the potential of an F word to attack his opponent.

"Potentially," he vaguely answered, hitting his son in the eye with a blunt piece of egg.

"Perhaps, you remember how she died?" Enrique fired a crumb spray at his dad's left cheek.

"Possibly," in return, his dad, shooting a small piece of bacon up Enrique's nose.

"Previously, wasn't Faith your girlfriend's name?" Enrique let one rip to the right jaw.

"Positively," his father sent a return to the bottom lip.

"Enough!" Enrique found a new weapon with the pronunciation of F, bombarding his dad's face.

"It is said this girl died from SHC. Remember her now?" Enrique bluntly asked.

His dad's eyes widened with a sense of fear and remembrance.

"Oh yes, of course."

"She didn't die from SHC. She was murdered."

"And? Your point?" Paul, his father, prompted.

Paul had shortened his name from the Spanish, Paulino. When he migrated from Spain, about fifteen years ago, he became Paul Elkato.

"You saw her that night, didn't you? You know what happened to her, don't you?"

"Look, it wasn't me. I didn't have control over myself. I was possessed by something."

"Muhasim?" Enrique suggested.

"Yes, but how did you know?"

"I have felt his power, too," Enrique answered. "We have to go to the police."

"They will lock me up for life if I live at all," Paul stated. "They may lock us both up in the funny farm."

"Why is he targeting us?" Enrique asked, sipping his coffee.

"My great grandfather, your great, great grandfather, made a deal with Muhasim," his father answered. "But Gran discovered sinister motives, broke the deal, and led police to the killer. Muhasim vowed revenge on Gran's bloodline and the other deal breakers for eternity." (Which is, in fact, by any account, a pretty long time indeed).

"And why Faith?"

"Faith was a descendant of one of the men that crossed Muhasim. The killer was also experimenting with black magic."

Enrique's eyes turned black.

"I will end your bloodline, that I may pass my spirit to the other side," the distinct, deep, foreign voice threatened.

Possessed Enrique hit Paul with a question, "Who's it going to be? You or your son?"

"Take me. Leave my son out of this."

"Wrong answer."

Enrique's eyes returned to normal. Paul's eyes turned black.

"Security, send in Doctor Von Schneiden," the distinct voice said through Paul.

Paul's eyes returned to normal. Enrique was confused with Muhasim's statement.

"We'll talk more about this, but I have to go to work now," his dad said.

***

A few days passed, and Enrique met at his father's office. As the head honcho of the APC, he was looked after. The office itself held some treasures on its walls. Picasso, Van Gough, over-priced just about everything, really.

Enrique sat down in the ridiculously priced leather reclining, vibrating, massaging, talking, do it to me baby, user-friendly, office seat while his father finished up a holograph call.

"... that's right. I don't care about their village. Knock it down."

Paul was seated, behind his desk, in his hugely overpriced executive professional chair. He faced away from Enrique, looking through the window at the marvellous view. The museum across the road was a three-story establishment, as the APC was. Above the rooftop he could see the hills reaching for the sky. He could also see the museum's neighbouring building, a ladies only gym. It is thought that Paul's sight was deteriorating as he purchased some binoculars, probably to see the hills. As he swivelled around to face his son, the blackness in his eyes revealed the occupant of that human vessel.

"Security, send in Doctor von Schneiden." Paul instructed through the intercom.

The words started to add up for Enrique.

Within seconds, two giant men bent under the doorway as they stormed the room. They immediately apprehended Enrique.

"Where is the doctor?" Paul demanded.

"He's having a sicky today sir," the guard responded.

"Umm ... sure," Muhasim said in disbelief. "Anyway, escort my poor son to the crazy house. He thinks he is possessed."

Muhasim took over Enrique's control once again.

"I can't control this spirit in me. I'm going out of my mind."

Muhasim swapped back to Paul.

"See what I mean?" Paul faced away, talking to the guards.

"We'll make sure he is delivered to the crazy clinic, sir."

***

Travis, Prudence and Gary contacted Paul a number of times to find out where Enrique had gone. Paul told them Enrique was seeking help with a personal matter and would not elaborate. Muhasim elected to keep Paul where he was, as his professional position could be an advantage over the other bloodlines that were to feel his wraith. Paul tried to see his son, but every time Muhasim would intervene. He told Paul if he tried to see Enrique again, a foreseeable accident would end his son's life.

I have no choice. At least he is alive, Paul thought.

CHAPTER 7

RODGER

Jeff, Enrique and Olly were joined by Rodger outside the shuttle. Rod was amazed to see prints of a life form on the new planet. He knelt down and analyzed the print.

"I'm sure it's human," he stated. "If you look at this front . . ." Rod then sneezed into the print, rendering it indecipherable.

Rod was not always a walking sneeze box. He was quite the inventor before his time at the nut farm. Rodger was responsible for some major inventions in this early 22nd century. The hover bus, the hover bus car park and a new range of Christmas crackers that hover then explode, were just a few attributes to his name. In 2119, it was Rod's final invention that landed him in the loony bin.

Rodger knew, from previous inventions, that an engine that runs on water was possible. He had an idea. If he could separate the H from the O and a 2 . . . there would be fuel and oxygen. He would need to split an atom. If all goes well, he could become one of the greatest inventors of all time. A saviour to the Earth. A world-changing idea that would bring all nations together, all joining as one, peace and harmony for our earth's occupants.

Of course, some powerful people in government were not particularly impressed with the idea of an individual splitting any atoms. Apparently, it is frowned upon to make an atomic bomb in the backyard. Tsk! Who would have thought?

"What's one little atom?", he pondered.

They let others have access to a Hadron-Collider about 120 years ago, in 2008. The team turned it on, not knowing if it would create the biggest black hole in Earth's history, or create enough harnessable power to turn on, say, a light bulb or two. Rodger had to rethink his strategy. He believed he could design a clean, free-energy device, using mechanics, hydraulics and the newly developed physics formulae as laid down by Professor Michael Watson. Rod set to work. There were so many decisions to be made. Rod had been known to spend several hours at the shelves, deciding on what shampoo to buy. A few years passed, and Rod had succeeded. Not only had he bought shampoo, but he had also built a working model of an engine that runs on water. This was a major breakthrough—no more burning fuel emissions. No more raping the Earth for its oil. No more power bills. No more tangles. This would undoubtedly change the world for the better, forever. Rodger was so excited he messaged his friend, telling him of his invention. Within two hours, there was a knock at Rod's front door. After fixing the knock, he answered the door to find four men of different nationalities in dark suits. The spokesperson was American and the biggest man amongst them, from New Zealand, towered over the Irishman, (who was little taller than a leprechaun), and a Korean, jingling the car keys in his hand.

"Rodger Phillips?" the front spokesperson asked.

"Yes," Rod answered.

"Let's be straight. We know you have a clean, free-energy device. We are prepared to pay you more than a generous amount for the rights."

"Who are you people? How did you know?" Rodger diverted his eyes to a black SUV parked on the street out front of his house.

"We are representatives of the oil and gas industries."

"So, you wish to mass produce my 'DROT'?"

"DROT?"

"Direct Result of Thinking, I called it."

"Hmm, yes, very droll, sir. Not exactly mass produce."

Rod considered what he was saying. Two of the suits stepped forward and opened a briefcase each, revealing an extremely hefty sum of cash.

"I didn't do this for the money. I did it to make the world a better place," Rodger stated. "And you didn't tell me how you know about my device."

"We, in the corporate sector of this world, are well connected. There are people at the highest level involved with what we do. We have contacts in government, the APC and National Security."

'What exactly is it that you do?"

All four men turned their heads quickly in Rod's direction.

"Rodger, for your safety and well-being, I hope you don't find that out," the spokesperson gave the death stare. "Mister Phillips, take the money."

"I will not be intimidated," Rod retorted as he slammed the door.

The four suits, filled with men, left Rod's premises. Just outside the front gate, the Korean was trying to retrieve the car keys he accidently flung into a hollow log, that was home to a numbat colony.

"Mister Elkato, sir," waiting outside the vehicle, on the holographic communicator was the suited spokesperson. "Mister Phillips has rejected our initial offer…Very good, sir. . . Yes, sir . . . I'll take care of it right away."

A few hours were history, and Rod wondered if he should try some oil in an effort to stop the door knocking. Then he answered the door.

The same four men returned (after their paintball game), bursting through the doorway in a whirlwind of suits and guns, apprehending Rod and enjoying another quick game, called peek-a-boo, before covering his head with a dark sack. Rod was forced into a vehicle, hands tied and blindfolded. After the Korean agent found the keys, the five drove away.

Rod had been drugged, but he knew he was at the APC building. He had participated in a few seminars at the APC establishment. A distinct smell wafted up his nose, past his initial nose hairs, some atoms probably attaching to mucus, down the nasal passage and the brain worked with this sensation, through a complicated network of electrical and chemical signals, to pinpoint the aroma. The smell of eucalyptus from the Australian gumtree that ran three sides of the building was unmistakable, at least for koalas. Also, a deep, unsettling bellowing from some of the koalas, was a recognisable sound that placed him there. Becoming fully conscious, Rod found himself strapped to a chair, guarded by two ape-like humans, who could have been mistaken for . . . apes.

"My name is Paul Elkato," a voice projected as he entered the room.

"Rodger, you have no idea what you are dealing with. This is some serious shit you're standing in. Diarrhoea from a curry-addicted Indian beggar, placed on the back of your tongue, would be something you should prey for, rather than the shit you are going to eat if you don't play ball."

"Let me get this straight. You want me to wish for a curry-addicted Indian beggar, with the runs, to lay a dribbly one on the back of my tongue?"

"Last chance, Mister Phillips."

Before Rodger stood a well-dressed Mediterranean man, with slick tied back dark hair, looking down and slightly squinting, arms folded and teeth grinding.

"What will you do with the DROT?"

"It will be shelved for now. We are aware that oil will eventually run out one day. We will continue to keep the balance of power and money where it is, for now."

"You are going to milk this until the earth is depleted of its resources and then reveal to the world a clean, free-energy source you have secretly kept for many years. Not only will you look good in the public eye, but you capitalise on the only power source available. Yet another corrupt monopoly already in progress."

"What will it be, Rodger?"

"I'm sorry. What was your name again?"

"It's Paul Elkato."

"Well, Paul Elkato, you can ram it up your ass," lifting his chin the defiant Rod cautiously negotiated.

Paul signalled one of the Neanderthals to open the door. A short figure clad in a musky smelling dark coat and Panama hat appeared slowly into the light.

"Excuse me; I have far more pressing matters to attend to. Doctor Von Schneiden will take diligent care of you now," Paul stated to Rod.

"This man is really getting up my nose. Perhaps you can find an appropriate treatment, Doctor?" Paul whispered as he left the room.

"You shoot be ein drummer vith timinngk like that, heir Phillips," the doctor, excelling in English and humour. "Vee hast bin experimenting vith the refined senses of zee volverine."

The serum was not yet perfected, but the good doctor was more than enthusiastic about injecting Rod with the trial Gene Enhancement Exercise Specialising in Ultra Senses or (GEESUS) serum. Rod's sight and hearing immediately deteriorated, and he began to sneeze more frequently over the coming weeks. His body odour was compared to that of an animal. Loosely translated and rumoured to have been recorded through history, the guard's conversation played out something as such:

"You know when you stick your nose up a cat's bum, right?"

There was a long pause.

"Yea", answered the other guard.

"Well, he smells exactly like the urine that came from that cat."

"Yeah, right," the second guard so intelligently answered.

The half-assed attempt at gene alteration had left Rod with an incurable frequent sternutation condition. The doctors of the psycho ward, who know better, declared otherwise.

CHAPTER 8

VENUS

Olly, Jeff, Enrique, and Rod were now joined by Venus and Reg, whose faces seemed a little flustered, and their hair was a little messy. Reg had utilised the first aid box, sporting bandages on his hands. Venus took a deep breath, with her back to the crew, stretched to touch her toes as briefly; the focus of attention lay, understandingly, not with the new planet.

Venus began her working years quite young, joining a travelling circus at the age of seven. She was a victim of the failed system. Her parents went absent amidst strange circumstances, and she fell into the hands of a caring family of circus performers. She was trained in trapeze, tightrope, contortionism, horse riding, acrobatics and more. Soon Venus became the 'star' attraction. Her rising fame also attracted the attention of one particular organisation, Fleece Individuals for Long Torturous Hours (FILTH). FILTH came about by the amalgamation of Profit Out Ways Everyone's Rights (POWER) and Profit Regarding

Individual Candidates Kicking Shit (PRICKS). So, in effect, POWER and PRICKS transformed into FILTH.

There was a change in the air in 2125. As the night's performance ended, Venus, returning to her trailer, deviated course around two men in suits, with their backs to the incoming target.

As she proceeded forward, one of the men called, "Miss Venus?"

"Yes," she turned.

"We are men of FILTH."

Inspecting them from head to toe, "You certainly are," Venus mused. "You guys stand out like a priest at a barbecue who volunteers to play, 'Find the Sausage on Me', with your kiddies."

"Ah . . . yes . . . very good, Miss. To get to the point, we have a business proposition for you."

"Well, that's a first," the sarcasm inevitable. "I've never been approached by two filthy men offering me money before."

"We are quite confident you have never been offered this sum," the man of FILTH pulled a cheque from his pocket, made out to Venus with a pre-written figure.

"I've had offers before, but yours is really huge," Venus gasped, looking down.

"For this money, we expect complete satisfaction," the man stated.

"Fear not. I'll have a hands-on approach," Venus returned.

"There is a particular item we are interested in."

"The clitoris?" Venus enquired. "Bondage? Anal?"

"Miss Venus, we request your assistance to retrieve . . . something . . . extremely valuable to our organisation."

"Why me?" Venus said, looking at them quizzically with her head tilted.

"The task involved requires a particular set of skills. Your skills. Our item lay in wait, in a safe, in the office of the thief."

"You are men of FILTH. Why don't you just go and get it?" Venus asked.

"The hand of our organisation has its fingers in many pies. This is not one of them. We, FILTH, cannot risk being caught and identified, or indeed, even being associated with this mission. Yes, we are FILTH, but we like to keep our hands clean...except for the pieces of pie stuck to our fingers."

The filthy man realised what he had said.

"Ha, ha, ha, ha, that's hilarious . . . the pie with fingers in . . . and . . . the whole hand thing . . . with . . ."

"Yes, very droll," Venus interrupted. "So, if I'm caught, you deny all knowledge?"

"There it is, Miss Venus. Are you in?"

Venus looked at the cheque.

"What's the plan?" she nodded.

***

Came the night of Venus's highest-paid performance yet. Shallow breathing, motionless, the prelude to the heist. A small palm tree rustles in a still corridor in the Museum of Ancient Artifacts. Our star emerges concealed in the planter box base. Two new plants were delivered late in the day to the museum, as a weak-as-piss effort to improve greenhouse emissions initiative, by our corrupt people-in-charge-who-know-better ruling body. In this year, 2125, the leaders of our species are still happy to watch forests levelled and rainforests become a thing of the past. But, in their defence, they are not shy of decorating lift shafts in hallways with a rubber plant on each side. FILTH posed as delivery men with two small rubber Australian gumtrees in planter boxes, positioning them each side of the lift doors and doing so, positioned a concealed and contortioned Venus.

Venus, dressed in tight black leggings and a tight hugging, unfortunately, not quite see-through top, proceeded quietly to access her equipment . . . hidden in the other planter box. If the security of the museum was measured by the size of a male animal that should be engaged as a raping tool for paedophiles, it only ranks around a pissed-off chihuahua. It is said you would need at least an angry donkey. Venus headed upstairs to the rooftop. The access door lock was not even a challenge for her. Part of Venus's circus performances included escapology. She picked the lock, stepped through to the night and closed the door behind her.

She made her way across the flat rooftop to a cable connected to the building across the road. Her rope walking skills would be put to the test. She pulled a weighty metal bar from her bag that she telescoped out to use for balance. On top of the three-storey buildings, she was set to walk the cable. Manoeuvring underneath the cable was not an option. The risk of exposure was too high. The cable height hung barely above the top of the floor-to-ceiling windows. On the pro side: It is an easy walk for her. The con: if she falls, she will probably die. And if she, by chance, lands on her head, her skull would probably smash open, likened to a pumpkin dropped from height and there would be lots of blood and brain matter, tissue and the like, scattered in a definitive pattern around the point of sudden contact. Pedestrians would probably be encouraged to detour around the body. However, it would surely be a sight to see—Venus colliding with Earth.

Venus positioned herself on the cable. And she did walk forth. A walk on the cable was . . . a walk in the park. She was halfway, about ten metres. She could hear a noise from above. She continued to move forward. A slight breeze progressively became a fierce wind. A helicopter, combating the warm rising winds from the street below, battled to descend upon the targeted building. The whirlwind became stronger. The cable swung from side to side as the pilot struggled to keep control and the base of the helicopter connected with Venus's balancing bar. It was knocked from her hands. The unpredictable cable quickly flung in a snake-like pattern. Venus began to think of pumpkins. She fell a short distance until her secured harness took her weight. Suspended by a lifeline to the cable, she hung vertically, peering straight into the huge window, fully exposed. The helicopter was meant to be her escape plan, however, the FILTH pilot, arriving fifteen minutes earlier than the planned time, made an individual, executive decision to abort the mission so as not to crash and ultimately die. The idea was about as appealing as tongue kissing his grandma. He swore he would never do that . . . again.

Venus suspended and looking straight ahead, through the floor-to-ceiling windows and into a huge office, observed a woman gagged and tied to a chair on the other side of the glass.

"I remember a night like that," Venus reminisced with a sigh.

Then, as a man came into view, she noticed he carried a funnel in one hand and a container in the other. He walked towards the woman. She apparently was not really down with the situation, and although her voice could not be heard, Venus could see her yell, muffled by the gag. She was struggling and thrashing her head from side to side. The look of horror and tears running down her red cheeks was also a fair indication of unpleasantness. The man removed the gag and immediately forced the funnel into her mouth. He then stopped. Motionless for a few seconds, he suddenly turned to look directly at Venus. Almost as if he knew she was there. Venus recognized him. He frequented the newspapers and recently gave his views of the future on public broadcast television. It was the CEO of the APC, Paul Elkato. FILTH had lied to Venus about her destination.

This was the APC building she was about to break into, and she was possibly witnessing the murder of Faith. Venus had to get out of there quick. She pulled herself up the lifeline and hung onto the cable. She turned around and shimmied her way back to the museum. Across the rooftop she fled. Back through the previously picked locked door, she hastily made her way down the stairs to the ground floor. Passing the displayed relics, she ran. Encased in glass were many items. A box of matches in one, a single gold bitcoin in another, documents of obscure laws from the 21st century, a bible, a lithium battery, and a prototype of the first mass-produced human robot were popular attractions for the museum. Disengaging the deadlocks on the museum's front door, the alarm was triggered as she burst through the main entrance and out onto the street.

Panicked, Venus had no idea where to go from there. She began to run down the almost deserted street. Her thoughts were a collective mess. The torture of the woman, Paul Elkato, FILTH, and the APC filled her less-than-settled mind. She ran, turning in only one direction, checking behind her the whole time. She had now lost her sense of direction. Venus was extremely hot from the unintended, fast-paced getaway, and she felt as if a huge cloud had covered her entirety. She was out of oxygen, and it seemed the whole universe was spinning in the opposite direction. Dis-orientated, she kept moving. Realising the gravity of the matter, she knew she had to seek refuge and hide from Paul and FILTH. Investigating her surroundings, she noticed a large sign. With limited options, Venus reluctantly entered the establishment.

"Hello, and welcome to The Fruit and Nut Friendly Psychiatric Hospital," came the receptionist's opening dialogue.

Venus, wishing to keep her new secret, declared she was a nymphomaniac and needed help. The bi-sexual receptionist was more than willing to admit her into the system. Venus would only stay a short time before the doors to freedom were unintentionally opened.

***

"Crikey," Jeff declared, with his eyes fixated on Venus.

"Quite a sight," Enrique added, staring past Venus at the new planet.

"I hope there are no diseases," Reg stated.

Jeff momentarily looked expressionless at the two commentators with his head slightly tilted and his jaw ajar.

Rod noticed; Olly appeared to be a bit concerned. He was looking around, head moving sharply from side to side, and a face overcome with distraught presented itself.

"OCD is there something I . . ." Rod began.

Just then, the kid appeared, standing on the access steps of the shuttle. Olly turned his back, perhaps rudely, on Rod and stepped abruptly toward the kid.

"Thank you," Olly, perhaps well mannered, gratefully acknowledging receiving of his suitcase from the kid's weighted arms.

Olly, quicker than fast, placed the case on the ground, opened it and started counting the case full of tiny marbles.

The kid took a step forward and planted both feet on the ground. Just then, a bright light in the shape of an arch encased the child.

"Oh, my God!" Rod exclaimed.

"Possibly," Reg answered the non-question.

"Aahh, fuck," Enrique added, in the same way a priest would reply when finding out a hidden camera was at the kindergarten he just attended.

"God, fuck me," Venus uttered.

For a split second, Rod, Reg, Enrique, and Jeff cast a glance at Venus.

"Not literally," Venus, in a condescending tone, replied.

"He looks like an angel," Jeff observed. "Titty fuck."

"72, 73 . . ." Olly continued with his obsession.

"Yep, real impressive kid, but can you turn that bright light off now?" Enrique enquired. "When does the darkness have its turn?"

The crew looked up to see the position of the sun. But there was a problem. There was no sun. The sky above was lit up, however, there was no source of light to be seen.

"Perhaps I'm caught in my own living hell," Enrique pondered.

"Shit face," Jeff opening his sentence. "No sun, yet light and no trees, yet oxygen."

Reg put forward an idea.

"I say, it's been a long . . . non-stop day. Shall we rest up, gather our things and explore this strange planet tomorrow, or what would be tomorrow if there was an end to today?"

"Well put, Reg. Let us return to our seats for a while," Venus prompted.

The crew agreed and all returned to the shuttle. Olly was last in. He shut the door, locked it, and put the keys back on the hook.

***

In the morning, or what would be morning if there was a night before, the crew did breakfast and gathered what they considered to be necessary items. The kid stood at the podium waving his arms around, grunting and appearing flustered. The bald child looked at the crew in a way that suggested something of a spiritual nature, a higher being's intervention, a knowledge of the future.

"He's giving us a weird look, isn't he"? Reg rhetorically questioned.

"Maybe, it's puberty," Venus optimistically said.

"He may be about to pass wind," Rodger said. "I get that look in my eye when I'm about to break silence."

Jeff, standing next to Rod, took a couple of retreating side steps.

"Who is this kid? How about we nail him to a cross?" Enrique suggested.

"Fart sucker," Jeff opened. "I think we should follow the kid's lead."

The rest of the crew agreed. After the child's light show, they realised this kid was special.

"How about we give the child a name instead of calling him kid all the time?" Venus insisted.

"Ass grape," blurted out Jeff.

"No, something rather more pleasant," Reg responded.

"Clitty tickle," Jeff impulsively yelled.

"The kid can communicate. What's your name kid?" Rod asked, handing him a pen and paper.

The kid wrote down the name Tasla.

After two years, the crew finally learnt the kid's name. With all that had transpired, his name didn't seem to be of any importance or relevance during that time.

"Tasla? I don't recall anyone by that name at the nut farm. Don't think I remember seeing you there either, Tasla young man. Where did you come from?" Reg asked.

Tasla just looked up, then back at the crew. Olly was inexplicably compelled to stop counting his marbles again and look into Tasla's eyes, as all the crew were. There was no need for any more words. The crew were overcome with a sense of calm, understanding and awe. They could sense the child had great meaning and purpose for whatever the future would bring. They knew, not for the reason, but for the feeling they must follow.

"Opossum piss," Jeff announced. "Everyone ready for whatever lies ahead?"

CHAPTER 9

NEW DISCOVERIES

Each crew member had a backpack with food, water and necessary items. Olly had not only a backpack but also a small upright trolley in order to carry his heavy case of marbles.

"You are bringing that?" Enrique enquired.

Olly replied, "I can't help it. It's not by choice. I have this condition. I'm not sure how I'm going to travel such a barren landscape with nothing to count. No rocks, no trees, no nothing."

"We can't stop and wait for you to count every so often," Enrique retorted.

"Pimple dick," began Jeff. "I have an idea. Let's make our way to the access hatch."

Reg was first to the door. He took the keys off the key hook, opened the door, and everyone stepped outside. All eyes were on Tasla to see if he illuminated again. There was no bright arch this time. Enrique was relieved. Reg locked the door and Rod continued sneezing.

Jeff asked Reg to give the keys to Olly. Olly looked confused.

"There are only three keys on this key ring. One for the hatch, one for the fuel cap and one for the glove box. I've already counted them. I can't keep counting to three all the time. This was a bad . . ."

Jeff interrupted concerned Olly. "Clip the keys to your belt guide, Olly. I want you to count how many times the keys jingle on your hip. Twat face."

Jeff had another undisclosed reason for Olly counting jingles.

With the crew prepared to explore, they all took note of their current surroundings. There was still light but no sun. No clouds. No trees. No wind. Yet they could not see their footprints or the remnants of the foreign prints from . . . the time they stepped out before. The surface was light yellow and solid but still impressionable from any weighted object. As they began to walk, Rod turned to see if they were leaving footprints. Not only did he observe footprints, but Rod also saw the wheel marks from Olly's trolley.

Rod had stuck pieces of toilet paper up his nose in an effort to control his sneezing for a while.

"Ah, Jeff . . ." Rod began.

Jeff faced Rod to hear his concern. Of course, Rod once again sneezed into Jeff's face.

"Anal lice," Jeff declared, pulling the used paper from his face.

"Yep, sorry, again, Jeff, but something weird is going on here," Rod continued.

"You think?" Venus intervened. "There is no sun, no wind, no water, no clouds, no trees, no shrubs, no rocks, no hills, and there are seven of us from a lunatic asylum on a strange planet. Weird, you say?"

"It's not that. We are leaving prints on the surface," replied Rod.

"What's weird about that?" Venus queried.

"Ball licker," opened Jeff. "He's right. Think about it. What happened to the prints from yest . . . ah . . . the last time we stepped foot on here?"

Confused, no one had any explanation.

"I can't go on," Reg confessed. "I've been trying to keep it concealed, but the Agoraphobia is overwhelming. I need to find shelter."

"We have only taken a few steps, Reg," Rod answered.

"Nine jingles, to be exact," Olly stated.

"I've got you, Reg," Venus coming to the rescue. She took her top off and wrapped it around the left side of Reg's head. "If your Agoraphobia kicks in, open your left eye. Claustrophobia, open your right."

Tasla gave a nod to Venus as if to say, "Well done. You are a good person."

The rest of the crew were happy, too. Venus was now reduced to shoes and socks, mini-shorts and a bikini top.

"My agoraphobia is kicking in, too, Venus," Enrique prompted, looking at her shorts.

"Nice try Enrique," she answered.

However, (in case they turn this book into a movie), Venus checked on Olly and his trolley, but as fate has it, ripped her shorts on a sharp edge of the trolley. Her shorts fell off. Venus was now reduced to shoes and socks and a teeny, weeny, tiny little mini white bikini against her bronzed body. The temperature seemed to be ideal for man.

The trekkers moved on. Jeff was the obvious leader, which no one even debated. He had that air about him. He was a solid build, clever, and brave and he kept Enrique in line. Venus followed second; Enrique, dressed in black, extremely close behind her; then Rod with toilet paper hanging out of his nose; Tasla dressed in a creamy coloured, all-in-one garment; then came Reg, in camouflage with half his face covered, and lastly, jingling Olly with his trolley.

The horizon they walked towards seemed so much further than they remembered, that of Earth. After some time, Jeff asked Olly, with his trolley (accompanied by a verbal outburst), how many jingles.

"12, 346," was Olly's reply.

Jeff stopped. Concerned about the others, still looking forward, he suggested they have a rest, initiated by a profanity. Jeff, a few steps ahead, about faced and sported an expression of utter disbelief. The others turned, and a similar expression was worn by all. They had traversed no more than twenty steps from the shuttle.

The Earthly phrase, "What the fuck?" was said, almost in unison by all, except, of course, the kid.

"How about we return to the shuttle and get out of this light for a while," Enrique threw out to the crew.

Everyone agreed. They were exhausted and apparently had not travelled far. Thirty seconds later, they had re-boarded the shuttle. As they rested, Enrique wondered if Muhasim would ever take control of him again. Everyone on Earth was now dead. This meant his vengeance was complete. His spirit could move on.

"Our laws of physics don't seem to apply here," Rod stated confidently. "What we are experiencing is quantum physics."

Six expressionless faces blinked slowly and stared straight ahead. It is said the crew 'blinked 182 times, as Rod spoke of particles, 'small things', atoms and the manipulation of reality.

"Donkey fuck," Jeff replied. "I think you are on the money, Rod."

After the crew had rested, they gathered more supplies and made their way to the access hatch. The same exit process was repeated; Olly clipped the keys to his belt guide. Again, all surface impressions had been erased, including Olly's trolley marks.

All noted the disappearance of the impression evidence, but not a word was said, except for Jeff who announced, "Scrotum flash."

Then everyone agreed.

Jeff peered at the distant horizon. Turning his head left and right, not knowing which way to head. It was then Tasla looked at Jeff, turned his head about fifteen degrees to one side and then back at Jeff. Again, no words were said, but Jeff knew they should head in the direction of Tasla's prompt. The last humans began their journey. They were in the same order as before. Unfortunately, Venus had donned more clothing. Reg wore a balaclava, with the left eye opening covered by fabric he had sewn on, while the crew rested.

"Tell us when we have made thirty jingles, Olly," Jeff instructed, with an added verbal outburst.

The insane ventured on.

Olly announced, "Thirty jingles."

Everyone stopped and turned to check if tracks were left behind. They could see the shuttle and prints clearly. They had walked further already than the time before. They were satisfied they were heading in the right direction and actually moving forwards.

"Did anyone else see that?" Rod asked, looking up at the sky.

After a brief moment's silence, Venus answered with a question.

"See what?"

"Oh, probably nothing. I thought the sky flickered for a split second."

"You are seeing things, Rod. I'll let you know if the darkness becomes known," Enrique informed. "And the darkness shall light the way," Enrique quoted from one of his cult books.

The child gave a glance that only enemies would share. Enrique's composure changed to a look similar to that of a defeated chess opponent.

The crew walked on, Olly jingling all the way. They occasionally stopped, taking a moment to eat and drink. They observed the shuttle in the distance and their tracks left behind them. They began to lose sight of the shuttle as they continued the expedition.

"Shit stain," Jeff began. "How many jingles, Olly?"

"153, 205," Olly replied.

"That's roughly eighty kilometres," Rod calculated.

"Let us camp here for the nig . . . err . . . for a while," Jeff suggested, with a "Fuck you," attached.

The weary travellers lay down after polishing off a pizza delivery, refreshed themselves and slept. When they awoke, they were surprised to see all the tracks had, once again, vanished. The shuttle also could not be seen.

"You better have this right, kid," Enrique conveyed in a threatening tone. "No tracks and no sight of the shuttle. No landmarks anywhere."

The child, once again, emitted a bright golden white light in the shape of an arch. Enrique suddenly had nothing more to say.

"Shall we push on, Son of the Devil," Reg smiled with a reply.

The seven got themselves together. Jeff looked toward Tasla. Again, the child nodded in the direction of travel. The group began to trek again.

"Counting jingles again, Olly," Jeff insisted. "Face fuck," he gratefully shouted.

After only several steps, Jeff, at the front, disappeared as though he had walked through an invisible, cloaking wall. Venus immediately stopped. Enrique, not paying attention, bumped into her rear, pushing her forward. She was stationary and halfway through the invisible wall. She could see Jeff, but the others could only see the rear side of Venus (which was somehow quite arousing). She walked forward to join Jeff and then the others lost sight of Venus as well. The remaining five just stood dumbfounded. Then came a hand, through the invisible wall, with one finger giving the 'come here curl'. They walked through the wall to join Jeff and Venus.

"I have to get me one of those," Rod stated.

"What? A curly finger?" Olly asked.

"Let us be extremely cautious. We have no idea what lay in wait for us," Venus advised.

"Rodger that," Reg confirmed.

"What?" Rod questioned.

"Twelve," Olly stated.

"Yep, Roger that, Olly," Jeff answered, followed by the inevitable outburst.

Rod again. "What?"

"Dribble dick. Everyone down," demanded Jeff.

Venus gave a shudder and smile as the crew lay face down. Reg retrieved a pair of binoculars from his backpack.

"You've had them all this time?" Enrique rhetorically asked.

"Well, yes, Chappy, but I couldn't use them as one eye has been covered the whole blasted time," Reg replied.

Everyone, including the child, gave a heavy sigh.

"What?" Reg asked, failing to see their point.

Enrique snatched the binoculars from Reg and broke them in half. He handed Reg one piece without making eye contact.

"Now you can use them," he said.

"What do you see?" Olly asked.

Enrique takes one half of the binoculars, (so . . . noculars?), squints to look into the distance, adjusts the lens, pushes his hair behind his ear, pulls his underwear from out of the crack of his ass, wipes his nose, (in that order, same hand. Yuk!), and if he had a tennis ball the Spaniard could have been bouncing it the entire time.

"It looks like a small city," Enrique replied, passing on half of the binoculars to Jeff.

"Oh, I say. Look!" Reg excitedly said. "There's movement. Life. People."

"Fart sack," Jeff exclaimed. "You are right, Reg, but some of them appear to be moving quite oddly."

"I have so many questions at this point," Rod declared. "How did these people get here? Where did the building material come from? What happened to our tracks, and what the hell was that we just walked through?"

"Unfortunately, it wasn't hell," Enrique answered.

Reg passed his telescope to Venus.

"I still don't see any trees. Where is the oxygen coming from?" she queried.

Olly received the magnifiers from Jeff.

"Oh yes, yes. Lots of people. There's one, two . . ."

Venus offered the sight glass.

"Tasla?"

The kid looked at Venus and back toward the city again. He held his arms out to the sides, palms up, closed his eyes, tilted his head up and took a deep breath. For a brief moment, he was encased in his arch of golden light again.

"No would have sufficed," commented Enrique. *What a show-off,* he thought.

"Are they friendlies, Tasla?" Reg asked.

The child shook his head in a concerning manner.

"Slut fuck," Jeff preluded. "Well, we can't stay here. It seems we don't have much choice if we want to survive."

"Olly counted our footsteps. Can't we just go back to the shuttle?" Enrique asked.

"According to my calculations, the chance of us finding another inhabitable planet in our lifetime is about four million to one," Rod stated.

There was silence as the crew contemplated the seriousness of their position. The undetected crew guessed they were about a kilometre or so from the small city. Returning to the shuttle, if it could be found, was not a promising option.

"Let's put it to a vote," Olly suggested. "I'll count the votes. All those in favour of heading into the city, say aye."

"Aye."

There were six and an affirmative nod.

"Very well," diplomatic Olly with his trolley said. "All those against?"

Crickets would have been heard if they were still on Earth before it blew up.

"Motion carried," Olly summed up.

CHAPTER 10

THE BIG SMOKE

The seven rose to their feet and reluctantly headed for the big smoke. They had only taken six steps, now walking side by side, when they noticed about thirty people from the city sprinting toward them, all dressed in red. These people took exceptionally large, loping strides, and they moved quicker than a dole bludger making his way to his crash dealer on payday. The crew noticed the clunking, loping strides of these people with human faces. There was something abnormal about these foreigners. They appeared human but moved in a way that suggested animal but mechanical. Within seconds, our seven were surrounded by the foreigners. There was still one more running toward them at a little slower pace.

"Duck fuckers," Jeff announced.

"Perhaps, I'll take control of the introductions, Jeff," Rod interrupted.

Jeff, realising he may not be the best choice of spokesperson, agreed with a nod.

"We come . . ." Rod began a sneezing seizure. His sneeze dislodged the toilet paper and it left his nostrils and flew into the face of the closet planet occupant.

"I'll speak, Rod," Reg offered.

Rod nodded before turning his head and continuing his uncontrollable sternutation condition.

"As my friend was saying . . . oh, no, I can't do this . . ." Reg's inability for public speaking outweighed his good intentions.

Olly, with his trolley, stepped forward.

"I got this, guys. Hello to everyone . . . and two . . . and three . . ."

"Planet of light!" Enrique taking the initiative. "I bring the dark side of . . ."

Venus put her hand over the dark prince's mouth.

Venus looked at Tasla.

The child is not about to speak up, she thought. "Take a breath ex-fruit and nutters. Allow me," Venus assured.

By this time the slower moving 'mechanical animal' had joined the group. It seemed the late one was the leader. All eyes from the thirty sprinters were on their man in charge.

"We come in peace," Venus began. "English?" she prompted.

There was an eerie silence. Venus was about to try her communication skills again when the leader spoke.

"Strangers. Welcome. We will escort you to our leader."

Enrique's head turned sharply, interested in who the leader may be. It was now apparent; this spokesperson was some sort of group leader. There was an unknown higher figure.

Being surrounded, the seven did not feel they were welcome or had a choice. Reg likened it to his days of capture during the war as Venus tried to open another dialogue.

"All questions will be taken to our leader," the spokesperson in an authoritative voice declared.

The planet's residents formed two lines, either side of our single filed seven, with the leader . . . leading. Our seven strolled as the residents marched in perfect unison. The thirty wore the same red coloured attire. They sported runners, shorts, and T-shirts. The leader wore the same, but a darker shade of red separated him from the others. They all appeared extremely fit, with much bigger builds, and they were sniffing, trying to find a scent from the planet invaders.

With several hundred metres still to go, Jeff tried to get a response. "Shit stain. What do we call ya' mate?"

"As we have just met, I'll do you the courtesy of disregarding your first comment. You can refer to me as Johnny Mercury. There will be no more answers until you speak with my superior."

"Nice to meet you, Johnny. I'm Enrique."

There was no acknowledgement from Johnny, who kept looking straight ahead. The seven realised this was an army type of mentality. The crew observed their surroundings. There were five, six-storey buildings situated in a pentagon shape and one large single storey in the centre. As they proceeded, they noted the absence of the people they were observing when they first came through the wall.

"Where did they all go?" Olly asked no one and anyone.

Crickets.

The group marched and strolled in between two buildings until they arrived at the huge doors of the central building.

"Wait!" Johnny demanded.

As he walked forward to the doors, the two lines of the 'red brigade' closed their distance to each other, leaving our seven virtually unable to move anywhere. The front two 'reds' moved closer together, shoulders touching, blocking any forward view for the seven. Closing the doors behind him, Johnny entered the building. A minute later, the two front reds moved forward and opened the huge front doors, and stood aside, creating a passage for the visitors.

At the other end of the giant hall, a man rose from his seat (which could only be described as a throne), with arms stretched out in a welcoming gesture, took a couple of steps forward and stood still.

"Travellers. Come on in. Please excuse Johnny. He is a great leader but lacks in the happy host department."

As the seven walked forward, the doors were closed behind them, and they spread out, visually investigating their new surroundings. The man from the throne appeared as an overweight, jolly, black-bearded king. There was, however, an air of distrust about him. Imagine a black-haired Santa with a bag of gift-wrapped genital herpes.

In the giant hall, rows of bench seats filled the floor area, leaving a clear aisle down the centre. It is said the hall could be mistaken for a place of worship, as they had back in the 21st century before religion was banned. Apart from Johnny, who had followed them into the hall, and the said king, there were two others.

"My name is Thomas Addison. You have already met Johnny, the leader of all tribes. May I introduce you to my son, Adam, and over there is Marsden."

Adam seemed to be quite normal. (Depending on one's views of normality). A wiry seventeen-year-old with slight acne.

"Hello, nice to meet you," he welcomed.

Adam, although disguising his emotions well, his body language told a story. His eyes would keep contact with the ground, raising them only to glance at his father and his bottom lip would quiver occasionally.

Marsden was an oversized giant of a man with peculiar facial features. It is as if everything was enhanced. Large eyes that darted around when a noise was heard, big nostrils, ears as big as . . . well, back in the 21st century they still had '78' records and a long tongue that would probably reach your stomach if he pushed it into your anal passage. Venus noticed his tongue.

"And please, who might you be?" Addison fished, ogling the eye candy.

"I am Venus. This is Jeff, Reg, Rod, Enrique, Olly and Tasla."

"Tasla? The Tasla?" Addison's eyes lit up.

Venus and the other 'nutters' were all surprised by the black-bearded Santa's response.

"Do you know him?" Venus asked.

"Tasla is renowned throughout the univ . . . I mean throughout this planet," Addison changing his wording mid-sentence. "Oh, but where are my manners? You all must be extremely tired. Johnny will lead you to the re-charging station."

"Tom, we have so many questions," Rod said. "Firstly, what happened to our space shuttle?"

"Ho, ho, ho," the said king laughed. "Your shuttle has probably disappeared, but I had nothing to do with it: your other questions, all in good time, my newfound friends. But refresh yourselves now and become merry. We will talk tomorrow. Everything will become clear then. Johnny, would you please escort these five lovely people? I would like a word with Venus and Tasla."

"King, respectfully, we are a group as one. So, whatever you have to say, you can say in front of them, too," Venus advised.

"No! You will do as I say. This is my planet. My rules." Addison raised his voice and smacked his hands on the arms of his throne.

Jeff could not hold back. "Buttocks breath. Our lady speaks for all of us, Addison."

With those words, Mars and Johnny immediately assumed a threatening pose.

"I will bring the darkness onto thee," Enrique threatened.

"Sounds like war has been declared," Reg stated. His phobias seemed to subside in this time of hostility. "I say, this is my game, chappies," he assured his companions.

"I'm with you, Reg. You can count on me." Olly put in his two bobs' worth.

"There is an answer my friend and it's 'blowing in the wind'," Rod declared, without really thinking about what he was saying.

Johnny Mercury, as quick as a necrophiliac does his business in a funeral parlour in broad daylight, ushered and bullied the five away from Venus and Tasla, pushing them towards the doors. Adam, the son, retreated a few steps, not wishing to be caught up in the heated moment. Marsden stood next to Addison as a protector. Tasla stood beside Venus.

So, to clarify, Venus was caught between the son, Mars and Mercury.

Addison gave a simple nod to Johnny. Immediately the doors opened. The red brigade rushed in. Once again, except for Venus and Tasla, the crew found themselves surrounded. They were quickly forced out of the building. They were no match for thirty. They were hardly a match for one or two of the reds.

"Kid. Do your thing!" shouted Enrique.

The child shook his head slightly, with an expression that said, "Not yet. Everything will be all right."

The looks of despair were transformed into looks of ease and understanding.

The five were marched to one of the six-storey, adjacent buildings. They were exiled to a large room on the top floor, the door shut and locked behind them. Inside the room was a buffet table covered in all sorts of delicacies you would expect to find at a feast for royalty. Water and wine were in abundance. An internal, smaller room had the necessary bathroom amenities. About forty prepared beds lay in wait. By all accounts, this was the best accommodation any of them had experienced in several years. The crew began to consume the overwhelming smorgasbord. Jeff waited a short while, recalling the meals tampered with during his incarceration. After he was satisfied there were no reactions from the others; he, too, chowed down, a ham and pea floater with mashed potato on the menu. One window overlooked the 'kings hall', and the other six-storey buildings were also in view. Hunger pains put to rest, the weary travellers selected a bed and rested. There was hardly a word said as they all contemplated the well-being of Tasla and Venus. They still had no answers.

"Wit of cock," Jeff, breaking the silence. "There was a band, back at the turn of the 21st century, that had a hit song. The lyrics certainly apply here. Something about so many questions in his head, without answers."

"Even if we were 'babies' at the time, we wouldn't remember that," Enrique added.

"We jolly well need to find answers, Jeff," Reg butted in. "'Isn't it time?'"

"Tom . . . wait . . . Addison . . . that name rings a bell," Olly trying to recall with his photographic memory.

***

Meanwhile, back in the huge hall, Addison was adamant he was going to get what he wanted at any cost. He was used to getting his own way.

"Marsden, take the lovely Venus to her quarters. Tasla, my nemesis, and I need to discuss a few matters."

"It's going to be a one-way discussion. The child doesn't talk, you know," Venus informed 'Santa'.

Mars did as the king ordered, although, this was unusual, as Marsden was the king's bodyguard and rarely left his side. Venus reluctantly left Tasla with Addison.

"I'll see you soon, Tas," Venus comforted.

Mars guided Venus to the same establishment as the others. She was placed in a duplicate room on the floor below. Neither Venus nor the others knew the whereabouts of each other. She, too, ate and rested.

CHAPTER 11

THE NEMESIS AFFAIR

Back at the smiling assassin's hall . . .

"I've heard remarkable things about you, Tasla. During WWIII, a young girl committed suicide. Before her body parts were scattered in an abrupt manner, she made a famous prophecy. She spoke of divine intervention in the form of a bald mute child. Legend has it you are a particularly bright person. You are enlightened and in touch with a higher being. What I ask of you is well within your capabilities. I would offer you a million credits to complete this task; however, money does not even exist anymore, and something tells me diamonds and gold has no value with you. Am I right?"

The child, standing before the self-proclaimed king, gave an affirmative nod.

"Excuse me, but I'm a tad deaf. When I was a child, I was struck in the ear by a javelin at the Olympic games. Did you say something? Of course. My bad. You are mute. Ha ha."

Tas just stared at lying, ruthless, credit-grabbing and shrewd, all wrapped up in one greedy, little, self-absorbed package of misappropriation.

"So, what I offer you and your companions is freedom to leave the planet, although your shuttle has probably vanished, which was not my doing, and finding another habitable planet is extremely unlikely, or a life here on my planet, I have deeply, affectionately called 'Miyanus.'

Tas, still appeared unmoved; on the whole, that is.

"You can come and go as you please on Miyanus, your companions as well. Miyanus is rather large, and there is plenty of room for everyone. Its sister planet is Uranus, but Miyanus is huge compared to Uranus. Maybe, I'll take you on a tour and show you all around someday. Show you the ins and outs and possibly rim the outskirts, feel your way around, then dive deeper into the guts of it all. Some parts can be a little hairy, but just follow your nose."

Tasla, stood as still as a straw in a bottle of your own warm urine and still expressionless. Addison spoke of promising words, but the child knew he was not to be trusted.

"I am in great need of electricity. An electric generator, to be precise. I have designed a generator, which is in use presently, but, alas, it has a few problems. It breaks down consistently, sparks, and I cannot run the current over a distance. It seems I need you as much as you need me. What do you say, Tas? Do we have a deal?"

Tasla was waiting for horns to protrude through Addison's head. There were not many options. He had already witnessed the ruthless businessman's anger and his attitude towards the other six. The child closed his eyes, lowered his head and reluctantly gave an agreeing nod.

"Wonderful. I will have you escorted to your quarters. You can refresh and get started afterwards. Everything you need will be at your disposal."

***

Venus awoke after a refreshing few Earth hours, aggravated by the sound of faint thumping from the floor above. She grabbed a broom and retaliated, hitting the ceiling with the stick end.

"Shut up, you bastards!" she shouted.

The thumping from above continued.

After several minutes, Venus thought, "Fuck this. I'll put my hair in curlers, don a dressing gown, pick the lock, go upstairs, knock on the door and give them a piece of my mind."

Then it dawned on her. This was morse code. It read, 'SOS . . . SOS . . . great farting galahs'. It was Jeff! Venus broke the shower door and managed to pull the hinges apart. She used the centre shaft and a well-concealed hairpin to unlock the door to the hallway. She quietly proceeded up the staircase and into the sixth-floor hallway. When she was directly above her room, she gave a discreet knock.

Reg's voice could be heard through the keyhole. "Venus?"

"Yes, it's me. Wait there."

Confused Reg thought, *Where else would I go?*

Venus employed her skills again and opened the door.

"Shh," she whispered as the six were reunited in the open doorway.

Olly closed the door behind her and the six were very relieved. They had a standing, group hug moment. Enrique was so relieved he gently moved up and down, pressing himself firmly into the wonderful, shapely, mouth-watering hips of Venus. Unfortunately, she decided it was a suitable time to check her flexibility. She bought her knee up, rather swiftly, into Enrique's groin. After a few moments, Enrique was again relieved.

"You guys took a significant risk. How did you know it was me?" Venus queried.

"Rod's sneezing seizures have ceased. He picked up your scent. It seems the wolverine is coming out in him," Reg explained. "And my phobias. All gone. I am a soldier once again. Bravo! I'd like to run into Doctor Von Schneiden right now."

"Von Schneiden? That low life, spat out, festering, anal passage expelled piece of flatulence debris?"

"Do you know him, Jeff?" Enrique questioned. "He destroyed the lives of so many people in my circle."

It is said he had the same effect as the ridiculous safety rules, on construction sites, back in the mid-2000s. Suicides from the workers were at an all-time high. Nobody could understand how safety outweighed common sense. It is fair to say a line was drawn between the two, and never shall they meet. For instance, the workers would operate a huge, bright orange cherry-picker with a flashing light and a deafening buzzer that rattled your brain against your skull every time it moved, but that was not enough. In case site personnel could not see this fluorescent "Gigantor" look-alike, it was enforced to place a tiny little witch's hat next to it. Apparently, this made it all safe!! However, if the projects ran behind schedule, all safety was abolished. It was widely believed that those responsible for implementing safety rules were not on any drugs, although there was a long, furious debate about that. Then, to exercise their power, the workers quite often would have to urinate in a cup. Not that this proved they were or were not affected by drugs, it just showed if they possibly had any within the last few months. Of course, that was only good for the poor marijuana smoker. The remnants in the bladder were detected. However, the harder gutter drugs were expelled in a truly short time. So really, to avoid detection it was safer to take harder drugs. How ludicrous! Other examples include the poor roof workers. They were forced to wear hard hats. As they looked up to the beautiful, open sky, they had a life-long question—for what? Perhaps emus were learning to fly? Perhaps the far less than comfortable 'safety hat' would save their lives if 200 tons of space debris fell on them? With all the silly safety rules being jammed down their throats, perhaps it was to stop them bashing their own heads in with a hammer that was incidentally attached to their wrist by a safety lanyard. So, following this mentality, they should probably have been forced to wear bulletproof vests, breathing apparatus, parachutes, a scarf and hat, a carrot and two currants in case it began to snow. As it came to light, giving up freedom for safety was not really about the welfare of the worker. It was all to do with legalities, lawyers and loopholes, and ultimately, (you guessed it), money. Records show one construction worker, carrying a flat wooden board, tripped over a small unnoticed obstacle in his path. He broke his leg in two places. The lawyers investigated the incident. Because he did not have his hard hat on, he received nothing in compensation. How would the safety hat have helped? Legalities, lawyers and loopholes.

"Sorry to hear that, Enrique," Olly stated as he took a break from counting the sheet threads on the forty beds.

"Faeces lips," Jeff opened. "We need answers. I have a plan— Enrique, with me. I need to find Addison's workshop. He must have some record of what is going on here. Reg, Venus and Olly. Have a scout around. See what you can find out. Keep an eye out for Tas. Rod, you are on lookout. We do not want to raise suspicion just yet until we can find a safe exit from here. To keep safe, we will use common sense, not scribble words on a piece of paper. We will meet back here in about half an hour. Be quiet and careful."

The plan was accepted, and the group cautiously descended the stairs to the bottom floor. Their doors of containment were the only ones locked, it seemed. Outside the building, Jeff and Enrique made a dash, straight ahead to Addison's Hall. Venus, Reg, and Olly headed to the structure next door, hugging the walls of the building. There was not a sound coming from anywhere in the compound. Not a soul to be seen. Rod waited in the doorway, scanning the area.

Jeff and the dark prince made their way to the giant hall. Creeping through the massive doorway, they began their (and to quote yet another band from the 21st century), 'private investigation'. Directly behind the throne, Enrique physically stumbled upon a locked hatch door, which obviously led underground. He made quite a noise. Not from the trip, but from the screamed profanities afterwards, which sounded as such: "Father fucker. I kicked my father fucking toe on the stupid father fucking padlock."

Jeff glared at Enrique, accompanied by a look of curiosity.

"What? Mum wasn't around much."

Jeff took a deep breath with closed eyes. "Shh . . ." followed by yet another product of Tourette's.

"Shh," Enrique returned.

"We need Venus. Let's go get her," Jeff whispered.

The pair left Addison's Hall in search of the others. They made their way to the building on the right. Cautiously entering the structure, their surprised faces could be likened to the expression you would find on the face of a Royalist enthusiast that realised the prince was involved in human trafficking, rape, kidnapping, extortion, indecently dealing with a minor, shaving his sister's pubic hairs and jaywalking. (Before the Earth's end, pedestrian crossing neglect was a serious offence).

There were hundreds, if not thousands, of what they suspected were people, all dressed in yellow, standing in perfectly straight lines. There was no noise—no movement, not even from breathing.

"Anal vomit," Jeff yelled rather loudly.

Venus and friends had snuck up on Jeff, tapping him on the shoulder. The six stood speechless as they waited to face the consequences from the decibel overload. After a few seconds, still nothing. No awakening, no sounds, no movement, no life.

"Yip, yip," screamed Reg.

The five looked at each other. Relief outweighed their curiosity. They broke into a happy dance, thumping the ground as hard as they could. Rod, hearing a commotion, appeared and joined in, not really knowing why they were dancing, but he went with the flow anyway.

"Let's tap dance," Olly encouraged.

"No, let's break dance," Reg trying his persuasion skills.

"Lap dance?" Enrique, putting his hands on Venus's hips.

Venus, obviously worried about her flexibility, swiftly brought her knee up once again.

"OK. Fun's over. Let's get to Addison's Hall," Jeff directed, followed by the expected.

The six traversed back to the evil king's hall, whispering about the lifeless people, dressed in yellow. Enrique was no doubt in prayer to his idol, as his hands overlapped each other, in contact with his groin, as he walked.

Venus opened the lock to the underground hatch. Reg led the way down the staircase.

"Tasla!! Jolly good to see you, old boy," surprised Reg announced.

There was another happy dance moment. Tas had a calculator, protractor and pencils and was working on Addy's request, taking a moment to join in the brief festivities. As the reunion cheer came to a halt, Jeff asked Tasla if he had seen any documentation of the bizarre world outside. Tas nodded in the direction of the filing cabinet, labelled 'The bizarre world outside'.

"Fuck me!" Jeff requested, analysing the paperwork. "Check this out, Rod."

Rod took a few seconds to process the reality of the facts. Being the engineering genius he was, he was taken aback with the discovery.

"Oh, shit," he professionally commented.

Rod and Jeff gazed in shock at each other. They handed the papers to Olly and his photographic memory, as there was not enough time to study all pages.

"You going to tell us?" anxious Enrique enquired.

Rod appeared to be performing some mental calculations.

"We need to get back to our room right now," he stressed. "We'll fill you in, back there. Tas, sorry, you have to stay here for the meantime."

The sweet angelic child with the face every mother would love, full of kindness and compassion for man, woman, other and child, nodded with a simple look that spelt, 'Yeah, I fuckin' know, dick shit'.

They hastily returned to their abode. Venus locked the hatch, raced to the fifth floor, locked her room and met the others upstairs in their sixth-storey, forty-bed, one-bathroom apartment.

Olly was beginning to act a bit strange. After all, he had literally lost his marbles.

Jeff, to the rescue, instructed Olly to count all the bricks on the buildings he could see, from the window. Rod initiated the tell.

"These, 'people' (Rod using a quotation hand gesture), are part human. In point of actual fact, they are hybrids. Some animal species' DNA has been scientifically melded with human DNA to form a human gene additive. The extremely fast red brigade is part Cheetah. The other animals include . . . ah . . . Olly?"

Olly had his fix and now joined the enlightening conversation, recalling with his gift, "Canis lupus, Ursus Maritimus, Panthera Leo, Panthera tigris—"

"In English, Olly," Venus suggested.

"I can only recall. I can't decipher," Olly explained.

"Vomit licker," Jeff intervened. "OK, Wolf, Polar Bear, Lion, Tiger and the list goes on."

"Wolves, lions, tigers and bears," Reg added. "They sound like vicious animals, oh my."

Venus, disgusted, asked, "What sort of a sick mind comes up with shit like that?"

"Dorothy?" Reg asked.

"According to the records, Jeff . . ." Olly stared at the Australian, 'Richardson.'

"Now I know how you knew the scientific terms," Enrique said.

The five gave Jeff a look similar to that of, possibly your female neighbour, when you are caught taking selfies, with her underwear on your head, that you stole from her washing line last Wednesday while masturbating outside her bedroom window, in an animal costume. So I am told.

"Fanny fart," Jeff defended.

"Hey, look all the . . . hybrids are in action again," Olly informed, peering back through the window.

The captives watched the hybrids going about their business. They were building another structure.

"They look so . . . mechanical," Reg noted.

Jeff filled the 'looks of death squad' in on how he became a resident of the nut house. They forgot he was Australian and a top bloke and were all apologetic for jumping to conclusions.

"No problem, Reg, ya' Pommy bastard. She's apples, too, Enrique ya' Spanish shit for brains, and you other fuckers can eat an oversized bag of undercooked dicks, too," he joked.

All except Reg and Enrique gave him more death squad stares until they realised the Aussie humour.

"It doesn't end there," Rod informed. "The technological advancements in robotics have made it possible for the hybrids to meld once again. This time with robots. These 'people' (again with the hand gesture) are a meld of human, animal and robot. I call them 'Tri-bots'. They do not consume food or water, breathe air or sleep. They recharge and are all connected, mentally to a common link."

"Have you noticed the electricity flickers quite often and occasionally cuts out completely?" Venus asked. "I'll bet that is why Tas has been separated."

"You'd be a rich lady from that gamble, Venus," Rod assured. "I caught a glance of Tas's workings. It was definitely an electrical system. Do you think that invisible cloaking wall surrounding the compound is also connected to it?"

"I don't think so," Olly, offering his opinion. "I haven't seen it flicker or disappear for a length of time."

"Ass reaper," began you know who. Putting it simply, "Olly...invisible wall."

The bashing from Rob's murderer had left Olly with a slight brain condition. Every so often, OCD seemed a little more unbalanced than usual.

"Yeah . . . ok . . . yeah . . . right. Invisible," the words finally making sense for The Count.

"The different coloured attire," Reg having a brain wave. "The reds are from the cheetah melds: the yellows, another animal. There were greens and blues as well. Five, six-storey buildings. Four distinct colours. Perhaps we are alone in this apartment block. There were no hybrids on our ground floor. Maybe this one is for visitors or prisoners like us, or perhaps . . . more colours."

"Oh, this is interesting," Olly calling on his photographic memory. "The invisible cloaking wall. Not just a wall. It is a dome, covering the entire compound. Tsk! No wonder I couldn't see it."

For some reason, all eyes with a blank stare were on Olly.

"What?"

"Anyway," Enrique broke the silence. "I still have a lot of questions. Like, how did all this get here? And if there are more colours to come, where are they coming from? And how come our Earth-to-space telescopes did not pick up any of this? And how long has this been here? And . . ."

"Slow down, Enrique. One at a time. I am reasonably sure the . . ." Rod was interrupted.

"Shush! Hear that?" Venus threw out. "It sounds like movement in the hallway. I hope the droids are not going to my room."

Olly peered through the keyhole. He caught sight of a human figure. Venus quickly unlocked the door. Reg opened the door slightly and quietly.

"Adam," he whispered as a wiry figure passed by.

Adam, briefly astounded by Reg's voice, about-faced and gave Reg a nod as if to say, 'Let me in. We'll talk'. Reg pulled the door in just enough for the thin-built Adam to enter, closing the door behind him.

"I'm so sorry you guys are held here. You all need to get back to Earth as soon as you can. Where's your spaceship?" Adam asked.

There was a deathly silence. Adam had been on Miyanus since he was a child. In fact, he had spent most of his life inside the dome. He had no idea Earth was but a memory. He was reduced to tears as the crew took it upon themselves to inform him of the destruction of their home plant. Venus comforted the young man, who appeared like a well-presented seventeen-year-old.

"I've been here for twelve years, seven months, one week and three Earth days. Of course, there is no night, so I keep a clock and calendar in my room. Dad told me I could go back to Earth on my eighteenth birthday if I wanted to. Apart from dad, who would not want to? I have vague memories of life on Earth. I was educated here and have seen many pictures of my home planet. I really wanted to see and feel the great oceans."

Adam realised his father had been lying to him for years. He broke down again. It seems child abuse was not just confined to physical or just to Earth. Recorded in history, as far back as the 20th century, artists became rich from releasing songs which were played on open airways, time and time again regarding little girls, the whereabouts of parents, the timing of the future offence, desire for a physical encounter with the young age bracket and so on.

Reg remembered the look of fear in Adam's eyes when his father was present.

"Has your daddy ever…done things to you that he shouldn't have?" Reg asked.

The seventeen-year-old broke down yet again.

"Bastard," Jeff blurted out while his Tourette's subsided.

"Have you ever had a woman, Adam?" Venus enquired.

"There was one woman here, but unfortunately, she developed a medical condition on the 'eve' of her birthday. She had an overcrowding problem with her ribs. She died. Hey, would you like some fresh apples?"

"Come with me. I've got something to show you," Venus directed, taking his hand.

The pair entered the bathroom and returned not long after. They both seemed a bit flustered, and short on breath and Venus's hair was a tad messy. They were probably trying to fix the broken shower door. They both let out a relaxed deep breath.

"Look, I have to get back to the hall. Dad gets extremely angry with me if I disobey. We'll talk more later," Adam said as he headed for the door.

"Wait. When do the droids recharge again?" Rod asked.

"They are only good for about four hours," Adam informed the crew. "Then they need to recharge for around sixteen hours".

Adam left the room, and Venus returned upstairs in fear of a spot check, and she claimed the detachable shower head was calling.

***

"Timing . . . the timing of it . . . timing," Olly muttered.

"What are you on to, Olly?" Enrique sensing comprehensible thoughts from someone so incomprehensible.

"I believe there were hundreds of shuttles transporting equipment to outer space. The materials would then be transferred to space cargo ships and sent here. That is how it started. Remember our history books? The third world war?" Olly prompted.

Crickets.

"One conspiracy theory was that the war was not about religion but control of space and a possible habitable planet. This planet. Miyanus!!"

"I think you are right, Olly. Addison, droids, the GEESUS serum, and building material. All sent here from Earth years ago. Twelve years, seven months, one week and three days to be exact," Rod clarified. "I also remember a space shuttle full of Korean scientists, that mysteriously vanished when they travelled in this direction to investigate the strange disappearance of yet another Korean space shuttle full of scientists. Rumour has it that they locked themselves out of the shuttle and had misplaced the keys.

There was a thoughtful silence.

***

Jeff appeared to be lost in deep thought.

"What are you thinking, Jeff?" Rod asked.

"Sheep shit," Jeff began.

"Really?" Enrique questioned.

Jeff ignored the Spaniard's comment. "The end of Earth was over two years ago. If the melded droids are still being manufactured, who or what is making them? Addison is obviously not clever enough. Adam is the only other human on this planet. I'm sure it is not him, either."

It dawned on Rod. "Holy shit! Artificial intelligence. The droids are making themselves and improving their product each time. Think about Marsden. He is not connected like the others. He is bigger and all his senses have been refined. If Tasla hands Addison the power of non-stop electricity . . ."

"They will surely make man. . . us . . . extinct," Reg realising the AI droid potential.

"We have to stop Tas!" the five said in unison.

CHAPTER 12

THE DEMISE

"What do you think Addison does all the time? We haven't seen him since our comforting introduction?" Reg asked the others.

"When he is not playing with his son's private parts and not eating yet another piece of chocolate cake, I assume he's sleeping or perhaps trying to work out how his generator could be improved, before Tas, a child, puts him to shame," Enrique answered.

There were still three hours of charge left in the droids. The five would wait until all Tri-bots returned to their charging stations before they ventured outdoors again.

"I can't get my head around a few things," Rod declared. "The cloaking dome. The flickering sky and our vanished trail. The source of light and oxygen outside the dome, also I know Addison is not to be trusted, but he seemed unusually sincere when he stated our space shuttle was probably gone and it wasn't his doing."

"Oh no. no, no, no," Olly panicked.

"What's up OCD?" Enrique asked.

"Well, what are we going to tell the Chief of Pukka Uppa? We were supposed to return the shuttle."

"Olly, what planet are you on?"

"Miyanus, of course. What a silly question."

***

As the time drew near, the reds, blues, yellows and greens marched back to their respective buildings, after another hard stint in the construction game, and plugged themselves into their charging stations. All seemed quiet. Jeff was about to thump on the floor to signal Venus when her voice pierced the silence. Her undeniably gentle, soothing, mesmerising to the ear, softly spoken and sweet-toned, fairy-like voice was unmistakeable.

"Nah! Fuck off, Johnny Mercurachrome!"

As the men looked through the bathroom window, they could see Johnny Mercury escorting Venus to Addison's Hall. They knew the king was in there somewhere. It was also a fair guess on their behalf; Addy was not having Venus delivered for a game of checkers.

Reg said what was on everyone's mind. "We have to save her."

"Shit ribs," Jeff offered. "Why is Mercury not recharging like the rest?"

"I think it has begun," Rod replied. "I believe he has had an upgrade."

Our heroes knew they would have to take on Johnny to save Venus. However, they also suspected Marsden would be lurking around, too.

"Right, so how do we get out of here?" Reg asked.

Jeff had a solution.

"Rectum reamer! How many threads per inch in the sheets, Olly?

"600. Why?"

"Freckle fucker! We are going out that way," Jeff, pointing to the window.

Venus and Mercury entered Addison's building, and shortly after, Jeff smashed through the apartment's bathroom window.

"We best move swiftly. We only have a short window . . . ha, ha, ha . . . escape . . . with the . . . window and . . ." Olly laughed, cracking a funny.

A roll of the eyes was in order for Jeff and Rod. The Spaniard and Reg had deadpan faces. The five pulled the sheets from the beds and began tying them together and creating large knots for safety. They decided against filling out paperwork and wearing uncomfortable hats. It took about seven sheets per floor, Rod calculated. They tied one end around the toilet and dropped the makeshift rope down to the ground through the window.

Because of his climbing experience in the army, Reg volunteered to go first. His phobias were no more. It was as if something had snapped in his mind. Here was a man that was confident willing and able. A real turnaround. A totally different person from what he had become. He was now more than just a shadow of his former self. He was a brave, 'Get out of my way, don't hold me back, I'm going to do this', sort of a soldier.

"It's an awfully long way down, isn't it?" Reg remarked, with his head through the window, staring at the ground.

For just a fleeting moment, the agoraphobia kicked back in. He was, almost over his phobias. The new Reg moved his head from side to side as if to shake off his fear.

"Right. Tally ho, here I go," he confidently said. "Tip, tip."

Reg, like a professional, began his descent. He had climbed two floors down while Jeff observed, head poked through the window, looking down.

Suddenly, a red flash sprinted towards the rope. It was Johnny Mercury. He was back much sooner than expected.

"Piss drops!" Jeff exclaimed.

Reg looked up and said, "Don't you fuckin' dare!"

"What? No, no. Mercury!" Jeff sending an alarm to Reg.

Reg looked down. It is said his response was something like, "This is jolly well not on. I seem to be in a spot of bother, chaps."

Johnny, the cheetah cross, the Tri-bot in charge of all Tri-bots, grabbed the rope and swiftly climbed. Reg could almost feel Johnny's deathly eyes staring at the soles of his feet and his bum as he wiggled his way back up the rope. Reg thought for a moment that maybe Mercury was sexually challenged. Mercury's weight was too much for the rope. The line broke just under Reg's grip. He scampered his way up to the top and, with Jeff's help, back through the window. Johnny had the look of a big cat that had lost its meal.

About twenty of our expired planet's minutes later, Mercury was seen escorting Venus across the compound, presumably, back to her room.

"Oh, poor Venus," Olly cried.

"Addison, you bastard," Reg said.

"What did he do to her?" Rod pondered aloud.

"That filthy, fart vacuum deserves every mouthful of shit that I can push out of the stomach of an infestation of overeating anal maggots," Jeff politely added as the others began to dry reach at the thought of his brand of justice. (At least the Tourette's seemed to subside temporarily). "Haemorrhoid tonguer." (And there it is).

Venus could be heard unlocking the door. She entered the guy's room with a smile on her face. No, she had not been checking the detachable shower head again.

"Venus! Are you alright? We were so worried about you," Olly concerningly asked.

"I'm fine," she replied.

"What happened? Where did they take you?"

"I was taken to Addison's lair."

"And?"

Reading their worried faces, Venus smirked, "We played checkers. I won, five-nil."

The men were relieved. The thought of Addy winning checkers was rather cutting.

Venus asked about the missing bed sheets. The five men filled her gaps in. Venus let out a huge sigh.

"We have to get back to Tas and stop him designing the 'you beaut' generator," Jeff stressed, followed by what had become the norm.

***

A mass movement was occurring outside. The Count, at the window, counted the Tri-bots as they entered the great hall.

"948," he told the gang.

'Faaark!' was on the tip of their tongues as the door burst open. Mars and Mercury were to take them to Addy's Hall. Across the compound, they marched. The Tri-bots sat row after row. The six were walked down the centre aisle towards Addison's podium and, with a simple nod to the left from Mercury, were directed to sit in the front row. Adam and Tasla were already seated in the same row. There was much rejoicing. They dare not leave their seats, but those closest to Tas put their hands on his shoulder and patted his bald head.

The podium suddenly tilted forward. This was his secret room, right next to the hatch to the room that held Tasla. Then Addison appeared, rising up from underneath, hands reaching for the supposed heavens with the look of a gospel minister about to give a sermon.

Addison stood behind the podium with his hands held high. He was about to make an announcement.

"My people and distinguished guests. I have done it. I have designed and built a new electrical generator and, indeed, a whole new electrical system, all by myself. I take full credit for the technical advancement. I've already recorded a patent here on Miyanus."

Our heroes knew it was Tasla's efforts that Addison was underhandedly taking the glory for.

"The next time you recharge, you will leave your charging stations stronger, you will last longer, and recharging will be quicker and less frequent. We will be able to expand, not only Miyanus, but further into our galaxy and, yes, the universe. Each new wave of designed droids become the next ones to create the next ones, advancing in intelligence every time."

This was Addison's master plan.

"This is cause for celebration. Go and get charged, my loyal subjects. Mercury and Marsden, stay here with our guests and me. We will get charged on champers. Ha, ha, ha. Champers . . . and charged . . . with the . . ." Addison attempting humour.

Nine hundred and forty-eight Tri-bots marched out in an orderly and fast fashion.

Tasla just stared at Addison as if to say, "What the fuck?"

"Adam, will you please make yourself scarce? I have some confidential business with our guests."

Mars and Mercury should have been 20th-century union reps, as their standover tactics were exceptional. Mercury, behind and towering over our seated seven. Mars positioned himself between the fearless seven and Addison. Addy did not say a word until Adam had shut the large doors behind himself. If looks could kill, Addison would have died a slow, torturous death seven times over.

"I can see you are not happy, but you don't understand our sense of humour on Miyanus. If Tasla completes one more task for me, to show my good faith, the seven of you are free to go or stay."

"What happened to our shuttle, Addison?" Rod asked, quite bluntly, a combative look in his eyes.

The bench seat creaked as Mercury pushed his knee into it, where Rod was sitting, as a warning to watch his hostile tone.

"Inside this dome, I am virtually a god. Outside the dome is not my territory."

The crew stared at Addison in disbelief.

"Look, approximately every sixteen earth hours; everything is wiped. Bigger objects take more time. All traces of life outside the dome are deleted. My shuttle disappeared a short time after my arrival many years ago. No one can see inside the dome, and we cannot see out. I say you were incredibly lucky that you all survived. It is my guess you, too, just happened to enter the dome before another total wipe-out. With timing like that, we should've all been drummers . . . ha, ha, ha . . . drummers . . . timing . . . with the wipe-out and . . ."

Seven deadpan faces. Perhaps Addison and Von Schneiden went to the same school of humour.

Jeff was about to speak when Venus put her hand over his mouth and directed Jeff's attention to Mercury, reasonably sure of what Jeff's opening comment would entail. Jeff pulled Venus's hand away from his mouth and whispered in her ear.

"So, how are you going to get your son back to Earth on his eighteenth?" Venus relayed.

"You and I both know there is no . . ." Addy stopped mid-sentence. "How do you know Adam wants out of Miyanus? What else did Adam tell you? I never sanctioned a talk between you and Adam."

Johnny informed Addison of the sheet rope. Addy assumed the talk was a result of that defying act.

"I think Johnny will have to spend a lot more time with our guests, at least, for the near future."

The bench seat creaked again.

"Mr. Addison," Rod so politely began. "Where do the water and oxygen come from?"

"Great question. I am glad you asked. Before I departed from Earth, I took out a patent on an artificial system that produces oxygen and water."

"So, in reality, again, you cashed in on someone else's brain power and arduous work," Rod clarified.

Johnny kneed the bench seat so hard he fractured the back of it. As Rod winced at the sharp back pain, he sent Mercury a sideways stare.

"Enough of Q and A, down to business," the black-haired Santa directed the conversation. "Tasla and friends, I want you to construct a tower, a communications tower. It will be built inside the dome, of course. Its range will reach far into other galaxies. Johnny will direct my people to assist you with the labour. You have, in Earth time, three weeks. Do this, and freedom is yours."

Addison instructed Johnny to lock the seven below in 'Tasla's workshop' to begin drafting the design while he had a 'private meeting' with Adam.

***

"Fuck, fuck, fuck, three fucks, what the fuck are we going to do?" questioned OCD, in panic mode. "As soon as the Tri-bots recharge, we are fucked. Nine hundred and fuckin' something super bots . . ."

'Easy, Olly," Venus comforted.

Jeff had a quiet word with Tasla and then the others.

"Anal slime, I've got a plan. Step one, the Tri-bots are all linked to a common source. Johnny Mercury. If we take him out, the bots should become unmanaged and free-willed. Or perhaps they die. Step two is a bit tricky but not impossible. We lock Marsden in this room because the hatch is the only way out. Step three. Save Adam and find out what Addison is not telling us. He would surely have an escape plan. Tasla, we need you to design that tower like now. How long will it take?"

Tasla closed his eyes and raised his arms to the sides, palms up.

"Oh, here we go with the arch thing again," Enrique, less than impressed.

The Golden Arch of Light was so intense this time that everyone had to turn away and shield their eyes. When the brightness dimmed, Tasla stood with a finished design of his tower as the others picked their jaws up off the ground.

"Well, that's pretty impressive, kid," Enrique said, between mouthfuls of humble pie.

"Olly, when we get out into the compound, we will keep Johnny busy. We need you to find your marbles. Once you have them give us a sign," Jeff instructed with an added, "Fuck suckers."

Jeff filled them in on the rest of his plan to save themselves and indeed humankind.

Reg bashed on the hatch. A short time later, Marsden allowed the seven to ascend back to ground level, where Addison awaited. Johnny Mercury was quietly poised behind the crew, ready to leap into action if necessary.

"That was exceptionally quick, Tasla. A bit like my wit, really. Ha, ha, ha . . . wit . . . quick," Addison amusing himself.

"Yea, that's about half as quick as me. I guess that makes you a half-wit, Addison," Rod amusing the seven.

When Rod became conscious, he realised Johnny Mercury had just given him a powerful backhander.

Addison inspected the design and believed it to be authentic. The Tri-bots were fully recharged and upgraded via the electrical integration, thanks to Tasla's efforts. Close in number to 1000, the super Tri-bots stood motionless in the compound, waiting for instructions from Johnny Mercury. The construction began. Our heroes were kept under tight security as they worked, ate, and slept. The tower was taking shape, and unfortunately, the opportunity to put Jeff's plan into action had not arisen. Improvisation was called upon. Olly had sighted his trolley just inside the doors of the green brigade's six-storey building but was not able to retrieve it after two earth weeks. More Earth days passed, and Tasla's tower was almost completed.

Addison had not been sighted since the construction began, but Venus physically bumped into Adam as the crew passed him in the apartment hallway.

Venus cunningly announced, "We are so close to completing the tower. I hope the generator holds out."

Adam knew in an instant; he would have to sabotage the generator in a soundproof room through an access door at the back of Addison's lair before Tasla's tower was finished. Johnny Mercury believed Venus was sincere as the seven kept up falsified enthusiasm for the duration of the project and added comments like, "As soon as we finish, we are free. C'mon, let's get on with it."

***

Adam had his own plan to stop the generator. He knew his wonderful father showered at a regular time, with his music playing loudly. Adam also knew shortly afterwards he would be summoned to the lair. Adam had the freedom to move about the compound unguarded.

Adam left his apartment, heading for the great hall. As he passed Tasla's tower, Johnny asked him what he was doing. Obviously, Addy had asked Mercury to keep an eye on him after divulging information to the seven.

"Dad wants me, as usual, Johnny," Adam stated.

Johnny gave him the nod, and Adam made his way to Addison's Hall.

Meanwhile, back at the construction site:

"Are you giving me the raw prawn? You fuckin' cube-pooing wombat," Jeff verbally attacked Enrique.

"Eeediot," Enrique retaliated.

"I say, leave the poor blighter alone," Reg defended Enrique.

"Nah, fuck you, Reg, Pommy prick," Rod shouted.

A scuffle broke out. Mercury had his back to Olly and the green brigade's building. Olly saw the opportunity. He quietly wandered off while the commotion kept Johnny's attention. Olly was out of view and opened his case.

"One marble, two marbles . . ." The Count in action.

Jeff had asked him to fill his pockets with marbles, not count how many he put in his pocket!

The scuffle had ceased. Olly was still counting. Mercury twigged that OCD was missing. Johnny began scanning the area.

"Fifty-six marbles, fifty-seven marbles . . ."

Rod knew it would be painful, but desperate times call for desperate actions.

"Seventy-seven marbles, seventy-eight marbles," Olly had two large pockets. "Seventy-nine marbles, eighty marbles . . ."

"Hey, Johnny fuckin' Mercury. Let us play a game. I'll pretend I didn't fuck your mama, and you pretend you weren't enjoying watching, from outside the window, taking selfies, masturbating with her underwear on your head, dressed in an animal costume," Rod attempting to provoke Johnny.

Mercury ignored the comment and started to turn his head as he scanned the area for Olly.

"Ninety-six marbles, ninety-seven marbles . . ."

Rod let out a sigh while looking at Jeff and friends. He then turned to Johnny, sprinted straight towards him and at full speed, jumped feet first into Johnny's chest. Mercury stood, unmoved, looking down at Rod, lying on his back.

"What the fuck are you doing?" Johnny questioned.

Rod was unable to answer as most of the oxygen had escaped from his lungs, and he was trying desperately to fill them again. He had become quite accustomed to breathing over the years.

Mercury spotted Olly returning to the tower.

"Where were you?" Johnny asked.

"I had to do wee wees."

"Why are your pockets bulging?"

Before Olly could answer, Addison, with a towel wrapped around his fleshy waistline, made an appearance, Marsden, the bodyguard, right behind him.

"Johnny! The generator has stopped. We need to get it back online immediately. Leave the tower for now. Bring Tasla and lock the rest in their rooms," Addison instructed in a voice that spelt, 'Fuck am I pissed'? Addison, not even waiting for a response, returned to his lair.

"Adam, good to see you again. I did not even have to summon you this time. I'll just finish up."

Addison was heard humming as he completed his ablutions, and Adam reluctantly waited, sitting on Addy's bed.

Tas stared into Johnny's eyes. The mute spoke no words, yet Johnny knew what he wanted. Mercury did not wish to disobey his master, but Tasla let him know he could not fix the electrics without the help of Olly and Reg. All Tri-bots had stopped construction. Just like the union showing up on a 21st-century construction site.

The more Johnny was upgraded, the more he thought Addison was an inferior intelligence and not needed. Mercury made his own decision. The generator was of foremost importance to the Tri-bots. Johnny gave a nod to four of the reds, who escorted Enrique, Rod, Venus and Jeff back to the apartment block.

Johnny marched Tas, Reg and Olly into the great hall, under the podium and into Addy's lair. Adam sat waiting and gave Venus a secretive wink as they passed by and made their way through the doorway to the generator room.

While Addison was busy, Adam had placed several large ice cubes on top of some electrical components. As the ice melted, the main fuse blew. Adam was not suspected as Addy saw his son sitting, waiting and singing with the music at the same time the generator stopped. Then, of course, the ice that became water evaporated, hiding all evidence.

Johnny left Tas, and the 'fix it' crew in the generator room, standing guard outside the door, and Marsden stood outside Addy's bathroom.

After an abbreviated time, Reg bashed the door with extreme force. Johnny could not hear it as the door, too, was soundproofed. Marsden, however, with his refined hearing, signalled Johnny.

"It's not running. What is the problem? Fix it," Mercury demanded, standing in the open doorway.

"It's a collapsed bearing. We are not strong enough to lift the main shaft. Can you lift it, and we will block it up?" Reg asked Johnny.

Tas was situated next to the opened control panel, inspecting wires. Olly and Reg were bent over underneath the opened and braced main electrical panel.

Knowing the Tri-bots' fate depended on the working generator, Mercury gave a nod and proceeded forward. As Johnny stepped over the six-inch-high doorway, he stepped down onto Olly's marbles. He scrambled, losing his footing, and falling backwards. Reg had rigged a wire rope loosely, just above the height of the access door, from one side of the room to the other, which caught Johnny and stopped his backward fall. Johnny, leaning backwards but still not on solid ground, smiled at Reg and Olly's attempt at capsizing the cheetah leader of all Tri-bots.

Olly and Reg picked up a wire rope which lay at their feet and returned the smile, grinning from ear to ear. Johnny's face changed from a 21st-century Emoji cheesy grin to a 22nd-century, 'I'm about to get fucked up here' look as he followed the wire rope with his eyes, around the room to a precariously balanced large, spare, generator fan.

Olly and Reg pulled the rope with little effort. A small wedge was dislodged from the giant balancing fan. As the fan fell to the ground, the rope tightened very quickly, catapulting Johnny into the electrical components. While he was airborne, Tasla hit the switch.

Johnny Mercury fried. The smell could be likened to . . . well . . . you know when you throw on the bar-b a cheetah, some mechanical joints, and a couple of someone's limbs, (and haven't we all?), it sort of smelt like that unforgettable fragrance.

"So, it's true. There is more than one way to skin a giant cat," Olly summed up.

Marsden had heard the commotion from the generator room but stayed outside the bathroom, guarding his master. You gotta hand it to the guy. His sole purpose was to protect Addison.

Adam had now walked over to the access door and could see Mercury reduced to charcoal.

Reg announced, "'We are the champions.'"

Tasla, Reg and Olly stepped back into Addy's lair.

Adam thought, "If Dad is the King, then fried Mercury's 'Queen'."

Addison was finishing, still humming, oblivious to it all.

Rod, Venus and Jeff burst into Addison's room.

"The Tri-bots aren't responding," Rod joyfully informed the room's occupants.

After Venus broke the four out of the apartment room yet again, they pushed one of the four red guards over. Enrique deviated to the yellow brigade's apartment as they made their way back to Addy's lair. There were rows upon rows of super Tri-bots, standing motionless, at attention. Enrique pushed one of the bots into another, and the domino effect amused him greatly. He then deviated to the greens and then the blues and finally the reds. He made his way to meet the others. Upon entering Addison's room, he spotted Marsden. Enrique's eyes turned black.

"I am Muhasim."

Tas immediately covered Rod, Reg, Adam, Olly, Jeff and Venus in his Golden Arch of Light, keeping them safe without the need for any online site-specific, safety inductions.

Enrique, occupied by the ancient serial killer after more than two years, made a beeline for Marsden. Muhasim had been lost between two worlds. The living and the dead. With the end of planet Earth, he had been searching the universe for the last of the bloodline that defied him.

Enrique levitated about three feet. Tasla was most impressed.

Addison opened the bathroom door. He was stunned, to say the least. There was Tasla and crew in a bright golden arch, black-eyed Enrique levitating and Johnny Mercury still smoking.

Marsden's attention was diverted to his master for a split second. That was all Muhasim needed. He flew forward, grabbing Marsden's head with both hands. He twisted with great force, using Enrique's entire body weight. More than the giant could handle. Marsden dropped, limp, to the ground.

Enrique returned gently to the ground. He could feel Muhasim's satisfaction as he left Enrique's body for the last time. Unbeknownst to Enrique or Paul Elkato, Enrique's mother had an affair and became pregnant with Enrique. This meant the Spaniard was not of Paul's bloodline. Tasla's light dimmed.

"Fuck nose," Jeff began.

"Fuck knows what?" Addison enquired.

"You, fuck nose. Where is your shuttle?"

"I told you; I don't have one. It vanished when the outside was wiped."

"One more lie from you and I'll make you vanish!"

Adam said, "Guys, I think I know where it is."

"Adam. Son. Please don't."

"You are not my father. Do you think I did not know you kidnapped me as a small child? I remember my parents well. You did your usual thing and swindled them for every cent they had, and when their money was depleted, you demanded payment in the form of me. I had to play along with your sick fantasy in order to survive. Now, you can . . . well, you . . ."

Jeff said, "Allow me. You fuck festering, anal felching . . ."

As Jeff continued with about every profanity that came to the Tourette owner's mind, the others walked outside.

Addison would be left with Tasla's unfinished tower, no electricity and no other soul stuck on Miyanus for the rest of his miserable patented life.

Adam had the keys to the Korean space shuttle Addy had parked in a secret underground space shuttle garage. The eight boarded the shuttle and flew through the cloaking dome. The shape of the dome could be momentarily seen in an outline of electrical sparks and zaps as the vessel penetrated the shield.

Inside the shuttle, Tasla spoke for the first time.

"Is that an emu I see? What a pretty emu. I'd like to marry that emu."

"What about the light source? The flickering sky, the wipe-outs and the cloaking dome?" Rod threw out to the gang.

"We'll have to wait for this moronic writer to explain it all in part three."

On board:

The last chance for man to exist.

PART 3

INTO THE OTHER WORLD

CHAPTER 1

PLAY LIFE

The year 2130.

"Another failed simulation, Professor Summers?" Candice Sweet, head of Retro-Tech, asked, (so loudly across the program sector, that employees in other sectors could hear), as she walked closer to the professor, running her fingers through her long, blonde-tipped brown hair.

"Mith thweet, we are getting clother. The more thimulathionth we run, we ditholve more problemth," Professor Summers said adjusting his white lab coat.

"Your speech impediment program is obviously working for you, Professor. You are talking much more clearly now."

"Yeth, thometimeth people don't even notithe. Maybe, thomeday I'll be public thpeaker for our thimulation program," the professor suggested, raising his shoulders and swivelling in his chair.

"Stranger things have happened. For now, though, we need to fix several glitches in the system. It was a bit concerning when one of the characters thought the sky was flickering."

"Yeth, we had a thudden power thurge. The main regulator blew, but it hath been fickthed, now."

"The cloaking dome was pure genius, Professor. We were able to monitor the events inside the dome, but from inside the dome, the occupants were not able to see out. We wiped all traces of activity; thus, our competitor's programs were unable to detect our progress on the simulated planet, 'Miyanus'. Being able to manipulate what and when we deleted people and objects was a fantastic advantage."

"Thertainly, and the input of divine intervention, in the form of Tathla, was quite an interethting eckthperiment."

"From all our 112 simulations, that one was the most satisfying and educational exercise to date. We witnessed the colonel and the best of humankind, The Golden Arch of Light, Tasla's Tower and the Tri-bots. I am expecting the next one to be extremely entertaining; however, we need to show our progress to the board of directors. Unfortunately, their interest is only directed by greed. They do not have the foresight or even care about the importance of what we do here. Unbelievable, is it not? The fate of humankind depends on our research, and all they give a damn about is how many credits they have. What good are credits when we are destined for destruction? 'At Retro-Tech, we give a damn.' What a joke. Do they think this is a game?"

"There are board memberth?"

"Well, yes. The board was established years ago. Are you all right, Sassan?"

"Ah, yeth, I'm fine. We will talk more about that in private later, Candith."

***

Jolene, Candice's personal assistant, entered the operations room. "Excuse me, Miss Sweet. Mister Eros is waiting in your office."

"What? Clint braved the Indian? Clint Eros is down here? Let's not leave him unattended. Jo, please tell Mister Eros I will play with . . . I mean I will see him shortly."

"No need, I've already come," Mister Eros announced as his eyebrows entered the operations centre, followed by the rest of a confident man.

"Clint! What an unexpected, pleasant surprise," Candice said, looking at this tall, dark- haired man.

"Unexpected surprise? Yes. Pleasant? Hardly," Clint answering his own rhetorical questions. "Mr. Sole called me. I am here to conduct a preliminary investigation on behalf of the board."

"Investigation? Investigation of what?" Candice asked, narrowing her eyes.

"What, why, when and who, to be precise," Eros correcting Miss Sweet. "It seems information about the simulation program is being leaked to our competitors."

"We have a mole? Mister Eros, I can personally vouch for everyone connected with this operation."

"And who can vouch for you, Miss Sweet?"

There was an awkward silence throughout the operations room.

Retro-Tech is situated on an unmapped, restricted island in the Indian Ocean, about halfway between

Madagascar and Australia. There is enough room for accommodation, a small runway, and the Retro-Tech Operations Centre. The four-storey building hosts the main operations room on the third floor. The floor itself is divided into two main parts. The cyber experts work in glass partitioned offices, gathering information, analysing data, and developing smaller programs or pre-programs for input and basic preparation for the simulation program.

The second half of the floor is devoted to the program in progress. Operated by staff, in the pre-program sector, there are seven small computers with various attachments, which are fed to the main computer, controlled by Professor Sassan Summers. In front of the professor is an exceptionally large holographic display, approximately eight metres long by three metres high, to view the current simulation in progress. In the top right corner of the image is an input box, which signifies items ready to upload into the running program. For example, Tasla's tower draft.

"Miss Sweet, Mister Van Real is waiting in the pre-program sector."

"Well, send him in, send him in," Candice, encouraging Jo.

"Roland! So good to see you. How are you?" Candice asked.

"Weally tewific. And you?" the boyish looking, thirty-two-year-old American answered and questioned.

"I'm very well, thank you. You know Clint."

"Roland," Clint greeted, his enormous eyebrows twitching. "Why are you here?"

"I've been asked to wun a pweliminawy investigation into possible corpowate espionage."

"How odd. Me too," Clint informed.

Jo politely waited for an audible gap. "Miss Sweet, Mr. Dunny has arrived."

"Candice. Looking mighty hot as usual," said Mr. Dunny, a hairy blonde with an unmaintained beard and bad breath.

"Oh, stop it, Dennis. Always a pleasure," Candice said, releasing the pin from her bun, her long, blonde-tipped hair dropping as she shook her head, running her fingers through her hair. She was once offered a hair modelling contract, which she was forever reminding people about.

"Roland? Clint? What is going on here?" Dennis asked.

"Excuse me, Miss Sweet. Doctor Bottoms . . ." Jo began.

"Candice!" Bottoms, a long black haired, pretty woman in a white see-through dress interrupted. "How positively delightful to see you again."

"Oppeniya. How long has it been?" Candice, greeted with a step forward and a kiss over the shoulder.

"Only a few weeks, really," Bottoms replied, then looked to the others. "Gentlemen."

"Oppeniya," Clint nodded, reaching for a scone. "Don't tell us. Arros contacted you. You have been called upon to run an investigation."

"Well, yes. But how did you know? It was supposed to be confidential."

"We've been asked to do the same thing," Roland answered for all.

"Do you know what this is about, Candy, my sweet?" Dennis enquired, spooning sugar into his coffee.

"Well, there are rumours that...," Candice started.

"Sorry to interrupt Miss Sweet, but Mr. Driver and Mr. Hail are here to see you."

"Send them in please, Jo."

As Jo with the girl next door appearance, was heading through the doorway, she bumped into the door. She stepped back and then forward, again, into the door. She tilted her head briefly and sharply, took a few seconds, then proceeded to go around the object.

"Max. How are y . . . I mean . . ." Candice stopped mid-sentence.

"Too late, Candice," Oppeniya said.

"Firstly, thanks for asking. I'm a little bit down, somewhat depressed, verging on suicide really, but contemplating mass murder and coming to terms with the very real prospect of facing inevitable consequences, that I may grab a large, jagged knife, viciously and brutally sawing the throat of the person, and woe to he, who makes it to the top of my 'who's pissed me off today' list."

"Sounds like you are doing much better Max," Candice acknowledged, then turned to Mr Hail. "Skip! Good to see you."

"Likewise, Candy," Mr. Hail said. "What's going on here? I've been asked to—"

Everyone said in a monotone voice, ". . . conduct a preliminary investigation."

***

"Oppeniya, gentlemen. The director, Mr. Arros Sole, has given me extensive and absolute power to conduct this investigation," Candy began. "He believes he has identified the department that harbour's the offender."

"This is most unusual, but, of course, Arros Sole always pushes shit downhill. So, if you are running this investigation, Candice, why do we, the board, need to be here? Seems you have it all under control," Clint stated.

Candice looked at them and noticed their curious, concerned expressions.

"Members of the board, it seems one, or possibly more of you, is guilty of corporate espionage."

There was an uproar from the board members. Diplomatic, professional phrases were heard to have been said, in the fashion of; "Nah! Fuck off!" and "Oh, for fuck's sake!" and "For the sakes of fucking!" and "Weally?" and "Can you tell I'm not wearing any underwear?"

"I'm not being subject to this. I'm out of here," declared Maximillian Driver, rotating his black driving cap from back to front. Max was smart, always seemed to be in control and wasn't afraid of chaos.

Candice signalled Jo. The assistant walked to the entrance of the preparation sector. She looked left, then right. Nothing was coming, so she proceeded to nod, then stepped aside. Through the entrance doors, making their way to the program room, four security guards unsettled the foundations of the building with each step. 'Buster,' 'Smasher,' 'The Red Man' and Rubortakov Trovoski, the Russian affectionately known as 'Robski' (although no one knew who would affectionately call him anything), ushered the board members into the glass-panelled, designated smoking area/conference room/children's play area, located to the side of the partitioned offices.

(Children were given ashtrays and butts to play with, but if they offended the smokers, rain, hail, or shine, they would have to stand outside, a minimum of five meters away from the entrance).

"Please be seated, and we will get this over with ASAP," Candice prompted. "Oh hi, Smasher. How long has it been?"

"It's been twenty years, 'Candy', give or take."

"'Well, I'm pleased you got out," Candice chatted as the board members 'pop'ped themselves into available seats.

Robski and Smasher stood in the conference room, arms crossed over their chests, either side of the entrance, facing the conference table, the glass doors now closed behind them. The Red Man and Buster positioned themselves on the other side of the room, either side of Candice. Any attempt to escape would have the same result as the chances of our ruling bodies admitting they have deceived us for many years regarding the confirmation of the existence of extraterrestrials. Not happening.

"Candice, how do we know with certainty that there has been a leak in our boat?" Skip, the ex-navy captain asked, dressed in navy shorts and a blue naval shirt, which was too small and exposed his navel.

"During our last simulation, a young girl had been uploaded, via an unknown source, into our system. She was a suicide bomber and managed to delete three soldiers who were of importance to the survival of one of our main subjects, Reginald Hargraves. She was also responsible for a prophecy relating to our input character, Tasla"

"Well, that doesn't prove a thing," Max interrupted, turning his cap visor to the front. "It could have been a glitch or an oversight or . . . who's in charge of this system, anyway?

Through the glass panels, Candice gave Jo a nod in the direction of Professor Summers. Jo whispered into the professor's ear. Through the glass walls, Sassan made eye contact with Candice and entered the room while Smasher and Russian Rob played a familiar tune of 'Bounce the Door'.

The professor was licking his lips, and frequently looking at the sweat on Skips forehead.

"Professor, you look a bit parched. Would you like a drink?" Candice offering Jo's services.

"I'll have 'Full cream dairy milk," Professor Summers said, prompting Jo to retrieve some milk and a couple of glasses.

"Professor Summers, please tell the board your name and position in this company," Candice requested.

"My name is Profether Thathan Thummerth. I am the chief controller of our current thimulation, known as 'The Program'. I anther only to Mith Thweet," Sassan clearly answered, standing next to Candice.

"Now please tell the board what the suicide bomber gave reference to, just before every cell of her DNA was distributed randomly and rapidly within a twenty-metre radius of the initial explosion."

"Thertainly. Her eckthact wordth were, 'For The Program.'"

Candice continued. "At first, we thought it was regarding the APC's designer baby program, but after Sassan ran a diagnostic, it became clear someone was trying to sabotage our simulations using a copy of our own program. As you now know, the proof is undeniable. This facility is under strict supervision, twenty-four-seven. The only avenue of outside communication is monitored by an independent security company appointed by Mr. Sole.

CHAPTER 2

SKIPPER HAIL

"So, to deal with this inquiry, Skip, you are first on my left," Candice initiating the investigation.

"Candice, surely you don't think I'm the mole?"

"As you know, Skipper, I gave that thinking thing up years ago when I decided gossiping with the other mothers outside the school was way more important than watching my blind, six-year-old cross the highway on her skateboard during peak-hour traffic."

"Yea, that's right. Of course. Yes, she did. I remember now. Weally? Are you sure you can't tell I have no underwear on?" came the assorted affirmations.

Skipper Hail loved the ocean and his preferred method of transport; his sixty-foot cabin cruiser, which he appropriately named *SS Extant*. He arrived at 'Retro-Tech Island' by way of his beloved cruiser. Before joining the landlocked Chad Naval Defense of North/Central Africa, Skip ran a charter cruise in the swamp lands of Paraguay, South America. After five days of digging, he realized it was a judgemental error and made the decision to set up shop elsewhere. Moving his business to the Gobi Desert, he believed, was a step in the right direction. Re-tracking his steps, he soon concluded that the lack of water was an oversight on his behalf. Skip then bought a map and had his cruiser airlifted to the heart of the Pacific Ocean. He hired another charter cruiser to sail out to his boat, thousands of kilometres off the coast of Vanuatu.

"Thanks for the lift, Captain," Skip rose from his knees in appreciation.

Skipper Hail sailed back to the east coast of New Zealand and began what was to become a thriving business called Cheap Sheep Ship Tours. The tiny island was host to tens of thousands of sheep. They were considered sacred, the same way Asian Indians considered cows to be sacred.

One eventful day, five passengers and his first mate Harrison set sail for the tour of a sheep's lifetime. The captain's navigation system and radar had erred three times recently, and each time Skip had it repaired by The Ferx Ert Bro, another successful NZ business. (The company had a sideline business selling, and quote, 'Churkins and iggs'). Believing his equipment was in good working order, Skip headed out, searching for an uncharted desert isle as an adventure for Harrison and his passengers. The excitement in the passenger's eyes didn't go unnoticed.

"Aww, look at Rosey," Harrison said to his captain.

Harrison thought Rosey was by far the prettiest passenger on board, and she should have been a model or actress or both.

As the *SS Extant* headed out to unknown territories, the weather turned nasty. The navigation system failed yet again. The ship was in the lost basket. A huge storm dictated the fate of the ship and passengers. They ran aground and were marooned on an island somewhere in the South Pacific. With luck on their side, the surviving crew and passengers were able to keep hydrated after the shipwreck by means of a flowing waterfall. However, there was not nearly enough food that could be scavenged or picked, and for some unknown reason, fish avoided the island. Skip guessed it might have had something to do with all the open barrels that had washed ashore, labelled, 'Warning. Hazchem. Toxic chemicals. Do not digest. Do not use as haemorrhoid cream'. Harrison thought he might be able to bottle it as an SPF 800 mother-in-law sunscreen.

Days passed by as Harrison and Skip realised they were in a desperate situation. The communications on the ship were destroyed.

Skip thought, "*I'll get the Ferx Ert Bro to take care of that when I get back to civilisation. I should have bought some churkins and iggs from them, too, whatever they are.*"

More unplanned dieting days resulted in a life-changing decision for passengers and crew. As there were no plastic straws on the island and no coins in any pockets, 'Paper, Rock and Scissors', became the mutually acceptable alternative.

"Best out of three?" Skipper Hail offered Harrison.

"Sure, Skipper," Harrison said, looking over the top of his dark tinted glasses, pushing his dreadlocks to the side.

Skip won, fairly, two in a row, claiming 'Dynamite' beats them all. Harrison had no choice. He offered his left leg as an appetiser. The captain gracefully accepted and, to show his good faith, offered Harrison the calf. After their stomachs were full, they threw the bones to the passengers. Skip retired for the night, and Harrison, too, hopped off to sleep.

As Harrison was quite attached to his limbs, he made a forsaken suggestion when Skip was noted eyeing off Harrison's right leg.

"Captain, how about we eat one of the passengers?"

"Oh, little buddy. I can't believe you even considered that. You know our duty of care is to the passengers first. What would happen to my business if potential customers found out we were eating our passengers?"

"Yeah, you are right, Skip. Well, I'm famished."

"Mmm, I could eat an entire lamb. Tonight, we will have steamed leg of Harrison."

"Let me know when it's ready, Skipper."

Captain and first mate enjoyed their meal before Skip retired for an early night. Harrison stayed up a little later and then finally dragged himself to bed.

The pair began their next feast with finger food for entrée. The captain had the night off from slaving over a hot fire as Harrison leant a hand. They ate until satisfied, and once again, it was time to call it a night. The captain was a little restless for a short time that night. He wondered if Harrison might try to turn the table and devour some of the skipper's anatomy. But then he realised, Harrison was quite armless.

The days rolled on. The passengers were looking rather plump from all the greenery they had consumed.

"You'll be happy to know the passengers are doing fine, little buddy, but now it's time for you to throw your heart and soul into your job. So long, my good friend."

With those touching last words of a loyal, caring, mutually devoted, fifteen-year friendship, the captain separated Harrison's head from his body. As there were no knives or sharp instruments to be found, Hail did as he had done on previous nights, and the last meal was prepared by tearing the body apart. He placed both feet on Harrison's shoulders, twisted and pulled until the head came off. Then with brute force, he smashed the chest cavity, creating ribs ready for a barbecue. The skipper ate well that night and drifted off to sleep rather peacefully.

He awoke the next morning to a gentle nudging from one of the passengers. She was directing the captain to the grounded ship. The skipper followed her to the lagoon's edge. Floating and tied to the hull was the emergency 400 hp, 20ft dingy with enough fuel to make it to the mainland bearing any direction.

"Well, aren't you clever?" the skipper threw out there. "I think I'll name you, 'The Teacher.'"

The captain retrieved Harrisons's head, checked tickets and boarded the passengers onto the large dingy. He gave the *SS Extant* a quick temporary fix, tied it to the dingy and towed the ship towards the first mainland he sighted. The day turned to night, and oddly two passengers howled intermittently at the full moon.

How weird, he thought. *I'll name them 'The Howlers'.*

So, there was the Skipper, The Teacher, The Howlers, Rosey, the should-have-been actress and the head of Harrison, all sailing back to the mainland. Captain Hail found himself mooring the dingy, freakily, in the same harbour he had departed from.

As the passengers departed, he farewelled with, "Thanks for sailing with Cheap Sheep Ship Tours. I hope you enjoyed the experience. Please come again."

Hail had the Ferx Ert Bro make the necessary repairs, and it wasn't long before he set sail again. This time he travelled solo. On his journey, he took the time to reflect on his previous trip. He cursed himself for what he had done. He knew if he departed from India, he would have had cows for passengers, and he and Harrison could have feasted on beef for a long time (as he had no intention of returning to India) before he had to consider devouring his first mate.

Destiny has a strange path. Again, a freak storm marooned the *SS Extant* in the same lagoon as Harrison met his demise. The skipper was prepared this time. He set up camp, hanging a hammock. He had eggs for breakfast and chicken for dinner. After he ate, he sat next to the campfire. He sat Harrison's head on a rock and indulged in light conversation. After three weeks, he found the chat was repetitive, and he felt he needed to change it up. He retrieved from the ship an Australian rules football stamped with the brand, 'Sherydan'. He sat the oval football, on end, beside Harrison's head. He had drawn facial features on it.

"Why the long face, Sherydan?" he asked.

Boredom had set in two weeks later, so he decided to have a kick on the beach sand, imagining: The final siren had sounded. Hail kicking for a goal to win the game and ultimately the Grand Final. He lines it up, allowing for the wind. It's a long kick from centre-half forward . . . Skip booted Harrison's head so hard his eyeball stuck to the skipper's big toe, but an amazing kick, all the same. 'Goal', the imaginary crowd went wild.

The captain picked up the onlooker, Sherydan, after a hot spell in the sun.

"What do you say, Sherydan? Let's go for a swim in the big blue?"

The pair frolicked in the Pacific Ocean for a while then, from out of the blue, a shark fought off some eagles, cats and bulldogs, for the right to grab the ball and run.

"Sherydan! No, come back. Sherydan," Hail was reduced to tears, shouting to his friend.

Try as he might, he could not encourage the shark to part with the Australian rules footy. His new-found friendship was suspended, sidelined indefinitely.

The captain was rescued by another charter cruise from India. It was a much larger vessel, carrying twenty crew and thirty cows. The crew appeared malnourished and had left their port, apparently, with twenty-five crew and thirty cows. The Indian ship towed the *SS Extant* all the way to Northern Africa.

"Thanks, captain," Hail simply said, wiping his chin.

Although The Cheap Sheep Ship Tours was successful, Skipper decided a change was in the air. He saw an advert for the Chad Naval Defence and applied for a position. He spent a few years with the Chad Navy, however, his time spent on the water was rather limited. He had made enough credits to invest in Retro-Tech, and later became a board member. To this day, annually, he honours his deceased first mate by kicking his stuffed head for an imaginary, game-saving goal.

***

"Skip, you have contacts all over the world. Primarily in New Zealand and Africa. Correct?" Candice asked, closing her eyes, lifting her hair and with beams of sunlight from the window, intermittently shing through as she released it, opened her eyes to look at Skip.

"Yes, those are two of a long list," he replied. "But I don't see what relevance . . ."

Candice interrupted, "And you would be able to transport just about anything, undetected, would you not?"

"I suppose that is a truthful statement."

"Have you ever transported hi-tech equipment?"

"Ah...not that I remember, Candice."

"Dementia? Alzheimer's?"

"I transport so many things and have done for so many years. No, I honestly don't remember.

Candice continued, "I have a copy of the manifest from your boat trip three weeks ago, captain."

Skip's composure changed from that of an innocent man to what could be likened to a nun being discovered advertising for a bestiality gang bang, stipulating minimum length and diameter.

"We will leave it there, for now, Skip," Candice setting a stage. "Roland. Even though you have changed seats, you are still next."

CHAPTER 3

ROLAND

Roland Van Real was taught by his father at an early age. Staring at his arrangement of trophies on the mantlepiece, Roland was keen to follow in his father's footsteps. His father was a well-built, strong man, feared by most at first sight. Roland had the perfect instructor and would gratefully accept any advice.

"No, No, son," his father, Sabian, said. "Left hand first, like so," (Sabian swiftly brought his hand down). "Then left again then right."

Roland practised that combination for some weeks, and then, pleased with his effort, he returned to his father.

Whack! Whack! Wham! "How's that Dad?"

"Not too bad, only hit a little harder, and now add the kick."

An hour later, sweating profusely, Roland called on his dad again.

Whack! Whack! Wham! Bang! Roland waited for a response.

"Your timing is out," Sabian criticized.

Overrun by frustration, Roland hit out as hard as he could.

"You'll break something if you keep that up, son."

Six months of gruelling practice and a bucket full of sweat had passed, Roland was learning more combinations and basics.

Kick! Left! Kick! Right!

"You have improved dramatically, son," his father stated as he entered the garage one evening. "Your basic skills and timing will prove to be a great advantage over your competition. You have developed good rhythm with your footwork, and your hand speed is exceptional. I think it has come time."

"Weally?" Roland anxiously asked.

"Yes, son. This weekend we will buy you your own brand new drumkit. Any brand preference?"

"Woland, of course."

They both laughed. Roland was on his way to becoming, unfortunately, another obsolete drummer. However, Roland did have the foresight to know that the electronic age was where music was heading; again, unfortunately.

Music has changed so much through the ages. Each new generation had its own ideas of what music should sound like. It is believed music originated from the chirping of birds. Sweet melodies from our feathered friends. The first instrument to resemble a guitar was recorded in history some 3,450 years ago. The drum can be dated back some 7,000-plus years ago. Even before that, prehistoric humans used sticks to hit objects, creating a rhythm.

Sticks have been used for many various tasks throughout the ages. Teaching children lessons by beating them with a stick seemed to be the best method for those who were not crash hot at parenting skills. It is widely accepted that the only lesson the child got from this method, was "Mum and dad are sadists". Some children misinterpreted the lesson as, "Run like hell. They are picking up a stick". Some parents realised the child was not bad and faced the harsh reality that the reason they hit their kids was due to their own frustration. They were not getting their message through clearly, to the child. So, altering their teaching technique made a lot more sense than beating their child senseless. It also saved on hospital bills. However, the truly narcissistic and/or sadistic claimed, "It's not as much fun."

These like-minded people were also heard to have said, "Let the children go first," as they evaluated the shark-infested waters.

Also, "Let the children go last," as they counted a shortage of parachutes in the crash-diving plane.

A more compassionate and thoughtful use of sticks was to dig a hole, half embed the sticks on end, and then camouflage the hole. Brilliant! Some other human ingenuity, for the use of sticks, came in the form of arrows, spears, poison darts, lances, torture tools, matches, witch burnings and crucifixion, to mention a few. Some less colourful uses include the non-returning boomerang and toothpicks. For Roland, though, it was all about hitting things with sticks. Mostly drums.

Music, through the ages, has surpassed classical, jazz, blues, rock, roll, soul, funk, metal, heavier metal, thrash, hip hop, doov-doov, punk, etc. Of course, in the late 2000s, heavy pop doov with sprinkles of classical B-bop was everyone's favourite. Progressing into this year, 2130, what we hear is a collaboration of high-pitched electronic squeals from a synthesiser, backed up by an underlining base that could be mistaken for a Harley Davison that sported an actual working muffler, a guitar noise that sounds like it's playing a totally different song, vocals that are over-sung in so many different keys, no one is really sure what key they should be playing and a drum sound that reflects an electrified, wet cardboard box.

At the age of twenty, with all the technological advancements, Roland found himself playing all instruments, on his electronic drum kit, in the city of Grand Rapids, Michigan. He had completed courses in high tech and was rather switched on, quite the bright spark with anything electrical. He called himself 'The Red Riva Rat.' The band, he, went on tour heading north, along the west coast. Sacramento, Portland, over the Canadian border to Vancouver and then, (where everything went south), Seattle. He had a reasonable voice, and the ten or so gigs he had played went extremely well. The novelty of a drummer performing the squeals and muffler sounds of modern music appealed to the young, not terribly bright, masses.

The people from Seattle were a little different to the other audiences. On this night, their sense of humour had taken a turn to quite bizarre and was fuelled by a few too many drinks.

"Good evening, everyone. I am the Wed Wiver Wat from The Gwand Wapids," Roland introducing himself.

The crowd were in hysterics. Roland didn't understand what they were laughing at.

"Hey, wat. What bwand is your dwum kit?" A smart-ass Roland would later learn was John Child, looked at his underaged brothers.

"Woland, of course, it's on the fwont of my dwum kit," Roland announced through his microphone.

The crowd lost it. Roland was seeing red.

"What's your name? Wobert?" the smart ass loudly asked.

"No, it's Woland," the drummer answered.

Some of the patrons were now rolling on the floor in fits of laughter.

"Woland van Weal," he yelled back at the ass.

More people began hysterically laughing.

"Weally? What is wong with you people?" Roland asked.

The ass continued with his shit storm, "Let me get this stwaight," he continued as more and more people hit the floor, tears running down their faces. "You are Woland Van Weal, The Wed Wiver Wat fwom Gwande Wapids, with a Woland dwum kit?"

Roland clicked as to the source of the Seattleite humour and could not contain his anger. He arose from the drumkit, pushing his drumsticks into his back pocket and walked toward the exit.

"Hey, look, ol' Wed is leaving," the talking ass continued dribbling.

You could have heard a drumstick drop as Roland stopped and locked the door. When the door was opened again, not a Child boy was standing; They were all on the floor, holding their stomachs and sides from laughing so much.

The night wasn't a total loss, however. John Child was taken to a care facility known as the Seattle Hospital for Internal Trauma (SHIT) with an obstacle stuck in his dribbling orifice. Roland had found yet another use for a drumstick before he left the venue. John would be able to sit again in a few weeks, but Roland spent some time in a prison cell for assault with a musical weapon.

***

Jail, for Roland, initially, was shared with one other occupant. The 'lifer' was covered from head to toe in tattoos. 'Leave children be', on his forehead, 'Don't hurt kids', on his right eyeball and 'I'll fuck you up if you attack young'uns', on his well-endowed digit, were just a few.

"What are you in for?" the evil, intimidating, red-haired man with an enormous penis asked.

"I sent a Child to SHIT," Roland answered without much thought.

It seems Roland was so impressed with the words of the latter tattoo he had them inserted into his anus after he was beaten to a pulp. When he got out of the SHIT, he was placed in another cell with a new lifer.

"What are you in for?" asked the dark-haired man, a lifer from a road rage incident. (The official report stated, "I saw him from 400 metres away. He did not use his indicator").

"J-walking," replied Roland, with his thinking cap on.

The lifer turned to a shade of green and seemed to grow into a huge beast. "I hate scum that dis-obey road rules," he announced, looming over him.

When Roland returned from the SHIT again, he was placed in a cell with yet another lifer.

"What are you in for," asked the curly-haired criminal.

"I . . . I . . . I'm in for . . . ah . . . have we met?" Roland answered, possibly saving his own ass from another SHIT trip.

"I'm known as 'The Woodster'."

"Yes, yes, you wewe in that gang, 'Connie and Snyde'. You tewowised staff at a fast-food outlet."

"You got me there. I was on that TV show, 'Worlds Most Hardened Criminals'. I had been on the run for three years before the law caught up with me."

"Yes, I wemember. What was it you said to that man at McYuks?"

"Well, it was most regrettable. I don't know what came over me. I said to the young man behind the counter, 'Excuse me. I know you are terribly busy with your phone game and message chat-a-long, but I ordered and paid for a dry bun with nothing in it fifty minutes ago. Nobody else has entered the shop, and no hover cars have come through the hover-through. Do you think it will be much longer?'"

"Ooo, you didn't?"

"As I said, regrettable. Unfortunately, there was a hostage situation in the next suburb. All twelve police hover cars and the Armed Response for Special Entities (ARSE) stormed the shop within minutes. I was lucky to have escaped. I wasn't coy, I slipped out the back and made a new plan."

"Hmm, eva thought about witing a song?"

"No, 'words don't come easy to me'. What about you, though? What's your name? What is your specialty?"

"Well, I'm Woland. I'm a dwummer, and weally, electwonics is my thing."

"You don't say? How would you like to make a dozen fwiends . . . I mean friends, instantly?"

"I could always do with a new fwiend, Woodsta. What is it you and your pals would like?" asked naive Roland.

"This jail is all run by electrics, thanks to Tasla. Electric pass codes, electric doors, electric toothbrushes, etcetera."

The reason for the friendship in want suddenly became clear to Roland.

"I only weceived a two-week-sentence. I don't want to jeopawdize my welease time."

"The thing is, Roland, I am trying to do you a favour, my new friend. If my pals find out, and they will, that you won't help them, they will do anything to make sure you stay for a very long time. Some of them are not as nice as The Woodster."

"I don't know, Woodsta. If I'm caught . . ."

The Woodster interrupted, "This is what friends are for. I have a feeling, well, it's 'more than a feeling' my friend 'Boston' could have you playing in the best venues in the States. We've got your back, Roland. Some of my friends are connected in extremely high places. You help us in here. We help you out there. What do you say?"

***

Candice continued her interrogation. "Before you became a board member, you were quite exceptional in the electronics field, were you not?"

"I dabbled a bit in my eawier days, Candice. It is not a secwet," Roland replied.

"Dabbled? You reconfigured every musical instrument and the entire sound system at the Central Resonating Artistic Performances (CRAP), an establishment for the musical cyber party of the century, did you not?"

"Well, I . . . yes, I did, a long time ago," Roland reluctantly answered.

"With that, we move on," Candice said.

"Where are you going with all this, Candice?" Max asked, rotating his black cap.

"All in good time, Max. We will get to you shortly." She turns to him, skewering him with a look.

CHAPTER 4

DENNIS

Like so many other wars, World War III of 2103 saw thousands of lives lost.

It is believed the conflict began with two innocent young boys. A seven-year-old from Russia and a six-year-old from Hungary were at the centre of the media-soaked dispute. Ukraine had fallen peacefully ten years earlier without a single shot fired, back under the rule of Russia. As seventy-five per cent of the Ukrainian population were Russian, there were not many to oppose. Russia and Ukraine became Russia again, and they all lived as one happy family, similar to that of a popular western family in the late 1900s, known as 'The Addams Family'. Although their day-to-day living and beliefs were quite bizarre, they had a harmonious existence.

"I smash you with bottle on head; you kick me in groin", was stereo-typical of the culture.

A wire mesh fence had been established as a dividing boundary of the two countries. Not quite the Berlin Wall look-alike from around 140 years ago, but the result was still the same; This side and that side. Tanks, ground-to-air missiles, soldiers and sticks could be found guarding the line for the opposing countries.

The families from both sides lived close to the separating boundary. Although it was not encouraged by both sides, the two boys had a unique relationship. They would meet along the fence after school and would share thoughts, conversation and laughs. The two became close friends after a few months of regular rendezvous.

According to history, the two boys met one decisive day as usual. On this day they agreed to play a game of 'Pick Up Sticks' (an alternative use for a small, light, slender length of wood). The sticks were set up, directly under the middle of the boundary fence, in a slight depression. The mutually acceptable rule was the sticks you pick up, without disturbing the others, are yours to keep. The winner was the one with the most sticks. The sticks had no value, and the loser would just collect some more from around their area to play round two. The Russian child had his turn, and then it was the Hungarian's. As the child picked up, using the tips of his fingers, the stick fell awkwardly through the gap of the wire fence, landing next to the pile but not unsettling the other sticks.

"Here, Frigyes," Rubortakov kindly said, attempting to pass his friend the stick.

Then, running towards the children, a Russian adult screamed, "No, nyet, no!!"

"What is wrong, Papa?" Rubortakov asked, quite shaken from the unexpected outburst.

"Stick on Russian soil. Stick belong to Russia."

"It's just a game, Papa. There are plenty more sticks."

Frigyes' mother was close by and saw the entire event. "The sticks were not disturbed. It's Hungarian stick."

"It's all right, Mama; Rubortakov can have it," Frigyes eased. "We have many sticks nearby."

"No, Russian must give it," she affirmed.

A Hungarian soldier had picked up on the increasingly heated debate. "Woman is right. Hand stick over."

Three Russian soldiers wearing the ushanka had heard the commotion. "Russian ground. We give, nyet."

Luckily for both sides (and the reader), they were able to communicate, using broken English.

More soldiers from both sides gathered as the debate escalated. Meanwhile, the two boys moved their game farther along the boundary line and attempted to play again.

The first known rifle shots of WWIII had been initiated. The parents from both sides were killed in the exchange. The boys ran for cover, and the turmoil of war dictated they would not see each other as children again.

For years after the event, psychologists, psychiatrists, war veterans, politicians, yoga instructors and teams of specialists were unable to determine how two young, innocent children from two different countries were able to dissolve a possible difference of opinion, in a matter of seconds, with no declaration of war, no casualties, no threats, no parental guidance and not even a sideways glance. It is hopeful that in the future, rocket scientists may decipher the mystery of how human beings can exist in harmony. Then perhaps, the mentally challenged can explain it to the fine examples of educated, war-mongering country 'leaders'.

With the movement of Hungary joining the Commonwealth in 2101, some believed war was a forgone conclusion, as Russia weren't terribly impressed with the idea. Russian leaders were hoping to take control of Hungary before they joined with other nations. The fifteen-year war was upon the Russians before they had planned. After five years of fighting, it became more of a cold war.

***

Dennis showed exceptional artistic skills at a young age. He excelled in subjects that related to his passion. With the onslaught of war, Dennis found himself in Hungary, under Commonwealth rule.

"Colonel, sir," the thinly structured, in touch with his feminine side lieutenant began. "We have located Private Dunny, sir."

"Well, very good man, show him in," Colonel Rigby of the English SAS ordered. The colonel, in uniform and handlebar moustache, held a strong English accent, however, he was born in a tiny, illiterate, uneducated town, (the same town 20th century English cab drivers were born). He was taught to use the word, 'what', to prompt a response.

A young Australian soldier presented himself to the colonel in the office of the Hungarian-based Commonwealth camp.

"It's common practice to salute your superior officer, Private," the colonel stated.

"Two things, sir. Firstly, If I salute you, I put a target on your back. Secondly, I'm Australian, and I don't care much for silly rules."

"By Jove, Lieutenant, I think we have our man. You are an artist, a good artist, Private. I understand you recently drew, free hand, a ten-credit icon which was passed into the American Federal Reserve, what."

"Yes, sir. It was a test for whatever this mission entails," Dunny said, turning his head slightly.

"Why did you agree to this mission, Private, what?"

"What?" Dunny scratched his head.

"Have you no ears?" the colonel asked, twirling his handlebars.

"As I understand it, sir, it could result in the end of the war."

"Jolly well, ol' boy. Let me lay it out for you. We need you to forge some papers for the release of a prisoner the Russians claim they don't have. The prisoner is the rightful Russian Tzar, Dominicov Lotokickbacks. If he is freed, a coup will overthrow the present dictatorship, ending the cold war, what."

"I can start immediately, sir, if you can provide me with the material and a copy of the required papers."

"Oh, I love the enthusiasm, Private Dunny, and I wish, for your sake, it was that simple."

"What aren't you telling me, Colonel?"

"You will need a recent photograph of his face, to attach to the official release papers and his signature. No one has seen him for thirteen years. We could simulate how he has aged, but if we get it wrong, I don't need to tell you what could happen."

"So, I need to be in the jail with him?"

"Now you have the picture, my good man. Ha . . . picture . . . release papers . . . with the photo . . . and . . . ha, ha."

"Oh, bravo. You are quite the comedian, sir," the lieutenant sucked, with a smile on his feminine face. The colonel smiled too.

"How will I get the release papers to copy, sir?" the straight-faced Dunny asked.

"We have our spy on the inside. She will access the papers and material you will need, what."

"Is there a secret phrase and response, Colonel?"

"Yes. She will say, 'Dunny'? You will answer, 'Yes'."

"Can't I simply use the papers she provides and attach the Tzar's photo?"

"She and the current Tzar, 'Fukuallski', are the only ones with access. It took ten years for her to get the Tzar's trust. We don't want to blow her cover, in case . . ."

"In case I get dead?"

The colonel and lieutenant glanced at each other.

"We will have Fukuallski busy with some other issues. It should be a reasonably simple exercise, what."

"When do I go?"

"That's the spirit. We have a fail-proof plan to get you in. Tip, tip, tally ho."

***

Dunny sat in a silent hover car with two English SAS professionals.

"Right, gov. See that geezer. Go and give 'im what for, then."

Private Dunny exhaled and let out a lot of wind, then proceeded to the mark.

As the SAS were gagging in the 'windows up', hover car, Private Dunny let one go to the nose of an important-looking Russian general. The general held his face, blood oozing down his chin, as two other officers escorted Dunny to 'the hole', but not before breaking his right wrist. His drawing hand was left incapacitated, but his left was right. So, to be absolutely clear, his right was left so that his left was right to write, so in effect, his right was now left to write with his left, which was right. However, if he were facing you, the left on your right would be the right to write as your left would be left on his right. Now, if there was a mirror involved, and he faced away, his left would be right, which was not right to write, so it would be left, and his right would be left to write with his left. Now, had he been writing a rite, you would find his left would be right to write the rite, and his right would still be left. However, in a mirror, facing away, he has the right to write the rite with his right that was left, and the right to his left on your right would be left to write the right rite. Simple.

"Dunny?", a voice quietly outside the jail cell door.

"Yes, and a wash basin, but no paper," the private whispered.

A voice, distinctly female, and the cell door is quietly unlocked.

"Shh, come with me."

The lady in a Russian uniform escorted Private Dunny to a cell ten metres further down the corridor.

She quietly opened the cell door to the captive, rightful heir to the throne.

"Here is your equipment. You have no more than two hours," the spy said.

"My wrist is broken. I'm not sure I can do this."

"Please," a voice from the cell begged.

"Thank you, Natasha," the heir said. "If we push hard, Dunny and I should be able to complete our business in time."

"You've got the paper. Don't forget to take a clear photo," she advised.

"Lighting is poor. I'm going to strain," the private said.

"Here. Take my torch," Natasha offered.

It is said another prisoner in the next cell had a peculiar look on his face.

It was certainly a challenge for the private, but after nearly two hours, Private Dennis Dunny had given it his best shot. Lotokickbacks pulled a cheesy, and Dunny took his picture. Natasha unlocked the cell door as the private finished up.

"Let me see," Natasha prompted. "Nice work, Dunny," she stated, checking the 'get out of jail free' card. "Nice texture. Feels right. No abnormalities that I can see. Oh, but the smell of it. We will have to do something about that."

It is said the captive next door was now dry reaching.

"Dunny, you stay here. Once the heir is out, the people will revolt almost immediately. I will let you out as soon as this happens," Natasha said.

As the cell door closed, the private couldn't help but wonder if this was the last time the world would hear of Dunny. He reminisced about drinking with his mates. One time in particular flashed through his mind. He had been drinking a lot and was full as a boot. He vomited that night, into a patron's beer jug. He used some of the hotel's napkins to wipe some of the vomit covered carrot from his face, leaving shreds of paper on his cheek.

"Garn for piss," the Australian so intelligently told of his immediate intentions. As he was at the urinal, a man next to him squirted some drops on the legs of Dennis' pants. Dennis went red in the face and clenched his fists.

By the end of an alcohol inspired night, someone had pissed on Dunny, he was covered in vomit and paper was stuck to his cheeks, and finally, someone had pushed his button.

Natasha locked the cell and escorted Dominicov to the front guardhouse. The guard on duty never liked Natasha and was looking for an excuse to 'Hit her head with bottle'. She pulled from her pocket a small perfume bottle.

"Do you like my new scent, Comrade," she asked the guard, spraying it plentiful around and close to the guard's face. "It's called 'Eu de Cell Toilette.'"

Natasha had filled an empty bottle with the prison's toilet water.

The guard's eyes started to well. As he teared up, Natasha presented the exit pass and Dominicov. The guard tried to focus through his watering eyes and struggled to keep the vomit from powering out of his throat and nasal passage, and although he couldn't quite see clearly, he filed the pass and was happy for the irritation, the ex-prisoner and the perfume to be on their way out.

Natasha delivered the heir to the leader of the rebellion. Dominicov was recognised immediately. After thirteen years in a prison cell, he regained control of his country. Natasha kept her word, returned to the jail and freed Private Dunny. She also unlocked the other cells, freeing those held captive by the tyrant, Fukuallski. The now-freed prisoner, from the cell next to the heir and Dunny, must have been extremely traumatised. He had no contact with another human being for several years, but as the gorgeous Natasha put her arms out to give the man a, 'welcome back to the world comrade', hug, he asked, "Have you washed your hands?"

***

"Sassan, please take a seat. I may call on you again," Candice instructed as she tied her hair in pigtails.

"Of courthe, Mith Thweet," the professor clearly answered.

"Dennis. You haven't always been Australian, have you?"

"No, as you know, I was born in Hungary but nationalised in Australia a long time ago."

"And you changed your name?" Candice prodded.

"That's correct. I was known as Frigyes Withu. Now I'm . . ."

"Frigyes?" the security guard interrupted.

Dennis turned and looked at Russian Rob.

"Rubortakov?"

Dennis stood up, and the pair moved closer, inspecting each other from head to toe.

"Frigyes, my old friend."

"Rubortakov Trovoski. Wow! Sunshine, you got big."

"And you got . . . Australian. I can hardly understand you."

The pair bought it in for a man hug.

"This is very entertaining, watching two grown men show their affection for each other, but how long are we going to sit here?" Maximillian asked, moving his cap visor to the rear.

Robski gave Max a stare that suggested he would be more than capable of penetrating Max's neck with his own designer pen attached to his shirt pocket.

"Once the dice are loaded, I will roll the end game," Miss Sweet said with a clever analogy.

"Dennis Dunny. What was your role in the war, Dennis?" Candy asked.

"I was a private, Candice."

"Come now. You were more than that, weren't you?"

"I helped out with paperwork, occasionally," the forger added.

"Important paperwork, wouldn't you say?"

"I suppose some of it was important."

Dennis sat down as Jo placed a tray of coffee close to Clint.

"Sugar, Candy?" Clint offered.

"Not for Candice, Clint. Candy is 'sweet' enough," Dennis answered for her.

Everyone except security laughed at the incredibly funny play on words. (You knew it was coming).

"And so, we move on to Maximillian Driver", Candice regathering attention.

CHAPTER 5

MAX

With a name like Max Driver, one could say his destiny was pre-determined. He would go down in history as one of the sport's best drivers. Hover car racing was his life and passion. His mother, 'Racey', had made a name for herself, being the first female to win the cross-country hover car championship, before Max was born. Max preferred the smooth track and set fast time records after his third attempt in the 'Big Race'. Changing with the times, the winner would pass through towers erected on either side of the track, with flashing lights and fireworks as opposed to the 21st-century checked flag.

Another older gentleman back in the early 2000s, had a different view on time and held a record for, and still stands today, the most expensive collection of timepieces in the world. The senile, erratic, aged country leader (which seems to be a pre-requisite for warmongers), had been rumoured to struggle with what year it was, let alone down to the minute. The great leader of men wanted to begin a war with a country, any country, about anything, but he fluffed and farted about and couldn't decide on when. It is said the heavy-laden daily decision of what gold timepiece to wear wore him down. Let's face it, with timing like that a metronome was not something he could keep up with. He should have taken a lesson from the indigenous Australians. Time was defined, within the minute, by a quick glance at the sun. It begs the question, 'If you can't tell time, why own so many time pieces'? Just throwing it out there, but perhaps the value of his uncyphered, expensive watches could have fed the starving masses for a few hundred years. However, there was probably a good reason for retaining a large portion of the country's wealth in his personal bank account.

As a young man, Max met a woman he wanted to spend the rest of his life with. She was free-willed, intelligent, funny and sexy and had all the traits he admired in a wonderful human being of the opposite sex. To clarify, he was a male. She was a female. Terms such as other or it, or trans-whatever, or asexual, or any of the other ninety-two politically correct bizarre gender descriptions were not relevant in this traditional human being relationship.

Thoughtless printer shop workers, pre-21st century, would only have two options for gender selection on any form. There was mass confusion, uproar, and hysteria when it came time to apply for anything that required a tick in a box.

Things were going well in the pair's partnership, and they decided to take the 'big step'.

"I bought us our engagement and wedding rings today. Mum paid for them, so you owe her 45,000 credits," Mandy casually mentioned.

"Remind me to thank your mother for that," Max, less than impressed, stated.

One fine, recently married day, Max and Mandy invited guests for dinner. The friends were from Mandy's circle.

"Let's get the most expensive champagne we can find for tonight, sweetheart," Mandy suggested.

"Do you think we should find something more to our budget, darling?" Max, the breadwinner suggested.

Mandy resorted to tears. "You don't love me. They are my friends, and I want to give them the best and . . ."

"All right. Ok, sure, get them what you want, if that makes you happy, love of my life."

The expensive dinner guests arrived, and everything was laid on for them. After dinner, some light conversation.

"Max didn't want to buy you that champagne," Mandy informed the guests.

The guests gave stares of death to Max. A couple of weeks later and Mandy gave Max a reluctant 'OK' to bring his best friend, Ray, over for a game of darts. At the end of the short night, Mandy said she didn't like Ray, and it would be best if he never came over again. Mandy also suggested Max should mow the lawn at her mother's house after he finishes work the following day.

"I suppose I could help her out, as long as I can get to her house before dark," Max weighed up.

"You don't love me. She's my mother. You should be thinking like me. You should be feeling that you always want to do things for her. She bought our wedding rings. She . . ."

"OK. All right, I'll take some flood lights with me just in case. I just have to move 10,000 credits worth of your unused gym equipment you desperately required nine months ago in order to get the lights. Maybe I could leave your gear to the side and actually use the garage to park the car in it?"

"I don't feel loved. You don't care about me. I'm sleeping in the lounge for a while."

The couple had bought a house through a hefty loan from the bank. The house required constant maintenance, especially in the yard. Max was not keen to buy that particular house as he realised the time involved in its upkeep was excessive. He wasn't much of a gardener, and he expressed his concern before purchase.

"I want this house. I will do all the gardening. I love gardening. You won't have to worry about it," Mandy whined.

Max continued to work, day after day, trying to make ends meet.

"Honey, are you considering joining the workforce again?"

"I don't want to be forced to work. You should earn more, as I want to be a kept woman. Oh, on that subject, I shouted the wives club at a restaurant today. You made me look so bad. The 240 credits bill was rejected on the credit card. It's ok, though, Mum paid for it. You owe Mum the money. I'm going to sleep in the lounge for a few more days."

"We have a credit card?" Max pondered.

Another evening, a dear old friend to Max dropped in out of the blue. The pair of friends had not seen each other for many years. Luigi had looked up Max's address and stopped in to say goodbye. He had been diagnosed with an incurable disease and was going, as he put it, 'into another world'.

"I don't want you to see that horrible little man again, ever," the kind spouse informed Max.

"That's one wish you are granted, my caring wife," saddened Max said.

***

Max's brother, Brodoe, paid Max a visit on a Sunday afternoon, which was Max's only time off work. He was out the front, weeding and mowing the grass, trying to get the yard under control.

"Hey, Max," Brodoe said as he pulled up in a hover car in the driveway.

"Hi, Brodoe, I haven't seen you for ages. How are you?"

"I'm good. You don't look so well, though. You need a holiday."

The continuous emotional blackmail had deteriorated Max's health to an alarming degree. He was black around the eyes, pale and had lost significant weight.

"Yea, tell me about it. What brings you out here?"

"I understand you are not keen to associate with mum or me anymore."

"What?" puzzled Max, who had been pruning the hedges in the shape of hover cars, stood motionless with clippers by his side.

"Well, mum said she tried ringing a number of times, and Mandy said you don't want to see us."

Max stared straight ahead at nothing, jaw agape.

"What do you say, just you and I go and get us one of those horrible McYuk burgers like we used to?" Brodoe asked his brother.

"Umm . . . just a second."

"Sure," Brodoe assumed Max would just tell his spouse.

"Mandy, am I hungry?" Max yelled to the open front door.

Brodoe's jaw dropped.

After a few seconds, an obese figure filled the door, wearing what could only be described as a tent.

"Oh, it's you," she said in a downhearted way. "I guess I could allow you to go out for half an hour. Get me some more chocolate cake while you are out." With those wonderful words, she slammed the door in his face.

Max was a changed man. He was no longer the happy, full-of-life, confident person he once was. His racing team had also noticed how distracted he was, as he placed around sixth and seventh through the towers for the last three races.

The brothers sat down on a park bench, threw their McYuk burgers in the bin and sipped on the watered-down soft drinks.

"Max," Brodoe began. "I need to be straight with you. The woman you married has been abducted by aliens and replaced by something else."

The brothers looked each other in the eye and laughed for a considerable time, resulting in tears running down their cheeks.

After years of torturous living, Max opened up. "She's been sleeping in the lounge room for years now. She has destroyed every relationship I have had with anyone, ever. She won't work. She spends money as if she was a millionaire. I suggested to her that she get help."

"How did that go down?" Brodoe asked.

"Imagine an evil witch with a hormonal imbalance that continually has PMS."

"Yep. That's bad."

"I've tried so hard to please her. It's like her preferred state of being is misery. She's only happy if there is a drama in her life, and if there isn't one, she makes one," Max analysed.

"Brother, trust me on this. It's the ring."

"What?"

"It's the ring. There is something evil about it. An unknown force to man. She was a lovely lady before she got that ring, wasn't she?" Brodoe asked.

"You know, you are right. She was a kind-hearted person, once. Since she put that ring on her finger, she has just slipped downhill. All self-esteem vanished, and she became the evil drama queen, ice dragon bitch from the bowels of hell that she has progressed to today."

"So, take it off. Get rid of it. Throw it away."

"You are so right. If she truly loved me, she could do without the ring. I must free her from its grip. Brother, how can I ever repay you for your words of wisdom?"

"Well, how about next race; I ride shotgun, like the old days?"

***

Max waited until his charming wife squeezed through the shower door. She always took her ring off on the odd occasion she showered. Max grabbed the ring and, with no hesitation, left the house for the Big Race with the ring in his pocket. He met his team, and as promised, made provisions for Brodoe to passenger the hover race car.

The pair sat in the vehicle, engine running. The start only minutes away.

"Here, Brodoe," Max handed him the ring.

Brodoe gave a nod as if to say, 'you've done the right thing'. Jesting, Brodoe fitted the ring onto his finger.

The race was underway. Max started in seventh position but was making ground, lap after lap. There were three laps to go in the Big Race.

"I don't think I really want any part of this with you, Max," Brodoe stated. His whole demeanour had suddenly changed.

"What?" Max said, looking sideways at his brother.

Then he realised Brodoe had put the ring on his own finger.

"The ring, Brodoe. Take it off! Take it off!"

"Oh, it's so bright and precious," Brodoe seemed to be in a trance.

Max slammed on the brakes. One hover car passed. As Max reached over to grab the ring, Brodoe avoided the hand tackle by raising it in the air and admiring this piece of gold on his finger.

Another car passed.

"So shiny," Brodoe said, falling victim to its power.

Max slapped Brodoe in the face. Brodoe shook his head and quickly took the ring off. Max planted his foot. 'Team Driver' gained on the front three cars.

"Sorry, Max, I don't know what came over me."

"It's all right, Brodoe. It's not your fault, brother."

"You should have just thrown me out."

"How could I leave you walking when there's room in my car for two?"

The last lap was in progress, and it was neck and neck as they approached the finish line. Max eased off the accelerator for a split second. He threw 'the ring' out between the 'two towers'.

Team Driver lost by a nose emblem attached to the hood of the winning hovercar.

"The fellowship of that ring means nothing when we have the brotherhood of the Drivers," Max putting it so well.

***

"Maximillian Driver. The hover car driver of the century," Candice opened.

"Well, I don't know about that, but thank you anyway," Max returned.

"You are too modest, Max. It is said you have been mistaken for being in two places at one time, due to the incredible speeds you travel, with your personal, super-powered hover car."

"Well, I don't like to brag . . ." Max snorted with approval of the rumours.

"That's all I need from you at this stage, Max," Candice played to his ego.

CHAPTER 6

OPPENIYA

As she listened and relaxed in her reclining couch chair, Oppeniya thought of the new direction she was heading. With degrees in psychology and psychiatry, many different avenues were available. She wasn't keen on 'Park' or 'Madison' but she did have her sights set on hypnotism. She had tried self-hypnosis and had been hypnotised by one of the great hypnotists of the 22nd century to date, Ms Clare-Lee Seizya, the 'Czechoslovakian Wonder Woman'. Ms Seizya conducted her therapy on Oppeniya to 'regain her positive affirmation'. Oppeniya Bottoms was born into wealth. 'Daddy's little girl' had everything handed to her on a silver platter, mainly because her father owned not only a silver mine but also a silver refining business, a shop that sold silver items (mostly platters), another sales outlet called 'The Hi Ho', that dealt primarily in figurines of a horse from a hit radio and TV series from the 1950s, 'The Lone Ranger,' and another outlet for miscellaneous silver items such as medals, rows of bells, subscription ranks, cutlery, gorilla backs, taxi tops, bullets and linings.

Oppeniya Bottoms' father, Iniya, of Middle Eastern descent, married at an early age to an Asian beauty called Upiya. The to-be tycoon had saved his credits and presented his wife with a diamond insert ring, nicknamed by the jeweller as 'The Crocodile', because of its diapsid (two holes in the skull), appearance. Upiya worked as a waitress while her husband began his career in mining.

She almost threw it in on her first day of waitressing. Inevitably, and more common these days, the restaurant played host to 'the wanker' customer. This customer was also a fan of a larger-than-life artist from many years ago. This fan was so obsessed he changed his name to Alton Hercules.

"Oi, Darlin', this shit's not whiskey!" yelled Alton, a notorious restaurant wanker.

"Sir," Upiya began, "That's because it's a bottle of wine in your hand sir."

Alton looked at his wife . . . Steven, then back to the gorgeous Upiya.

"When I want some lip from you, I'll undo my trousers."

"Well, that's a tiny threat, sir," Upiya with a clever, degrading come-back.

Alton arose from his chair and closed the gap between their faces.

"You think you're pretty good, don't ya'? Dancing around the restaurant, strutting your stuff. I've danced with some of the world's finest. I'll speak to the manager, and you'll be danced out onto the street."

Upiya raised her right fist.

"Any closer, 'tiny dancer', and I'll bop you with this 'crocodile rock'."

***

Iniya, too, had a rough start. He signed up for some land located on the side of a mountain with mining rights. To safeguard his wife, he put the lease in both names, Upiya and Iniya Bottoms. He bought gold detectors, underground radar scopes, and new-age gold finders and went to work. After a few days, it seemed he was not the lucky miner he had hoped to be. He packed his gear up and made his way back to the opening. He returned to the office of the land leaser.

"Ain't no gold in them thar hills," Iniya bluntly stated in a language the redneck would understand.

"Gold?" began Honky Cat, the redneck. "Will, arl be. Yur even dumber 'n ah thote. That, thar is a silver marn you idjit."

And so, 'twas the beginning of a silver mining magnate.

***

"Hmm? Oh yes, yes. Your therapy is certainly helping, Dr. Lecture. If you remember, when you first came to me, you wanted to eat people. Now, you only want to create dead bodies. Quite a significant improvement, I'd say," Oppeniya replying to Dr Lecture's question, 'Doctor, are you awake'?

"Well, with all my knowledge and pieces of paper in frames hung on my office wall, I'm saying you are all cured. Oh, you seem to have something stuck in your teeth. It looks like a penis. Let me handle that for you."

***

Dr Oppeniya Bottoms returned home after a long day of sitting in her office couch chair and sat down in her couch chair. After an hour or so, she arose and performed her daily good karma routine, which involved sitting down in her couch chair for one hour. Under her own psychiatric advice, she then arose and began her positive affirmation exercises. This required her to chant the words, 'I am good. Good things will come to me if I am good', while sitting in her couch chair. After half an hour, it was time for her to self-analyse her psychological well-being. She had arisen from her couch chair and concluded she was over-run with work pressure. After her self-diagnosis, she prescribed herself a remedy, which entailed relaxing in her couch chair.

Oppeniya boarded the plane, destined for Czechoslovakia. She was scheduled to meet the Czech wonder woman as her pupil in the art of hypnotherapy. Oppeniya was guided to business class, passing a young couple playing a game while waiting for lift-off, and the stewardess, wearing a standard airline checked scarf, settled her in with a beverage served from a silver platter. As soon as the pupil sipped the airline's champagne, a huge fear came over her. After Oppeniya had delivered her baggage to check-in, she checked her purse to see if she had the cheque for the Czech. It was missing. She had sighted it ten minutes before. The two young passengers paused their game as they realised she was panic-stricken and offered to help find the missing item. The couple that was playing checkers checked for the cheque for the Czech after check-in. The stewardess, checked boarding passes in her checked scarf, closed the doors, and cross-checked, then helped the players of checkers check for the cheque for the Czech after check-in. More people joined the effort, searching the backs of seats and seat pockets, overhead storage compartments and even the hippies were searched, so as to leave no stoner unturned. So, after the stewardess had checked boarding passes in a checked scarf and cross-checked, she then helped the players of checkers and now more checkers check for the cheque for the Czech after check-in.

The pilot, Captain Checker, had heard a commotion, delayed departure, and exited the cockpit, leaving the door open. Captain Checker checked on the flight attendant that checked boarding passes in a checked scarf, then cross-checked, but now helped the players of checkers and other checkers check for the cheque for the Czech after check-in. Co-pilot, Charles Checkerton, had checked all aeroplane functions, heard the term 'recheck' and then quietly closed the cockpit door.

Oppeniya exited the plane, and Clare-Lee was in wait, to greet her at the Czech airport.

"How was your flight?"

"A bit unsettling. I'm so sorry; I had your fee in cheque form, but I seemed to have misplaced it."

"Did you check your purse?"

"Yes, of course, I did."

"Have another look," Ms Seizya suggested.

Oppeniya opened her purse, and the missing item was in plain view. She looked up at Seizya, eyes wide. "I don't understand. It wasn't there before."

"Dr Bottoms, I had you under hypnosis," the Czech woman said, her unique eyes like circular rainbows were mesmerising. "I wanted to show you how powerful it really is. I knew you would be back. When you were under my control, you confessed to yearning for the ability to conduct hypnotherapy. I suggested to you that after you sipped your airline drink, you wouldn't be able to locate your prewritten cheque."

Bitch! Oppeniya thought. "Oh, how clever of you," she stated. "But how come the other people didn't see it in my purse?"

"I can only suggest they were too busy looking through your white see-through skirt, which clearly shows you are not wearing any underwear."

The ladies, of female gender, caught a hover taxi back to Clare-Lee's office. On the journey, six motorcycle enthusiasts roared past, revving their engines between gears (because that's what you do when you ride a bike, although not necessary), creating a deafening sound likened to that of (well, you know when you super glue the side of your face to a base amplifier that is stuck on warp ten? And haven't we all?) — the same as that.

"They are probably on their way to buy mufflers," Clare suggested.

The taxi hovered along, arriving at Wonder Woman's office.

"I have two patients due shortly," Clare said. "I will show you how to hypnotise, and then you can treat the second under my supervision."

Dr Bottoms agreed, and before long, the first patient arrived.

"Hello, Evan please take a seat on the couch. Oppeniya, can you please get off and give Evan a seat?"

Bitch! You are nothing but a control freak, Bottoms thought. "Certainly, my pleasure," she said.

"Evan, what is your profession, and what are you hoping to get from this therapy?"

"I deal in stocks and shares and hope to be cured of my overwhelming fear of donkeys."

"So, Oppeniya, what we suggest to our patients is something they are comfortable with and combine their ailment."

Fuckin' know it all, she thought. "OK, understood clearly, Clare-Lee," she said.

The wonder woman pulled an item out, attached to a string and with the pendulum, she told Evan to focus on it.

"You want me to watch your swinging tampon?" Evan asked.

"Oh, sorry about that. My bad. I'll just put it back where it came from."

The professional therapist turned her back and appeared to be adjusting something, then pulled from her pocket a watch attached to a chain.

"Deeper, deeper, relax, deeper."

"Are you talking to me?" Evan asked.

"My bad again. Just adjusting my item. Now, focus on the watch. You are getting sleepy. Deep breaths. Your body is tired. Relax, sleeeep."

"Evan, you are a donkey dealer. One, two, three. Wide awake. How do you feel?"

"Quite disgusted after you waved that tampon inches from my nose," Evan replied. "I'm out of here."

Evan returned to his work desk, surrounded by other desks, with share traders sitting behind them. He then rose from his swivel chair and loudly asked the other swivel chair occupiers, "Does anyone have an ass for sale?"

The floor was filled with hush and concerned looks.

"Buy an ass? Anyone looking to buy an ass? Come on, let's do a deal. My ass for yours?

Other traders' eyes lit up as a drag queen made his/her/its way towards Evan.

***

Meanwhile, back at Wonder Woman's hideout:

"See the way it's done, Dr Bottoms?"

Condescending bitch! she thought. "Yes, I think I've got it, thanks, Clare", she said.

Andy was on time for his appointment with the mind-altering pair.

"Dr Bottoms will treat you today, Andy. Ready Oppeniya?"

What does it fuckin' look like, bitch? she thought. "Yes," she said.

Oppeniya stood and turned her back and appeared to be adjusting something.

"No, no, that wasn't part of the process, Oppeniya."

I'm following what you just did, bitch! she thought. "Oh, OK," she said.

"What is your profession, Andy?" the doctor began. "And what are you hoping to get from this therapy?"

The communicator rang, and Clare-Lee excused herself for passing wind and then answered the call.

"I'm a full-time kleptomaniac, and I have a fear of superheroes," Andy stated.

"Oppeniya pulled out Clare's watch on a chain and told Andy to focus.

"You're getting tired. Relax, sleep. Deep breaths. Relax, sleeeep."

"You are a cat burglar, and you will steal everything from Wonder Woman's hideout," the good doctor smirked.

"One, two, three. Wide awake. How do you feel?"

"I'm feeling good. Well, I have plans for tonight. Best be on my way."

The Czech wonder woman returned to the room.

"Oh, sorry about that and the call. Where did he go?"

"Andy said there was an emergency. He also said in lieu of the cancelled appointment; we should go out for dinner tonight. His treat. If you get the bill tonight, he will fix you up tomorrow."

"Oh, wonderful," said Clare Lee Seizya.

"Got you, bitch!" Oppeniya said. *Oops!* she thought.

***

"Oppeniya Bottoms," Candice Sweet dived in.

The doctor, unusually, stood up from her comfortable chair.

"Sit down, please, Doctor Bottoms."

Oppeniya misplaced her weight, losing balance and subsequently, Bottoms sat on Dunny. (Again, you knew it was coming). The doctor apologised, but unfortunately, not before sneezing and spraying Dunny. The doctor manoeuvred back to her seat, pulled out a tissue and wiped up the mess that she had just created on Dunny.

"Oppeniya, you are a Doctor of Psychology and Psychiatry, correct?"

"Yes, that's right."

"Where did you study?"

"I've told you before. I studied at Oxford University."

"And you received your professional degree?"

"Yes, two, actually."

"Ah ha, ah ha. Then you learnt hypnotherapy?"

"Oh, well. I dabbled . . . and . . . ah . . ."

"Isn't it true, you were trained by the Czech wonder woman, Clare-Lee Seizya?"

"Well, yes, but . . ."

"That will do for now. Thank you, Oppeniya."

CHAPTER 7

CLINT

As a criminal law judge, Clint was a man that demanded respect. He was, as you would expect, a no-nonsense professional, however, some say he was a little too lenient, and then there were those who said he was a little too harsh.

"You crossed the road with blatant disregard for the safety and wellbeing of all other road users. A zebra crossing was in sight, no more than 800 metres from where you crossed over, clearly shown in the evidence," Judge Eros stated, holding up photo evidence from the street camera, his huge eyebrows raised, almost covering his forehead.

"Your file says that you saved thirteen children from a burning orphanage, running in and out of the building until your foot was burnt off but kept going on the stump of your lower leg."

"Your Honour, I have to use a walking frame as I'm missing one foot (no one has stepped forward with it), and the other has steel plate inserts to stop it from falling off. It has weakened over a period of time and needs to be tightened, but my pension doesn't provide the cover," the frail eighty-four-year-old replied.

"Kevin, do you think a 'Foot Loose', is an excuse to break the law?"

"No, Your Honour, however, it was 2.45 a.m., and there was no traffic to be seen."

"Oh, so there is a right time to break the law?"

Kevin sighed, "No, Your Honour."

"What could possibly have been more important to you that you would disregard the correct lawful procedure of crossing a road from one side to the other, hence resulting in a very serious jaywalking charge, hmm?"

"My great grandson is two years old, and he suffers from asthma. He needed a puffer, or it was certain death. I was going to the 24-hour chemist while my ninety-two-year-old wife, who is wheelchair-bound and mute, comforted him through his asthma attack, which was brought about by the toxic fumes from the government's new greenhouse emissions incentive factory, which incinerates rubber trees, that until recently, could be found on both sides of lift shafts."

"Oh, so it's the government's fault, is it? Choose your next words wisely, 'stumpy'. No one would get any great enjoyment from front kicking you into a bottomless pit."

Kevin sighed again, "No, Your Honour, I guess I'm at fault."

"Let me take the guesswork out of it for you. Guilty! Five years hard labour on the hover train rail. Next case," the judge smashing his mallet down.

"The court versus Jarred Pork," the bailiff announced.

"Another serious offence. Jaywalking again. Unbelievable. What have you got to say for yourself, hmm? Well? Speak up, speak up," the judge said, his thick and fearsome eyebrows alternating up and down.

"If the court pleases, Your Honour . . ." Sid, the defence lawyer, started.

"I'm not too pleased so far but 'carry on, Sid'."

"I'm the accused's attorney. I will speak for Jarred as the accused is mute."

The judge gave a heavy sigh and adjusted his black gown.

"Very well, continue."

"Jarred went out looking for his husband, as he hadn't returned with an asthma puffer for their great-grandson., Wheelchair-bound, Jarred left the child with a trusting neighbour. As Jarred left their tiny unit, the red-bearded, dreadlocked kiddies friend, Molly Lester sang a kiddie song, and everyone assumed the child was safe, sport. (It is said Molly was heard on the phone: Hey, Dad! Bring Bill over. I've got another one. Presumably, another child to nurture, teach and explain what fine examples of human beings they are).

"I've heard enough from that man's/woman's/its mouth. Guilty! Throw away the key, like a rapper!"

"Next, and this better be good, Johnny," Clint said as Sid swapped out and Johnny became the new defence lawyer. "You sure are a weird lawyer Johnny, but I like you."

"The court versus Harlett Sexton Action. The Honourable Judge Clint Eros presiding," the bailiff stated.

"Oh, you poor thing. What have they got you in here for?" the judge showing compassion to the DD's.

Harlette continued chewing gum as she spoke, "Well, Clinty, I'm pretty sure it's a case of mistaken identity. I was on my way to make another porn movie, and the next thing I remember was a police officer saying I hit something or something."

"You have a very strong defence Miss Action," the unbiased judge claimed. "Let the prosecution begin."

"Your Honour, the accused . . ."

"Don't refer to her as the accused. It makes her sound guilty. This is a fair trial. Refer to her as the improbable defendant or the unlikely," the judge demanded.

"Very good, Your Honour. The improbable defendant drove her sports hover car into seventeen school children," the prosecutor Judy Judge opened.

"I'm sure the collateral damage was minimal, Johnny?" Eros prompted, raising one of his, (some say caterpillars), eyebrows.

"Twelve children died from the impact. Five are still in critical care," Judy intervened.

"That seems a tad unbelievable. School zone speed limits are set at 30 kph," Eros stated.

"The unlikely was travelling at 180 kph, Your Honour."

"I can't imagine her doing that, really," the judge said, stroking the underside of his chin.

"The unlikely had a blood alcohol level of 2.7."

"Well, we all enjoy a little drink now and then."

"The acc...the improbable defendant has no driver's licence, and her hover car is unregistered," Judy continued.

"Just the facts pertaining to the case, Judy."

"There were forty eyewitnesses, Your Honour."

"We know that eyewitnesses are not reliable. DNA is solid proof these days."

"Your Honour, one of the deceased children had their teeth embedded into the bumper of the hover car owned by the unlikely."

"Were you driving the afternoon in question, Ms Action?" Judge Eros asked.

"Haha, I was so drunk and high I don't remember. I don't think I was." The blonde bimbo slapped the wooden front of the witness box, then brought her hand to her cheek, tilted her head and stared at the ground.

"That's a mighty powerful defence, Johnny. It's easy to see, someone borrowed your hover car, Ms Action, and ran into those children. Let this be a lesson for all the jaywalkers and children that are still in critical care. Don't play on the road. Not guilty!" the judge smashed his mallet down, splattering an unsuspecting earwig.

"I'll see you in my chambers shortly, Ms Action. We'll discuss your compensation claim against the dead's parents."

"Te, he, he, OK, Clinty."

"That was a good defence, Johnny. Next."

"The court versus Cardinal De Seever."

"The charge? And let's not forget, he is a fine and upstanding citizen who would never take advantage of anyone."

"Sexual relations with minors, Your Honour."

"Did you do it, De Seever?" the judge asked.

"Well, yes, but it was only oral."

"I think the best thing to do is let you run away and hide under the oversized robe of the Pope. We won't send the authorities after you. We would prefer it was hush, hush. The children and their parents will probably forget all about it, and I'm sure the public will be more than happy to see you live out the rest of your days under the guise of the richest organisation in the world, even though their true leader's teachings, says exactly the opposite. You should take comfort when you look at the starving masses, that you are part of a company that has yet to be proven criminal."

"Guilty! But with leniency."

"Time for one more, then it's smoko."

"The court versus Max Betts."

"The charge is multiple counts of fraud."

"Guilty!" Judge Clint Eros declared. "Life imprisonment in solitary confinement, for you, any and all associates. The court will also seize all assets and family funds related to the guilty parties."

Online casinos grew very popular from the early 21st century onwards. There was already an abundance of physical gambling venues, ripping off the honest people who perhaps had a dream of 'the big win', or a smaller amount to enjoy short term, or indeed, those unlucky ones affected by addiction. The advantage of gambling at these venues was the instant payouts, as opposed to the lengthy delay tactics the online sites had adopted.

As a case example, Lisa's story is highlighted. Lisa is a bi-sexual female. For all intents and purposes, she had long wavy hair, beautiful facial features, large breasts that bulged out of her push-up bra, a fantastic figure, extremely sexy, often wore very little, and had the hots for readers and writers, all of which is irrelevant, but with that pleasant mental picture in mind, the story will continue.

Alone and bored one evening (and why she was alone is still a mystery), Lisa found an appealing cyber site and took up one of the promotional offers. She filled out the necessary identification requirements, popped in her payment details and deposited $100. With the added bonus, she had a starting figure of $500.

She began to play, and after a couple of hours, she had a balance of $2,000. Happy with that result and time to call it a night, she visited the cashier and prompted a withdraw. Knowing there would be an initial processing period, she waited two weeks before checking her bank account balance. The funds had not appeared in her account. She returned to the site, and contacted live chat, which informed her that she had not yet met the wagering requirements that accompany the bonus. Even though she had no desire to continue with the gaming, for the payout, she did so. After another few hours, she had met the requirements and once again pressed withdraw. Lisa allowed another two weeks for processing and checked her account. No payout again. She returned to the site, and live chat informed her she would need to provide identification criteria. She then uploaded all requested documents. Lisa waited another two weeks. Still no payout. Again, she returned to the site. She was informed she would need to download a copy of a credit card authorisation form, fill it out and send it back. She clicked on the provided link to find the form was a jumbled mess of not quite words. She returned to the site and explained the problem. There was no explanation from the casino; they simply sent another link. Lisa again downloaded the form, filled it out, returned it and waited another two weeks. Payment still had not been honoured. Yet again, she returned to the site and was informed that one of her documents was not clear. She sent the same document through a second and waited two weeks to find the payout was still not honoured. Back to the site, she was told an independent company would contact her for a facial recognition verification. A few days passed, and she followed the procedure after being contacted. Waited two weeks. Again, checking her account, no added funds. Contacting live chat for the umpteenth time, she was advised that the funds were waiting to be approved. Two more weeks and no funds were deposited in her bank. More than an umpteenth time back to the site, she was told it had been approved and now waited for processing. Two weeks passed and of course, no funds. Again, back to the site, who explained it would take twenty business days to process. In layman's terms, one calendar month.

The end result: Almost five months later, she received a payment of $150 of the $2000 she was owed. Furious, she clicked on the site to find that the site was no longer available.

A deposit was made instantly by an individual. A part-payment by a team of people from an online casino took five months.

Lisa opted to join a task force, investigating on-line theft. She applied for a position as arresting officer but was rejected.

“You are not qualified for this position, Lisa,” Super Intendant Terry A Newone stated. “We are only trying to help.”

“I don’t see how you are doing that,” Lisa replied.

“What do you mean?”

“Well, right at this point, I’m considering driving to a gun shop, buying a machine gun, coming back here and blowing half of you fuckers away.”

“On second thought, I think you are a wise choice,” Terry summing it up.

***

“Coffee and cake?” Jo offered the room, wheeling in a tea trolley. “Sweet, Clint Eros, anyone else? Max, Bottoms, Smasher? Dunny, Buster? Really, Red man? Hail, Robski?”

“Thanks, Jo. Now, Clint. You have been a judge for a long time?” Candice continuing her interrogation.

“Yes, that’s right.”

“And in that time, you have had many criminals to cast judgement upon. Had you met anyone from this room prior to being a Retro-Tech board member, in or out of the courts?”

“No, Miss Sweet.”

“And that’s all I need from you, thank you.”

CHAPTER 8

CANDICE

"Last name first, first name last."

"Sweet Candy," came the reply to the recruiting officer from Restricting Independent Gambling Halls Taskforce Subsidiary, or (RIGHTS).

Basic training was mandatory for all cadets, even though most of the cyber division of RIGHTS was conducted from the safe atmosphere of offices. Candice's dream was to be part of the team to physically take down the corrupt individuals responsible for the theft of millions of credits from the unaware fair gambler. Australia had been targeted for many years as an easy con. Not only were overseas casinos cashing in on the gullible, but there were also many scams designed specifically to rip off older 'Aussies'. As an example, back in the early 2000s, a supposed company called, 'Jarrah Hill Australia', fleeced the Australian residents for, again, millions. The posing company was set up in Malaysia. Some of the 'cannibals' were, surprisingly, Aussies. Candy's department sought retribution from the gambling aspect of the less than reputable organisations.

Training was complete, and a celebratory night out was on the cards for the fair justice department. 'Millsy' had excelled in basic training and befriended Candy. The pair became close after the six months of association.

"What do ya' reckon, Candy? Wanna' go see a comedian tonight. Maybe have a laugh or throw a few tomatoes?" Millsy suggested.

"You 'bet'!" replied Candy.

"I've heard of a comedy night held at a hotel in Fremantle."

The small venue welcomed the 'stack' of recruits as they joined an almost 'full house'. Candy was feeling a little 'flushed' and took a deep breath before entering.

"I'll be 'straight' with you, Candy. I've heard some great things about one of the acts here tonight," Millsy said.

The 'pair' were in anticipation, of the first act.

"Hi . . . oh, I see some of you already are."

There was a huge roar of laughter from the entire audience, except for one individual.

"We'll just let the cogs spin on that one for our ol' mate, right there," the entertainer nodding in the direction of the 'few cards short of a full deck' patron.

"Look don't feel stupid. Children sometimes struggle with comprehension. If at any time tonight you don't understand, don't get it, please stand up and say, 'What'? We will all stop and stare at you and simply think to ourselves, what a fuckin' moron."

"My name is Lost, Darryl Lost. No, that's not my real name, but with a name like Alfred Hermowitz, it doesn't really have that zing, that comedy bling. And wherever Alfred is, I feel sorry for him, 'coz he aint ever gonna get on a fuckin' stage like this. With us, Cogs?"

The patron smiled and nodded.

"For those of you that don't know me . . . I'm guessing you've been living under a rock. I've had quite a successful career in the comedy industry." Darryl looked down at his wrist. *"For all of . . . ah . . . forty-five seconds now."*

It was a comedian's dream crowd. They 'lost' it.

"Still with us, Cogs," Darryl looking toward 'Mr smile and nod'.

"For those of you who do know me . . . well . . . they really should have been here by now," Darryl perusing the audience.

"I'm so lost. Look, thinking doesn't come easy for some," Darryl took a brief pause and stared at Cogs. *"I gave that thinking thing up years ago. I say, be the total idiot that you can be. Excel! Take full advantage of your options, remembering failure is always an option."*

The crowd, now in hysterics.

"Mind you, I have never failed at sex. Even if the child is crying."

There was a laugh of disgust and some booing.

"Oh, you sick people. I was talking about the faint echoes from the apartment, two doors down."

Tears of joy were hitting the urine and vomit-soaked carpet floor.

"Cogs?"

"But honestly, thinking comes in many forms. For instance, If I'm looking at a gorgeous woman, I'm thinking I would really like to touch her tits. However, if I'm thinking to her, I'm thinking I'd really like to touch your tits."

Some people were now rolling on the floor, amongst the urine and vomit, in uncontrollable seizures of laughter.

"Wow! You are a wonderful audience. To be honest, last night's gig wasn't the greatest. But I give credit where it is due and thank everyone for coming. Both of them seemed happy with that. It was just unfortunate mum fell asleep, and my sister drove her home."

Darryl stared at Cogs, who assumed a blank expression.

"Oh dear," the comedian putting his head down and moving it from side to side.

The comedian continued for some time, creating an extremely fun night for all, but unfortunately, closing time was upon the venue.

"Thank you; you've been an audience. And last chance, please grab a book written by a great author on your way out."

Candice, Millsy and the other cadets returned home for the evening. Some months later, Candy had passed all written and practical exams and was accepted into the task force. To her disappointment, she manned/womaned/personed the communicators. Most 'newbies' began this way.

Candice answered a call.

"My name is Miles Stone. I recently invested my retirement funds into a company called 'Advantage Retirees'."

"Sorry sir, this is the RIGHTS department. You will have to contact another subsidiary for fraudulent misappropriation of investments. I'll give you the number . . ."

"I am just getting the run-around. I have called one department after the other. I knew I shouldn't have taken that gamble."

"Did you say gamble, sir?"

"Indeed, I did."

Candice had found a loophole. *With the mention of gamble that should be enough to follow it up,* she thought, picking up a pen from the desk.

"How much did you invest, sir?" Candice asked, tapping the pen on the desk.

"350, 000 credits. All my savings. I was due to retire in three years. Looks like I'll have to keep working, shovelling cement at the age of seventy-six, even though I've had triple bypass surgery and now sport a pacemaker."

"So, you were swindled out of your life savings? Some people just don't have a heart. I will investigate immediately, however, there is only a slim chance of your funds being returned, as the culprits usually spend it or hide them in other affairs. I have your contact details, Miles, and I will keep you up to date."

***

Candice spoke with Millsy, and they were determined to help the desperate man.

"It's an all too common, sad story, Candice. Unfortunately, the offenders reside in Nigeria. Our ruling body, again, unfortunately, does not wish to make any waves overseas. Take the case of Cardinal De Seever, for instance. He was permitted to run away so as not to embarrass the church any further and instead of Australian authorities extraditing him back to Australia to face his sentence, he was left to continue sailing along with his life on smooth waters. As history shows, it is more than probable he will be noted as a repeat offender. I feel sorry for the children in his company of wherever he is now," the super intendant informed Candice and Millsy.

"Don't we, as Australians, have an obligation to those innocent children he is probably targeting as we speak?" Candice morally questioned.

"Just like his probable current victims, our hands are tied."

"So, as Australian authorities, we are unable to do anything about the Nigerians who are targeting helpless Australians? What? We just turn a cheek, bend over and take it a bit harder?"

The bald lieutenant never had a hair out of place. Uniform always ironed, teeth always clean, fly always done up. "Watch your tone, Candice," with a stern look.

"Is there no one with enough guts to take on the criminals that attack Australian citizens?"

"One more word Candice Sweet and you will have the record for the shortest service in RIGHTS."

"RIGHTS? What a fuckin' joke. Here's my resignation," Candice Sweet holding up both middle fingers. (It is said her intentions were not to point out the shabby paintwork on the ceiling).

***

Candice boarded a plane bound for Nigeria. She noted a couple playing checkers and a woman in a white see-through skirt, obviously not wearing any underwear.

With the help of Millsy, she obtained a location on the scammer's whereabouts. She hired a motorised car, as hover cars were not plentiful and readily available in Nigeria. She sat outside the boundary line, observing the human traffic entering and exiting the small portable donga made in Australia to add insult to injury.

Candice secretly took pictures of the offenders and sent them to Millsy, who, with RIGHTS technology, identified the Nigerian international criminals. Candice followed one of the guilty parties to his home, but something didn't appear to add up. Why was this man living in squalor? Chickens were scratching in the dirt of the front yard, and his home was little more than a shack. If he had credits to burn, he could be living like a king. Candy decided to watch and wait. After a few hours, a hover car pulled up out the front. Only the rich and powerful would have a hover car. This was possibly the only one in the country. A suit filled with a man exited the vehicle. He was greeted at the door and stayed only a moment. He walked out carrying a small bag, which happened to split open as he swung it too close to the jagged fence. Thousands of credits fell onto the ground. He scrambled to pick up the small fortune.

It then twigged. Candice put the puzzle together. This was the recipient of all the swindled Australian credits. This figure oversaw the scam. Perhaps he paid the contacting swindlers a small wage? Perhaps he threatened them? The reason is unclear, but the head criminal was identified.

Candice battled to keep up with the hover car as she tailed the crim to his place of refuge. The overweight man entered what could be described as an 'out of place' palace.

Candice returned to her resident motel. The next day, she made a stop at a chemist, the local hospital and an STD clinic, then proceeded to the ringleader's palace. The head crim returned, and Candice waited until the darkness of night. She crept into the palace and into the head criminal's room. As he lay asleep, Candice jumped on top of him and immediately forced Rohypnol, that she had bought at the chemist, down his throat. The effects of the modern drug were instantaneous. Subdued, the head crime boss lay on his huge bed, eyes barely open and a stupid smile on his face, as Candice pulled a nail file from her pocket, sat down and manicured her nails. Six minutes later, there was an expected knock at the door. Two paramedics that Candice had paid off at the hospital, were there as arranged, to take the crim to the airport. The cover story was the patient was on his way to receive an organ from a donor. A piano was out of the question. The Nigerian crime boss was escorted back to Australia by Candice. Millsy met Candy at the airport with all the appropriate paperwork, stating that the offender was now nationalised as an Australian citizen. Millsy took the ex-Nigerian to the Australian authorities.

Millsy's friend Daniel was on duty.

"Book him, D man!"

CHAPTER 9

THE STAGE SET

"Firstly, it seems all of you are lying members of the board," Candy began, with a stern look in her eye, scanning the individuals.

Another huge uproar from the members followed.

"What do you mean?"

"I've been honest?"

"Weally?"

"Honesty is the best policy".

"Are you kidding?"

"I feel so liberated not wearing underwear."

Candice folded her arms, closed her eyes and put her head down. "Does anyone wish to confess to the director, Mr. Arros Sole, their part in the corporate espionage case at hand?"

A murmur from the party followed.

"Where is he?"

"Weally? I don't see him."

"Is he coming here?"

"Dennis, please don't mention your underwear anymore."

"My point, exactly," Candice confusing the members. "Mr. Arros Sole is right in front of you. Let me unravel this mystery." Candice took a deep breath.

"More refreshments? Oppeniya Bottoms, Driver? Hail, Dunny, Smasher? Real, Red, Clint Eros? Robski, Buster?" Jo bustled in with the tea trolley.

"Thanks, Jo," Candy acknowledged.

***

After Maximillian's failed marriage, he went on a six-month bender. He found himself at a raging party one early afternoon with all sorts of celebrities. Drugged and drunk, he got cosy with one of the (assumed) female guests.

"Sho, you are a movie shtar?" Max asked.

"Te, he, he. I've been in hundreds of movies. Some were even legi . . . legiti . . . some made it to the screen," she intelligently answered, eventually.

"I'm a hover rashe car driver."

"Te, he, he. And your name is Driver. Te, he, he."

The intellectual stimulation continued for a short time.

"I've got a sports hover car. I bet you could drive really fast," the blonde braless bimbo said, shaking her shoulders swiftly left and right. It is safe to assume it wasn't her shoulders Max was looking at.

"I could drive you fasht and hard. Watch your name, shweety?"

"It's Harlette Sexton Action."

Max looked towards the sky. "Thank you," he mouthed.

"Let's go riding," Harlette prompted.

Some say the run to the sports hover car was the fastest Max had moved in six months. Max gave the engine a rev (because that's what you do when you drive a sports hover car, although not necessary), then threw it into gear as it roared down the road. Neither had buckled their seat belt. The pace picked up, 100 kph, faster they went, 140 kph, 160 kph, reaching a speed of 180 kph. Some obstacles on the road left no reaction time for the high and drunk speed demon. Max hit the school crossing, loaded with children. The first victim was hit with such an impact that her teeth were embedded into the bonnet. Her eyes stayed in the same GPS location for a microsecond until the windscreen connected with them. For a fleeting moment, Max could see a pair of eyes and a mouthful of teeth in front of him. He collided with sixteen other pupils. Then the car rolled several times, and the driver and passenger were thrown around inside the car. Finally coming to a rest, the driver and passenger lay unconscious but uninjured in opposite seats, giving the impression that Harlette was the reckless speeder.

Max found himself in a jail cell, looking through the bars at the judge, Clint Eros.

"I know it was you driving, Max. The penalty for your crime will be at least twelve consecutive life sentences. I could make this all disappear. You only have to do one little job."

"What is it you want me to do?" Max asked.

"Drive," Clint simply answered.

***

"Roland Van Real. Do you know how much trouble you are in?" Clint rhetorically asked.

"I'm only in this pwison for one more week. Who might you be?" Roland asked, handcuffed to the table's steel bar.

"I might be your only chance of ever leaving this place. You have made a booking in my courtroom," Judge Eros said, knowing full well, two dead caterpillars glued to the bottom of his forehead would be a vast improvement on the unsightly eyebrow impersonating bushes he had growing at present.

"What do you mean?"

"Roland, Roland, Roland. It's not every day six prisoners escape from an electronic fortress. I know you waved your electrical wand, (in the shape of a stick), and set them free. The penalty, in my courtroom, is extremely severe."

Roland looked down and gave a heavy sigh (the same way a one-footed man would look down and sigh if he was charged with jaywalking).

"There may be a way out for you, though," the judge suggested.

"What do you want fwom me?"

"I want you to do what you are good at."

"I don't suppose you mean play dwums?"

"You supposed right. I have an electwical pwob . . . I mean, I have an electrical problem. I need you to fix it."

Roland thought of The Woodster's words.

"So, you help me; I help you?"

"Now you've got it," Clint confirmed.

"Fwiends?"

"Yes, sure, I can run with that."

***

Dennis answered the knocked door. The door had little else to say, but the man behind it had plenty of words to speak. Pushing the mute door aside, Dennis observed a suit, occupied by a distinguished gentleman, with caterpillars above his eyes.

"Hello. Dunny?"

"There's a thunderbox in the *Sail and Anchor* hotel next door," Dennis informed the man.

"What?"

"Thunderbox. Next door . . . the crapper."

"No, I mean is your name Dunny?" Clint asked.

"Yea, do I know you?"

"I am Clint Eros. May I come in?"

Dennis gave a welcome gesture.

"Have a seat."

Clint looked down and gave a double take.

The pair sat down on novelty dining chairs shaped like toilets.

"Let's talk, Dunny," Clint began.

"You look a little 'flushed'. Would you like some water?" Dennis asked.

"No, thank you. Seems you are quite the artist."

"I'm good at what I do," Dennis replied.

"So I have heard. Is it true you copied, freehand, a ten-credit icon that passed into the American Federal Reserve?"

"Well, I don't like to brag, but yeah, I sure did."

"Yes, you see. That's a bit of a problem."

"What are you on about? Clint, was it?"

"Judge Clint Eros, Dunny."

"Are you pissing in my pocket?" Dennis asked.

"No, Dunny, I'm not pissing on you at all," Clint answered, not too sure of the Aussie slang.

"I think it's time you left. The way out? I'll show you Clint Eros," Dennis standing up.

"Don't be too quick to judge," said the judge. "Sit down, Dunny."

Dennis knew there was more to Clint Eros than met the eye. Dunny sat down again.

"You see, when governments are taken advantage of, they won't rest until the culprit is caught. They want you extradited to the USA to face a heavy sentence. As opposed to a mere child molesting priest or con artists taking individuals for everything they have."

"It hardly seems fair. I draw one item, and they will go to extreme lengths to punish me, yet repeat offenders they don't worry about?"

"No one said the law is fair," Clint winked and prompted a caterpillar to move.

"What's more is, I did what I did at the request of the united forces. My contribution stopped the war, saving thousands of lives."

"I feel your pain, Dunny, but in this year 2130, our ruling bodies of Australia are terribly wishy-washy and won't stand up to another country's demands. It has got worse over the past 100 years or so."

"So, you are here to warn me?" Dennis asked.

"In a way, yes, I am warning you. If you do something for me, Dunny, I can make all this float away."

"Oh, rightio! I get it. Forgive me, is this termed blackmail or extortion? If I don't play ball, you are going to send good ol' Dunny down the shitter."

"You can call it what you will. The facts remain," the judge declared.

***

"Ahoy, Captain. Permission to come aboard?"

"Permission granted, fine sir. Are you after a charter?" Captain Hail enquired.

"I . . . most certainly am. Can we retreat to your cabin and talk?"

"Sure," Skipper said, thumbing the direction of the cabin (as if a person can't work out where the cabin is on a cabin cruiser).

"I am Clint Eros."

"You look a little wet there Clint Eros."

"I got sprayed by some NZ seaman," Clint said, dressed in his out of robe attire, a wet white collared shirt, a wet real expensive looking jacket, wet blue pants and wet-look, black shoes.

"Yes, they have a weird sense of humour. I'm Captain Skip Hail. Oops! Don't step on my churkin iggs!" the captain panicked.

"Your what?" Clint asked.

"Sorry, my chicken eggs. It's the local accent rubbing off on me. It can be a bit irritating sometimes. Have you been rubbed up the wrong way, Clint Eros?"

"No. No, I am a judge, though. I deal with pricks all the time," Clint began. "Skip, what is that on your shelf?"

"That is the head of my first, first mate. He's stuffed now."

"He sure looks it. So, how did that come about?"

"I had to eat him."

"You ate your first mate?"

"He was also my best friend."

"You ate your friend?" Clint froze briefly, turned to look at Hail, then the stuffed head, (dreadlocks still intact), then back to Hail. "Do you know how many laws you have broken?"

"Whose laws would that be?"

"Well, I'm sure NZ would frown upon cannibalism. Was he dead when you ate him?"

"Not initially, but after a few days . . ."

Clint was shocked at the confession.

"It happened in neutral waters. No country's laws apply."

Captain Hail went on to explain how he kicked his head for a goal once a year.

"It's about time I relaced his mouth; his tongue is hanging out."

"Excuse me," Clint said as he barfed over the side of the boat.

"Seasick, hey? You sure you want to charter a boat?"

This is harder than I imagined, the judge thought.

The judge knew Skip was fond of his ship and becoming more creative; he appealed to the captain's sense of pride.

"She's a unique vessel, Captain. It would be a shame if you lost her."

"What makes you think I would lose her? Who are you?"

"I am your worst nightmare. I'm a judge with friends in high places. I could have your boat impounded indefinitely. Your ship would be pulled apart, piece by piece."

"There's no need for that. What is it you want?

"As I said, I wish to hire your services."

***

Doctor Bottoms answered the frequently knocked office door, dressed in her usual white see-through dress.

"Clint Eros?"

"Yes, I can see. I mean, yes, I am," Clint finally looking at Oppeniya's face.

"Please, take a seat. I am Doctor Oppeniya Bottoms. Psychologist, Psychiatrist, and Hypnotherapist."

"Well, I do believe I'm talking to the right person then."

"Yes, as you can see, I have lots of official-looking pieces of paper plastered all over my office wall. Now Clint, when we spoke on the phone, you said you were interested in hypnotherapy."

"Yes, does it work on everyone?" Clint enquired.

"There is a small percentage of people it has no effect on, but I am yet to meet such a person."

"Is there such a thing as group hypnosis?" Clint asked.

"It is in the category of difficult, but with the right preparation, I believe it is possible. Why?"

"I have a goal to achieve," Clint stated.

"Look into my eyes," Oppeniya said.

"No, I don't want you to hypnotise me right now."

"No, I mean, please lift your eyes. Stop perving at my see-through dress!"

"Hmm? Oh yes, yes. Sorry . . . it's mesmerising. Hypnotic, one could say."

They both laughed (the same way one was to laugh at a 2020 parking inspector, who had just given you a ticket and then stepped in front of a cyclist who had been holding up traffic for two blocks), and the connection was evident.

Parking inspectors were given a licence to graffiti motor vehicles, pre-2000s. Tyre black cost a pretty penny, and the grey-uniformed parking inspectors ('grey ghosts') would put a large white chalk mark on the tyres of parked cars. They would return and check tyres to see if the vehicle had been parked in a bay too long. Show car owners were furious. However, one little tasty painting on a wall would see the layman with a fine if the artist had to park up to express his talent and parked too long-double whammy.

Post-2000, motor vehicle drivers were forced to leave at least a one-metre spacing when overtaking a cyclist. The trouble with that was, when you were stuck behind a cyclist in a single carriageway, you couldn't lawfully overtake. Approaching a set of lights, where the road widens to two lanes, seemed the only way to complete the manoeuvre. The trouble with that was that catching a red light meant the cyclist would ride up the inside (not allowing one-metre clearance) to the front of the traffic, and all vehicles were again stuck behind the cyclist. Perhaps the reason for bull bars?

"Doctor Bottoms . . ."

"Please, Oppeniya," interrupted Bottoms.

"Oppeniya, I have a proposition for you. You can name your price."

Clint had no dirt on Dr Bottoms, not from a lack of looking, though.

"I don't need money, Clint. I come from wealth."

"So, what is your motivation?"

"My work is my life," Oppeniya stated.

Clint made an offer too good to refuse for the mind specialist.

"What if I offered you a constant supply of the mentally disturbed, with no alternative but to do as you say?"

"No. I've had my share of cyclists."

"No, I mean those with life-changing mental distortions," Clint clarified.

"I'm still thinking cyclists."

Clint let out a mini sigh.

"Tasmanians? Scientology enthusiasts? ~~Editors~~? Road and traffic planners?" Dr Bottoms trying her best guesses.

It is understood that studies were done all over the world to incorporate the best traffic management plan into Perth, Western Australia's roadways. Notorious for its lengthy travel time, Adelaide Terrace comprised of what seemed an endless line of traffic lights. You could drive for forty-five minutes and only travel six minutes up the road.

"I mean serial killers, child molesters, rapists, parking inspectors," Clint defined.

"How can you promise that, Clint?"

"My courtroom, my rules. Psychic evaluations are required more and more often. I can recommend the offenders are assessed by Doctor Oppeniya Bottoms."

"It sounds like we have a deal, judge."

CHAPTER 10

THE UNVEILING

"Please take a seat. Thank you all for coming," Judge Clint Eros welcoming his five guests to the Retro-Tech board room, Adelaide Terrace, Perth, Western Australia. "Allow me to do the introductions. Roland Van Real, electronic cyber genius, Dennis Dunny, master forger, Skip Hail, boat captain, Maximillian Driver, hover car racer, and Dr Oppeniya Bottoms, hypnotherapist.

"It's not like we had a choice," Maximillian said.

"You all had a choice. You chose to be here. You can walk out right now if you wish and spend the rest of your days behind bars. Make your minds up right now," Clint firmly stated.

There was nothing but silent glances amongst the members.

"Lady and gentleman, Retro-Tech has something every capitalist and country leader in the world would kill for. Literally. With the inevitable destruction of Earth, this simulation program is the most precious item in the world. It is a matter of life and death. Whoever controls this program controls their own destiny. Therefore, you will all become board members, giving you access to the project's main control building. We are going to copy the software discreetly."

The reality of humankind's doom, lay heavy with the enlightened group.

"Destwuction of ouw pwanet?" Roland asked.

"It has been kept a secret from the public for obvious reasons. The scientific world and a selected few have been informed that the giant asteroid, 'Epilogue', is on a direct collision course with Earth, entering our atmosphere in approximately five years."

"So, we will all survive the collision with the asteroid?" Skip asked.

"If we are successful with my plan, we stand a far greater chance. Let's not forget, Retro-Tech is still experimenting with it too. It has become somewhat of a race."

"Now, that's my language," Max warming to the situation, turning his cap visor to the rear.

"You will enter the Retro-Tech building, posing as board members. I will keep Candice Sweet, the overseer, occupied while Dr Bottoms hypnotises Sassan Summers the chief controller, allowing Roland to copy the program. Dennis and Max will stand guard at and near the main control room doors. Skip, you'll be on your ship keeping lookout, engine running."

"What is your relationship to Arros Sole?" Oppeniya asked.

"Arros Sole, the company director, is an eccentric and an extremely private man. He is just a figurehead, a money man, who has very little to do with his company. Our only communication has been via audio calls. He has rejected every attempt to meet in person. I helped Arros out of a tight squeeze. He made me a small percentage partner in Retro-Tech as payment. I still have not met him face to face. The situation he was in was rectified by communication with his lawyers."

"So, let me get this straight. You cleared up the shit from a tight-squeezed Arros Sole?" Dunny clarified.

"Mr. Dunny . . . Clint closed his eyes and shook his head.

"Analogy withdrawn, Your Honour," Dennis interrupted, smirking to the others.

"Roland and Dennis. You need to work together to create electronic passes to enter the establishment for all of you, including Skip. I will lend you my identification pass to copy."

There was a brief silence as the 'board members' took in everything they had learnt.

"Questions?"

"If we are considered legitimate board members, why don't we just get proper passes?" Max asked.

"Because you are not legitimate board members. I will, however, introduce you all, except Skip, because it is not necessary, as board members to the head of Retro-Tech, Candice Sweet."

"Is Candy in sweet with Arros?" Skip asked.

"I believe Candice and Arros have never met or even talked on the phone. I am the middleman and have been now for about three years."

Eros gathered up some papers, getting ready to leave. "Oppeniya would like a quick word with you all. I really must leave now. I am due in court in one hour, and I have no option but to travel half a kilometre down Adelaide Terrace. I should just make it. I'll be in touch soon."

Cint Eros stood up and left the conference room.

"I want you all to concentrate on this," Dr Bottoms began, taking out a teabag.

"You want us to stare at a teabag?" Dunny asked.

Oppeniya put the teabag back in her pocket and pulled out her hypnotic charm.

"Oh, sorry. I mean this special watch of mine. Focus on the watch. You are getting sleepy. Relax. Deep breaths. Sleep, sleeeep."

Max, Dennis, Skip and Roland were under the hypnotist's spell.

"Mr. Arros Sole was present at our meeting today. You all saw him. He made you board members. One, two, three, wide awake."

"Where did Awwos go?" Roland asked.

"Mr. Sole had another matter to attend to," Dr. Bottoms answered, quite happy with her first group hypnosis session. The group were not wise to their mind alteration.

The supposed board members began filtering out of the conference room, after a friendly, light-hearted, 'get to know your accomplice', talk.

"I'm not only a cyba electwonic expewt, I'm also a dwumma. Unfowtunately, I went to jail, just fow a little while."

"You? You went to jail? What for?" Max asked.

"I stuck my stick in a child boy's wectum."

The group looked at Roland with disgust. (The same way one looks at you when your silent wind finds its way to the nasal passage of the only other person in the lift. So, it is understood).

"You know Roland, speech therapy is readily available these days," Dr Bottoms pointed out.

"Why awe you telling me that?"

The group stared in silence at Roland for a few moments.

"I am somewhat of a celebrity in the hover racing sport. I too, did a short stint in jail for smashing into a few moving objects," Maximillian stated.

"What sort of moving objects?" Dunny asked.

"Human," Max replied.

The group looked at Max in a way that suggested he should be chained to the inside of a lift with the offending rider.

"Some people held me responsible for the start of WWIII," Dunny said, puffing out his chest.

The group looked at Dunny in a way that said, "Your nose should be sewn to the anus of the offending lift rider."

"What about you, Skip? What's your story?" the doctor asked.

"I don't have anything of that nature to confess. I only devoured my best friend, and once a year, I kick his stuffed head for a goal."

It is believed looks of "You should have your nose sewn to your own anus while riding a lift" were present on all faces.

"And you, Doc?" Skip prompted.

"Well, really, I don't have a story that even comes close to those. I'm a wealthy career woman who wears see-through dresses and rarely has underwear on."

The looks from the gentleman suggested they would volunteer to have their noses sewn to the anus of the sexy doctor while riding a lift.

Dr Bottoms was the last to leave. As she entered the lift, a familiar face stepped in at the last second.

"Clare-Lee, how wond . . ." Oppeniya was cut short, as a woman with 'rainbow eyes' entered the lift.

Clare said some mystery words and tapped Dr Bottoms' shoulder. Oppeniya was under a hypnotic spell.

"You didn't see me today. You did see Arros Sole, and he conducted the meeting. He made you all board members," Clare-Lee stated.

The lift opened, and Clare stepped out, leaving an air of anal passage expulsion.

"One, two, three, wide awake", said Clare as the lift closed its doors.

Clint stayed out of sight as Bottoms hit the ground floor, gagging and left the building. Another passenger who had caught a ride two floors up gave Bottoms a disgusted look. Clare and Clint met near the exit.

"How did it go, Clare?"

"No problem."

"What do I owe you?"

"Consider it a gift. That deceitful bitch deserves to eat whatever shit pie you are cooking."

Clint flew by helicopter, as usual, to the island, and the others sailed with Skip at the helm.

"Why did you bring all that food, Max?" Hail asked.

The group stared at Harrisons's head.

"Oh, just in case we get hungry. It's a long trip," Max replied, turning his cap visor to the rear.

***

Waiting outside the Retro-Tech establishment, Clint greeted the new board members. Dunny and Van Real were successful with the production of the electronic passes. Two guards stood on either side of the entrance doors as Clint led the way, assuming the role as a guide for orientation.

"You'll notice security is extremely tight," Clint spoke as the members followed him into the building.

The guards observed, as one by one, the small group scanned their passes, and then proceeded through the only access, a turnstile with a swipe monitor. Cameras were mounted in the small entrance foyer and nearly every ceiling corner throughout the entire four levels. Employees numbered ninety-eight, including security guards.

The board members summoned the lift, and all passengers were accounted for as the doors shut.

"What's that strange odour?" Max asked.

"Smells like a dunny," Roland said.

"It wasn't me," Dennis stated. "It smells like something from a bottom."

"It certainly wasn't me," Oppeniya slightly offended. "It's a real stink."

"What? No, I didn't do it," Roland added. "That's offensive to the max."

"Hey? No, not me," Maximillian said.

Clint stood silent, facing the doors with a grin on his face.

The lift doors opened, and the group hastily exited, taking an overdue deep breath.

Seven pre-programmers could be seen through the glass partitions, busy on their computers. In the other segregated main control room, Professor Summers sat in front of his large computer and screen. Candice was in her office, standing, looking at the main program screen.

"Hello, Clint. Who do we have here?" Jo questioned as the group headed for Jo's desk, between the lift and the control room.

Clint introduced the board members.

"Would you please wait here while I inform Candice of your presence?" Jo rhetorically asked.

Jo walked into Candy's office as two security guards situated outside the control room kept an eye on the guests. Jo returned after a brief moment and escorted the members into the conference room/smoker's lounge/children's play area.

"You look a bit dry, Clint Eros. Can I get you refreshments?" Jo asked.

"Yes, thanks, Jo."

"Bottoms, Driver? Real, Dunny?"

"Yes, that would be nice," Bottoms answered for all.

"Thank you for looking after our guests, Jo," Candice said as the pair passed each other in the doorway.

"Hello, Clint Eros. A nice surprise."

"Good to see you, Candice. Allow me to introduce our board members. Real, Driver and Dunny, Bottoms. Another member, Skip, won't be joining us today."

"Hello to all of you. I'm Candice Sweet, head of Retro-Tech. I've been expecting you," Candice said, pulling a pin from her bun, letting her hair drop. Then she ran her fingers through her hair and shook her head.

Real, Dunny, Driver, tilted their heads to the side and looked at Candice with puppy dog eyes.

"I thought it would be a good idea to show the members around the establishment, to see what they are actually board members of. Arros gave his blessing by phone, as usual, at our last meeting," Clint informed.

"Yes, yes, I was aware of that," Candice said.

Jo returned with drinks and nibblies for the members. Real and Driver rejected the offered napkins, but Dunny and Bottoms took one each to wipe with.

After the group had refreshed, the tour continued.

"If you would like to follow me, I'll show you the pre-program sector," Candy said, leading the way.

"Here are our pre-programmers. The seven computers feed information to the main control room. Our latest simulation has just ended. We are simulating . . ." Candice stopped mid-sentence.

"Clint, do they know . . ." Candy whispered in Clint's ear.

"Yes, they all know Candice. You can speak openly."

"We are simulating the inevitable asteroid, 'Epilogue,' colliding with the world. Our goal is to find the best scenario to save as many people as we can. So far, a group of seven, less than desirables, and another group of seven, six of them from the mentally insane asylum, seem to be our only hope for the continuation of human life."

The board members appeared quite upset with the situation.

"Hey, chins up. It's only early days for the simulation and remember, 'At Retro-Tech, we give a damn,'" Candy reciting the company motto. "Now, if you'll follow me into the main simulation control room, I'll introduce you to Professor Summers."

The 'board members' were getting closer to completing their mission.

"Professor, may I introduce, Real, Bottoms and Dunny, Driver. Board members of Retro-Tech, and you already know Clint."

Sassan turned from the big screen and greeted the guests.

"Candice, may I have a word with you in private?" Clint Eros asked.

"Sure. I'll leave our guests in your care for the moment, professor. Maybe you can replay some of the interesting events of our last simulation?"

Sassan's eyes lit up at the thought of a captive audience. In his office chair on wheels, he skated three metres one way, collected some software and skated back again. He connected fibre-optic cables to his computer, disconnected other adapters and generally piss-farted around.

Sweet and Clint walked into Candy's office. Candy, behind her desk, could see the professor and guests, with Clint Eros in the foreground, sitting in the office visitor chair. Clint fabricated some lame questions about Arros Sole as a distraction tool. He stood up after a minute or so, blocking Candy's view of the professor, guests and part of the simulation screen.

The board members began their plan.

"Sassan," Dr Bottoms caught the professor's attention. "Look at my new watch. See it swinging. Mesmerising, isn't it? Relax. Breath deep. You are getting tired, sleepy. Sleep. Sleeep."

Sassan was under the doctor's spell, and Roland went to work. Max stood between Sassan and Candy's view from the office to limit the chance of being discovered. Dunny stood back, close to the entrance. For anyone that happened to catch a glance, everything looked normal. Roland injected a piece of high-tech equipment into the professor's computer. The device was copying the entire simulation software. The mounted cameras did not have a clear view as the human traffic was blocking all views.

"When I count to three, you will be wide awake. You won't remember us being in the control room today," Dr Bottoms fed Sassan.

Roland's equipment had completed its task. He ejected the item and pushed it back into his pocket.

"One, two, three. Wide awake."

"Who are you people?" the professor asked, looking around wildly.

"We are the board members, Professor Summers. Are you all right?"

"Oh, I mutht haved dothed off for a thecond. Yeth, I'm fine."

"Can you replay some of the last simulation, please, Professor?" Max asked.

The professor put their request on the big screen, and everything looked as it was meant to be. Clint finished his conversation with Candy, and the pair returned to the control room, where all members were gathered in front of the screen as if nothing had happened.

"Have we all seen enough?" Clint asked.

"Yes. Sure. Yep, done. No one knows I haven't any underwear on," came the assorted responses at the same time.

"Thank you, Candice and Professor Summers. It was most informative," Clint declared. "We will be on our way."

Clint, again, summoned the lift.

"Ah, let's use the stairs," Dunny suggested.

Everyone was eager to follow Dennis' lead. As the group verged on exiting the building, one of the security guards stopped them.

"Protocol states we must scan you for possible hidden paraphernalia. Clint, you know the rules," the familiar guard said.

"Oh, yes, of course. Dr Bottoms, why don't you go first?" Clint offered.

"Where's the dunny?" asked Dennis to the other guard.

"You can't wander off on your own, sir," the guard replied.

"Oooh, I think I'm going to shit myself right here," Dennis desperately said.

"Ok, Ok, I'll show you to the toilet, sir."

As soon as Dennis and the guard left, Dr Bottoms again used her gift on the only guard left, by the exit. After that, everyone walked out and waited outside for Dunny.

"All good, Roland?" Clint asked.

Roland smiled and nodded to his new friend.

Dennis exited the establishment, and the group smiled and laughed as they headed to the pier to meet Skip aboard the *SS Extant.*

'How did it go?" Skip asked Clint, greeting the thieves on the pier.

"According to plan, captain."

"Where are we headed, judge?"

"Back to Western Australia, Skip. The best place in the world. Apart from Adelaide Terrace. And the ignorant cyclists . . . and parking inspectors . . . silly safety rules . . . and . . . you know what? Let's go straight to New Zealand."

Max Driver had his hover race car parked at Fremantle, ready to zoom across Australia, which would have been a much quicker trip, to take Clint and the copied program to Cape Tribulation in the northeast of Australia. Then a short boat ride to New Zealand.

The *SS Extant* took the western and northern coastline route to New Zealand. The sights were amazing for all passengers. The forty-mile stretch of crystal-clear ocean and beach of Broome, and the regular, magnificent thunderstorms of Darwin, Northern Territory, were highlights for the sailors. All aboard were ecstatic with the short travel holiday. There was plenty of food to keep the captain from eating anyone.

The captain moored at his usual port in New Zealand.

"So, board members and Skip. You need to return to Perth and carry on with your daily lives to avoid suspicion. Hang on to your passes in case we need to cover up any unforeseen problems—Max, with me. I'm going to need a lift. I'll be in touch with the rest of you."

"What awe you going to do with the pwogwam, Clint?"

"I have my own, Retro-Tech, hidden underground in Ruapehu. The room requires no heating, for some reason. I'll run the simulation program from there. My team are excellent cyber whizzes."

With those words the thieves parted ways.

CHAPTER 11

THE TELL

"I put it to you, Clint Eros, that you are the ringleader of a criminal operation. You witnessed Tasla's character forming in the pre-program sector. You uploaded the suicide bomber, and she had passed on information, reaching Addison by way of the cargo shuttles, about the unique Tasla," Candice accusing the judge. "In our simulation, Addison said he had heard about Tasla. How was that possible? The only way is through our program. The one you stole."

"Preposterous," Judge Clint Eros in denial.

"More refreshments?" Jo asked.

"Enough with the refreshments, Jo. They don't deserve it," Candice snapped.

Jo, the robot, and personal assistant returned to her desk outside the control room entrance.

"Clint Eros blackmailed you all."

Well, that clarifies my question about extortion or blackmail, Dunny thought.

"Except for Dr. Oppeniya Bottoms. I am sure a deal was made between you two."

"Being sure is not proof, Sweet," the judge stated.

"I'll get to that, Clint."

"Roland was blackmailed for his electronic genius," Candice continued.

I thought we wewe fwiends, Roland thought.

"Max for his driving ability."

I dropped Clint off as more like a taxi service, Maximillian thought.

"Skipper Hail as the get-away and delivery source."

Yes, likened to a leisurely cruise, the captain thought.

"And, of course, Dr Oppeniya Bottoms, hypnotherapist. Would you like me to tell you what gave you away?"

There was yet, another uproar. "I don't know what you are talking about. Say what, Candy? Weally? It's all bullshit! I hope my churkins are alright. Maybe crotchless is the way to go."

"Dr Bottoms had hypnotised me, prior to your 'orientation', with you so-called board members. As fate has it, I had a booking with another hypnotherapist to reduce my anxiety of the future the following day. The other doctor picked up immediately that I was already under hypnosis and told me the 'spell' was related to board members. You imitated security passes, probably from Clint's valid pass, hypnotised the professor, and Clint distracted me, while Roland copied the information from Sassan's computer."

"But we are board members. Arros Sole declared us as such," Oppenyia argued. (And how unusual for a woman to argue).

"Clare-Lee Seizya, Dr Bottoms. The woman with rainbow eyes, at Clint's request, hypnotised you after you put your spell on the four men."

Bitch! Oppenyia thought. *I knew that odour in the lift was familiar.*

Bitch! thought the four men of Oppeniya. That didn't alter their decision to volunteer to have their noses sewn to her anus, though. (They are men; What can I say?)

Bitch! thought Clint of Candy Sweet.

"Bitch!" Jo, the robot, in artificial tears from 'snapping Candy'.

"The program you stole from Retro-Tech was designed to work only once. A virus was planted into it. We tracked you to New Zealand. Your equipment now, Clint, will be worthless. We kept up appearances just in case you had another inside player. We gave you enough rope to hang yourself, which may be a better option for a judge that is destined for jail."

"Blah! Blah! Blah! Candice. Where's your irrefutable proof?" Clint questioned.

"Oh, almost forgot. Thanks, Judge. Here is a separate piece of paper for you all, not to wipe with, and a pen. Red, Smasher, Buster and Robski. What will you do if you see them look at the other papers or hear a whisper or even a glance amongst them?"

"I will bust them until their faces have the appearance of a smashed crab," Buster kindly offered.

"I will smash their teeth so far down their throats they will have to floss their ass-holes," Smasher gently added.

"I will turn their bodies red and black and blue," The Redman colourfully explained.

"Robski?" Candy prompted. "Feel free to express yourself."

"I not know."

"You not know what, Russian Rob?

"Use designer pen or pencil to force into jugular?"

"How about both?" Candy suggested. "One in each hand."

Robski smiled, ear to ear.

"Eyes down for bingo lady and gentleman. You all claim to have met Arros Sole. Write down a description of him. You included, Judge. They should all be the same, should they not? Also, your name and signature."

"Eyewitnesses are not reliable in a court, Candice," Judge Clint Eros declared.

"Point taken. I'll accept similar."

Nobody was writing anything.

"The world ends in only five years, people. Write or Robski adopts a bigger grin."

The six thieves reluctantly wrote and handed their papers to Candy.

"I think now is a good time for Mr. Arros Sole to read the descriptions."

Sitting quietly through the entire interrogation, Professor Sassan Summers, stood up. Arros was such an eccentric and recluse he opted to be part of his company incognito. A computer genius with an exceptional IQ, he portrayed the role of "Thathin Thummerth" to avoid unwanted contact with just about everyone.

"It's all on you, Dad," Candice said.

"Dad? Clint Eros, you fuck tool!" Dennis Dunny observed.

"And Clint Ewos is exposed," Roland Van Real added.

"How to sink a ship, or the man in the boat, by Clint Eros," Captain Skip Hail stated.

"Men will say, 'Where's Clint Eros?' Others will answer, 'Who cares?" Dr. Oppenyia Bottoms offered.

"You'll be, 'Dried up, old, wrinkled Clint Eros', by the time you make another appearance," Maximillian Driver submitted.

"Gentlemen, take these thieves to my good friend, Millsy. He will escort them to the D man," Candice Sweet, head of Retro-Tech ordered. The room cleared.

"Let's have a look at my descriptions, shall we, Candy?" Arros Sole asked.

"The first says, 'He is brown', the next, 'He is clean shaved', 'He is hairy', 'He has piercings', 'He has a bleached appearance', 'He was dribbling'."

The pair laughed so hard Arros Sole dribbled as his piercings glistened against his bleach-spotted brown skin, and his beard bounced up to his bald head.

"Dad, the people in our simulations. They believe they are alive?"

"Well, by all accounts, they are alive. They have feelings; they have all senses, sight, taste, sound, smell and touch.

And they think. Therefore: they are."

"So, what happens to them when they are deleted?"

"My educated, best guess is that their minds are still active, but they are thrust into an eternal darkness. No light or sound, smell or taste. They have no body but are still very much aware. A consciousness floating in a void of infinite blackness."

"One final question, then. How can you be sure we are not merely a simulation?"

FOR THE MUSIC I THANK

AC/DC
THE BABYS
BLINK 182
BOSTON
COLD CHISEL
F.R. DAVID
DIRE STRAITS
BOB DYLAN
ELTON JOHN
MEN AT WORK
IGGY POP
QUEEN
RAINBOW
KENNY RODGERS
PAUL SIMON
DODIE STEVENS
VAN HALEN

Thank you – Jacko, Kelly and Zoe,
for being a rock in your role.

Lightning Source UK Ltd.
Milton Keynes UK
UKHW051552130223
416650UK00012B/943/J